"I D...

Maddie felt as if a weight had been lifted from her once she'd said the words. She grabbed Rowan's hands, and he matched her smile with his own. "Now I'm not going to go overboard on this or anything. Time travel is as much as I'm willing to declare magical right now."

Rowan drew her even closer. "You talk too much, lass."

Maddie found she couldn't look away from his gaze. A shiver ran through her, leaving a hot ache in its wake. Rowan ran one hand up her back, tangling his fingers in her hair. Warm sensations spread through her as he gently drew back her head and kissed her. The pressure of his lips against hers was insistent, and she answered it with an eagerness that surprised her.

Published by HarperPaperbacks

One of These Nights

 Susan Sizemore

HarperPaperbacks
A Division of HarperCollins*Publishers*

HarperPaperbacks
A Division of HarperCollins*Publishers*
10 East 53rd Street, New York, N.Y. 10022-5299

This is a work of fiction. The characters, incidents, and
dialogues are products of the author's imagination and are not to
be construed as real. Any resemblance to actual events or
persons, living or dead, is entirely coincidental.

ISBN 0-06-108132-9

HarperCollins®, ®, HarperPaperbacks™, and
HarperMonogram® are trademarks of HarperCollins*Publishers*, Inc.

Cover illustration by Jon Paul

First printing: June 1997

Printed in the United States of America

Visit HarperPaperbacks on the World Wide Web at
http://www.harpercollins.com

❖ 10 9 8 7 6 5 4 3 2 1

*For Lois Greiman—who truly understands
that England and Scotland share a border.
And because she graciously put up with
a lot from me on this one.*

One of These Nights

Prologue

"Face it, honey, this is your last chance."

Even though her mother was on a ranch in Montana and Maddie McCullogh was on an island off the coast of Scotland, her mother's voice came clear as a bell over the phone line. A warning bell. One she'd heard often and was finally considering heeding.

Maddie had spent years ignoring all the advice and criticism and admonitions from her mother, her sisters, her cousins, aunts, and every feminine female in her overextended family. She had had to go her own way. She'd never listened. And where had it gotten her?

"Twenty-eight years old and never had a date," her mother spoke the answer for her.

"Of course I've had dates," Maddie countered. Not many, it was true, and no romance to speak of. "I'm not a complete failure with the opposite sex."

Her mother's laughter was mocking. "Honey, I don't know what's going to become of you if this last chance with Toby Coltrane doesn't pan out."

Toby Coltrane. Maddie's heart skipped a beat just at

the sound of his name. She was shocked at her strong reaction. She attempted to sound cool when she said, "Now there's a name I haven't heard in a while."

Her mother laughed again. "You've had it bad for Toby ever since sixth grade."

Maddie didn't deny it. The Toby she remembered was handsome, athletic, sweet, charming. Everybody in town had known how she felt about Toby. Except Toby. He always treated her like his best friend. That was her problem. Every man she'd ever met had always treated her like one of the boys. She was beginning to think it was her own fault.

"Where'd I go wrong, Mama?" The question slipped out before she could stop it.

"Well, look at the way you live, honey."

"I like my job."

"I blame your father for that. Treated you just like a boy, and you ended up acting like one. Now, there's nothing wrong with you being an engineer. Lots of proper young ladies are engineers. You just took it to extremes. Took it to the ends of the earth, you did."

Maddie couldn't argue with that. She did spend her time in remote areas. She had loved the wild places once, loved solitude. She still craved the adventure, but she was getting dangerously lonely. So lonely she thought she was going crazy from it. She'd never thought it would come to her wanting someone to share her life with, but it looked as if her emotions were aimed that way. She had to admit that she hungered for someone special more than she wanted to see new places. The desire for a normal life, for a man of her own, a marriage, was eating at her more and more lately. She wished these feelings would just go away; they were impractical and inconvenient. Probably hormonal. Maybe there was something she could take for it.

Her mother interrupted her thoughts. "You have to do something to get Toby to notice you."

"What?" she asked, instead of protesting that she wasn't interested.

"Get yourself back to civilization first, honey. No reasonable man is going to want a woman who works on an oil rig in the middle of the ocean and then goes digging in the dirt on remote islands on her vacation."

She was spending her vacation as a volunteer at an archaeological dig, but her mother's call, with the information that her lifelong love was flying in to Glasgow for a business meeting, threatened to change all that. Her mother had promised Toby that Maddie would meet him at the airport and show him around the city. Then she'd called Maddie to tell her to get down to Glasgow.

Maddie should have been annoyed at this interference in her life—this matchmaking. Instead, she was unreasonably grateful. She'd spent too much time staring out to sea recently, gone for too many lonely walks, been too restless and dissatisfied. She had to make some kind of major change, take some action. Toby's visit might be a godsend.

Or it could prove to be the most embarrassing few days of her life. It could go either way. She might indulge in a fantasy of a whirlwind courtship, but she was a hardheaded, practical woman well aware that indulging in fantasy was dangerous.

"You put on a dress when you meet Toby at the airport. You hear me, Madalyn?"

"I don't own any dresses, Mama."

"Then get yourself one. A nice one. Fix yourself up. You're such a pretty girl."

Maddie snorted. "I've got frizzy red hair and freckles over eighty percent of my body."

"You've got a nice figure."

"My boobs are too big."

"Men like big boobs, honey."

Her mom was probably right about that. Her mother was right about all sorts of feminine things. Her mother had managed to marry off three other daughters. Maddie was the only holdout, the only McCullogh girl who'd ever resisted the matrimonial urge. An urge she now knew was as strong in her as in any woman in the family.

"Gotta be a pill for that," she muttered. "Prozac, or saltpeter or something."

"Do you want Toby Coltrane or not?"

Maddie sighed. She gave in. "I want him, Mama."

Or at least somebody just like him.

"Put it on."

Maddie looked questioningly at her friend Kevin, then at the necklace. She didn't welcome the distraction from the archaeologist seated beside her. Her mind wasn't on the dig, but on the man she was to meet in Glasgow.

"Go on," Kevin urged.

"I don't think so."

The roaring of the little plane's engines must have drowned out her words, or Kevin simply chose to ignore them. He leaned closer; considering how small the airplane cabin was, he didn't have far to go. When he whispered, "It's all right," in her ear, it sent a shiver down her spine.

Somehow, she didn't think it was all right, but she was tempted. The necklace was beautiful. Far more beautiful than something that had been buried in the ground for hundreds, perhaps thousands, of years, should be. It was made of two strands of intertwined chains. One was obviously gold, the other looked like copper. The perfect condition of the gold made sense, but the copper should have tarnished or rotted away long ago. Instead, it was bright as a new penny. Which was impossible for an object that had recently been excavated from an archaeological dig. Kevin was taking it to the University of Glasgow to run some metallurgical tests.

In the meantime, he was tempting her. He'd been getting everyone he could to try it on ever since they'd taken it out of the ground. He said he had this compulsion to see how it looked on a beautiful woman. This was the first time he'd asked her. The necklace resting on the unfolded square of chamois tempted her, too. She didn't know why.

"I don't wear jewelry."

"Maybe you should."

It wasn't that it was incredibly beautiful. Except for its age, it was hardly unique. It was an artifact from a long-gone place and time. That was what was so tempting about the thought of wearing it.

Kevin gave her a boyish smile. "Go on," he urged. "I won't tell."

He was right. Maybe she should wear jewelry—and perfume and short skirts and makeup and all those other things Mama had ordered her to acquire. She had agreed to follow at least some of her mother's instructions. Might as well start now, and get some practice in before she made a shopping trip in Glasgow.

She shrugged and took the necklace from the smiling archaeologist. By all rights the clasp shouldn't have opened, but it worked just fine. She had the slender, twined chains fastened around her throat within moments.

"I don't think it was meant to be worn with a gray sweatshirt."

"It looks great," he told her.

Maddie's answer was drowned out by a sudden roar from outside the airplane. Then the plane lurched sideways. For a moment Maddie was afraid an engine had fallen off, then she saw the lights outside the windows.

They looked like fireworks. Maybe it was a meteor shower. Noise howled around them, too loud for Maddie to even hear herself scream. The sky went dark, but inside the darkness, something moved.

Then the bright fireworks explosions filled the darkness.

The plane began to dive.

She knew she was going to die. She'd never have a chance to see Toby Coltrane again. She'd never have a chance to find love.

It just wasn't fair.

Life isn't, her practical side reminded her, just before the world went completely dark.

1

Scottish Highlands, 1210 C.E.

Rowan Murray looked up at the pale morning sky, glad that the day had come. He'd been more than a little worried that it would not. He adjusted his plaid around his shoulders, took in a deep breath of sea-tinted air, and silently thanked God that dawn had come after all.

When the great howl like heaven's own pain had come out of the night, he'd rushed outside with all the rest of his people, his sword in his hand, half-awake and terrified. He'd looked up to see a great fiery glow in the night sky, bright as a thousand full moons, more vivid than a hundred sunsets. Then the noise faded, and so did the lights, and his people crowded around him as though he could protect them from whatever creatures waited out in the night. And so he would try, he knew, for he was chieftain and laird of all the Murrays of Cape Wrath.

Though they manned the walls through the rest of

the night, nothing supernatural came out of the cold, swirling mist to harm them. And no Harboth, either, for it was soon whispered that the unearthly noise and light was some trick of the rival clan. Now that day had come, Rowan nodded once to those who watched him, to indicate that he declared the danger over, and turned to climb down off the outer wall.

His brother, Aidan, put out a hand to stop him. "I think," the lad said, "you best have a talk with the White Lady about this."

Rowan considered. He was much troubled, and not only by the night's odd occurrence. The others had been urging him to consult the wisewoman of Glenshael since the message had come from the Lord of the Isles. He didn't like to, for he preferred real answers to magical ones. He was the only one of the clan who seemed to. If he was going to do it, now was as good a time as any.

Though not until after he'd had his porridge, he decided.

"So you've come to ask my help at last, Rowan Murray?"

The White Lady of Glenshael did indeed have white hair, but she was no bent-over old crone with gnarled hands and warts on her nose. Indeed no, she was fair of face and form, though hardly young, with bright eyes and soft cheeks and all the pride in the world in her manner. Her hair hung down to her waist in thick plaits, and her dress was of purest white wool. A golden, jeweled brooch fastened her plaid mantle at her throat. Her house was small, tucked neatly beneath an overhang of rock on a ledge high above the glen. Rowan thought that it perched like an eagle's nest above the trees and peaty stream below. It gave a fine view, not just of the valley, but of the hills to the north and the wild sea beyond.

Rowan had had a hard climb up the narrow path after leaving Aidan to watch the horses. He stood before the White Lady a few moments while she watched him and he caught his breath. Finally, he nodded in answer to her question and followed her into her house.

A fire burned at the center of the room, lighting and warming the interior of the stone structure. A pot simmered over the fire, full of a rich, meaty broth seasoned with herbs. Whatever the White Lady was cooking was no doubt for her dinner, and not some arcane love or healing potion. Her greatest gift was in seeing the shape of the future. Her wisdom was so revered that any who came to her had to vow to obey her advice or risk being eternally cursed.

He disliked spells and curses and magic riddles, though he didn't shun their usefulness. He disliked making promises before he knew what was asked of him, but still, here he was.

"Last night's portent was too much for even your dour stubbornness, I see," the White Lady told him as they took seats by her fire.

Rowan was a man who preferred keeping his thoughts to himself. Words did not come easily to him, but he gathered as many as he could together and spoke his concerns aloud. "We Murrays have troubles. The Harboths and the Norsemen raid our cattle and crops, and the land and sea have been hard enough on us these last few seasons. Now the Lord of the Isles comes within two months' time to trouble us."

The White Lady nodded. "You have many a mortal care, Rowan Murray. And a few magical ones as well."

Rowan nodded his head. "The fair folk are troublesome," he admitted.

She laughed. "I spoke of the would-be wizards and wisewomen within your own walls."

Rowan's habitual frown deepened. "I come here not to discuss my family, but seek advice for our troubles. Nature has been hard on us this year," Rowan told her. "Fires, storms, sickness. The lights in the sky last night seemed a dread omen to me."

She stabbed him with a proud and angry glare. "What do you or any of yours know of reading omens, Rowan Murray? Have you the gift, or have I?" she demanded.

He ducked his head. "You do, Lady."

"That I have, so you let me decide what that noise and fire was all about." Her expression grew softer. "I saw your fate last night, Rowan Murray. Shall I tell it to you?"

"My own fate is not so important to me," he answered. "I fear the Lord of the Isles plots to destroy my clan. My people need help and hope, and I know not where to turn."

"You are their hope, so your fate is tied to theirs."

He considered, then nodded.

She stood. He rose with her, and though he was far taller than the White Lady of Glenshael, it seemed that she towered over him as she spoke. "Hear me, Rowan of the Murray clan, laird of the seafaring people. Hear and obey, or lose all that you hold dear for your defiance of my aid."

Rowan knew what was expected next, though no one had ever told him just how the vow was made to the White Lady. He bent over and slipped a small dagger out of the top of his boot. With the sharp tip of the blade he pierced the skin of his hand, just enough for a few drops of blood to seep onto his palm. He held up his open hand. "With my own blood I swear," he told the wisewoman.

She pressed her palm flat against his, the small prick of pain dissipated at her soft touch. "Your blood speaks true."

She stepped back, her magic as thick around her as a dark cloak. Rowan could practically breathe it in, like scented smoke. A glance at his palm showed him that the small wound had already healed.

"Very well." She crossed her arms and closed her eyes. "This is the way to save your people," she said.

"How?" Rowan leaned forward intently. He held his breath.

"You'll meet the future standing in the middle of the road on your way home. You must marry her."

He had not known what to expect. He'd hoped for some brilliant plan to defeat the Harboths once and for all. He'd hoped for a spell to make the weather more friendly to his fields and flocks, or some trick to make the fish more abundant in Murray nets. He'd hoped for foreknowledge of what the Lord of the Isles intended. He was prepared for anything but what the White Lady told him he must do.

"What?"

She looked at him, far too much merriment in her gaze for his liking. "You must marry the first woman you meet on your way home."

"What?"

"Are you deaf, man? Should I be more specific? You'll know her by the golden necklace she wears about her throat. Besides, she'll be the only woman you meet on the way back to Cape Wrath."

"I've no mind to marry."

"And I've no care what you have a mind for." She pointed toward the door. "You made your vow, now live by it, Rowan Murray. Now be gone and get yourself married. Name the first girl babe after me," she called after him as he hurried angrily out. He heard her laugh as he slammed the door behind him.

Twice he nearly stumbled and fell headfirst off the cliff as he hurried down the path. Anger always made him heedless, though he was not quite so angry as to fall to his death just because he didn't like the woman's advice. Advice he was oathbound to heed. He was more angry at himself than at the White Lady. She was half mortal, half fairy born, and fairy folk were too mischievous for any mortal's good. He knew that well enough.

It didn't help that Aidan's silvery green eyes were narrowed with perpetual amusement as Rowan approached him. "You've not got goat's feet, brother," he said. "You should remember that when you're leaping down mountains."

Rowan frowned at his brother in answer, and mounted his horse for the long ride home. Aidan's laughter followed him down the track, then after a little while, so did Aidan.

When the lad caught up to him, Rowan said, before Aidan could ask what the White Lady had predicted, "Ride ahead to Cape Wrath. Tell Walter to send his daughter Meg out to meet me at the ford."

"Why?"

Rowan didn't answer. He knew Aidan had his own designs on pretty Meg, but those designs were not the honorable sort. Rowan's were.

On his hurtle down the mountain Rowan had considered just how to deal with the White Lady's foolish requirement for him to marry the first woman he met. He'd decided to take his fate into his own hands and arrange the match himself. Meg was fair and mostly biddable—the Lord knew there were few enough tame women among his clanfolk. If he must have a wife, the one thing he required was meek obedience from her. Besides, Meg was gifted with the sort of hips that told a man she would make a fine mother.

The wisewoman was right in that it was time he sired an heir, whether he wanted to share his life with a woman or not. Meg would do. For the most part, he was cursed with a tribe of spell-chanting amazons. Was it any wonder he hadn't sought a wife before now?

Still, he feared that the White Lady had her heart set on his marrying a woman from the Harboth clan. In a few hours he would have a bride from among his own people. He didn't like practicing deceit to fulfill an oath, but if that was the only reasonable way he could fulfill it, then deceitful he would be.

"Just have her meet me," he told Aidan. "Go on."

Aidan gave him a disgusted look, but rode on ahead. Rowan decided to take a longer way home to give Aidan time to carry out his mission, and turned off to follow a side track through wooded hills that would lead him eventually to the river ford. The stony way he chose was more often used by deer than people. He had no fear of meeting any woman he didn't want, with or without a gold necklace.

"Don't worry. Everything's fine."

Maddie spoke aloud to reassure herself. Actually, nothing was fine, and Maddie didn't know what to do about it. She knew she was somewhere on the mainland, but she didn't know what had happened to Kevin Macleish or the pilot of the of the small plane they had taken out of Stornoway the night before.

There were a lot of things she didn't know, and quite a few that were very mussed up in her memory. She remembered flashes of bright light in the sky, like fireworks or a meteor shower. She remembered the plane starting the long, dizzying, spiraling plunge through the lights toward the ground, and knowing that she was going to die.

Then she woke up. The plane was on the ground, intact but perched on a steep hillside instead of properly resting on the flat ground of a runway. The pilot was gone, and Kevin was gone; she was the only person on board. She couldn't imagine Kevin or the pilot going for help without waking her first. Nothing made any sense.

The plane's radio didn't work, nor did the engines, though nothing seemed to be damaged. So far no rescuers had shown up to help them from the plane that wasn't actually wrecked. It looked as if she was going to have to get down off the mountain and find help herself. She'd waited long enough, cowered, actually; it was time for some decisive action.

Outside it was cool and damp, but she'd gotten used

to that since she'd come to work in Scotland. Thick mist hung above the craggy peaks of nearby mountains. When she stepped out of the airplane door, the ground beneath her feet was rocky, scattered with patches of gorse and wildflowers.

She heard water trickling nearby and headed toward the sound. At the tiny stream she discovered a sort of beaten earth track. It wasn't exactly a road, but it was a sign of habitation. So she followed it along a narrow ridge that led down into a wooded valley. Just as Maddie reached a slightly wider path, a horseman appeared from around a turn.

He had long brown hair, was bare-legged, wore a thigh-length dark yellow shirt and a plaid cape. The hilt of a claymore was visible over his left shoulder. He was dressed, in fact, exactly like an ancient barbarian Highlander.

Maddie peered at him for one confused moment. Then she put her hands on her hips and demanded, "Toby Coltrane, what are you doing in that getup?"

He looked about as out of place in modern Scotland as the small airplane back up on the hillside would have been in the Middle Ages. Besides, Toby was from Montana and didn't have a drop of Scots blood in him, as far as she knew.

"You're supposed to be in Glasgow," she reminded him as he continued to glower down at her from his incongruous presence on the big horse.

He was leaner than she remembered. His features were sharply chiseled and far too dangerous-looking for anyone's good. He glared at her out of ice blue eyes. Those unfamiliar eyes flicked over her, coldly assessing. "At least you're not a Harboth."

She had to be dreaming.

Dream or not, Maddie considered running for it as he got down off his horse. She backed up a pace as he stalked toward her.

Rowan Murray grabbed the red-haired woman by the arm. She was a stranger to him, dressed in odd gray clothes. She wore a close-fitting necklace around her slender throat. It looked to be twisted strands of thin gold and copper chains. The necklace was proof that she would fulfill the White Lady's prophecy.

"Are you wed?" he demanded as he pulled the woman close.

Maddie looked wildly at the angry stranger who had to be Toby. "What?

"Are you wed?" This time the words were even fiercer.

She was annoyed despite her sudden terror. "You know very well I'm not."

"Have you a man of your own?"

This was insane. All of it. The meteors. The plane crash. Especially finding Toby dressed like a Highlander and asking strange questions.

"No," she told him. How could he, of all people, ask her such a thing?

"Well, then," he said, voice rough with fury. "I suppose I'll have to marry you."

2

"What?"

Rowan tugged the stranger toward his horse.

"What are you talking about?" Her voice rose to an angry shout. "This isn't funny. Let go of me!"

Rowan grasped her around her waist and settled her on the broad back of his mount. He had questions for her, but he kept them to himself for now. He wanted to be inside the stout gates of his stronghold before he encountered any more strangers. The chances were there were armed men about, from some raiding ship moored on the coast, he guessed. For he could think of no other way this stranger who was to be his bride had come onto his lands. The White Lady had not said he would have to fight for the woman, but he didn't intend to take the chance that she'd left that little part out of the prophecy.

He showed her his dagger, and said, "Be quiet."

She gasped at the sight of the bare blade, but said no more. He mounted behind her, put one arm around her waist, and kicked the horse into motion.

"Why should I be quiet?" She snarled the words after a tense pause. He could feel her body tremble in his embrace.

The woman was spirited but frightened, and he could well understand her feeling. Understand he might, but there was nothing for it but to get on with what needed to be done. He kept his attention on reaching safety, but couldn't ignore the feel of soft, womanly curves beneath his hand, or help but notice the bright color and springy texture of the thick hair that brushed his cheek. Hair that was but a bit below shoulder length, far too short for his liking. He'd have her grow it out when they were wed.

Maddie fought her confusion, as she had for hours. She did her best to keep calm as the horse hurtled down the track, not because of the threat of her captor's knife, but because concentrating on staying calm helped her not think about the knife. The sword. The strange clothes. Or the hard-muscled body so close to hers. She was almost too aware of the steely arm around her waist and the bare thighs that brushed against her hips.

She had dreamed about Toby many times, but never like this. Well, she'd had erotic thoughts about how his body would feel, but the weaponry had never been part of her fantasies. This had to be a dream, a phantasm, but Maddie was fully prepared to deny that she was the one having it. She was too practical to conjure up anything so outrageous.

He had said something about marrying her. That was certainly something she wanted Toby to say, but this was hardly the time or place. What she needed now was a logical explanation of everything that had happened. She wanted to ask him some questions, but he'd been rather adamant about her keeping quiet.

Then again, who was he to give her orders? Other than a possible figment of her imagination, and armed to the teeth. She decided not to let these considerations stop her. "What's going on?"

"Hush."

"No."

His grip tightened. He leaned close. His breath brushed across her ear. The intimate nearness sent a shiver through her. *Fear,* Maddie told herself, as he said, "Obedience is a virtue in a wife."

"I'm not your wife." And she wasn't going to be, no matter how much she'd always wanted him, if he kept being rude to her. "We have to get a few things straightened out first."

"I have spoken my intent," he answered. "That is enough."

"Being enigmatic is not a virtue in anyone," she responded.

Rowan stopped the horse and dragged the woman to the ground. Not to continue the conversation, but because of what he'd heard coming up behind them. This was no time for talk. The Hunters were on their trail.

Though they moved almost silently, Rowan's hearing was trained to detect their approach. He knew the swords they carried were silver, or crystal, or obsidian. They feared the cold iron of his own weapons, but their blades were sharp. And there were at least three of them. No doubt they had their black hounds with them as well.

He shoved the woman to the ground. "Stay."

Rowan thought of the strange lights of the night before, followed by the appearance of this strangely dressed woman, and now the presence of the beings behind them. Somewhere there was a connection. The White Lady had sent the woman to him for his clan. Rowan would not let the fair folk interfere with his saving his people.

He could feel her glare against his back as he hurried to his saddlebag. He drew out a pouch of salt mixed with herbs, then sent the animal on its way with a swat on the rump. He must not face the Hunters on horseback, but with his feet on the strong earth of his own land. He turned back to his bride. She sat where he'd put her, arms crossed beneath her ample bosom. She looked confused, but at least she was obedient for the moment.

Rowan quickly sprinkled the salt in a circle around her. "Don't move," he warned, "and they won't see you."

Maddie was thoroughly frustrated. "Who they?"

He turned his back to her without bothering to answer. She watched the play of muscles in his arms as he reached up and pulled the long sword from the sheath on his back. It came out with a dangerous metal rasp. He leaned forward slightly, the claymore held before him in a two-handed grip.

Who was he prepared to use it against? What was going on here?

She nearly shouted, but then the circle he'd traced around her started to glow, and the light shot up around her in an enveloping arc. Then it turned a shimmering, lustrous white. For a few moments she felt as though she were trapped inside a pearl. Then she felt nothing as her senses went blank once more.

Rowan faced the trio of Hunters squarely, though the sight of them was disturbing. Theirs was a beauty that inflamed the senses, though he had no desire to mingle with any of their immortal kind. Still, to merely behold the fair folk straight on was an invitation to commit every sin of sensual indulgence. Images of warm naked flesh and the musky scent of lust teased at his controlled emotions. He recognized that he was being drawn into a spell even as his blood warmed with hot need, sang with longing. The nearness of the woman in the charmed circle called out to him. His body craved her touch, even though he forced his mind to concentrate the business of the moment.

"The sunlight belongs to me and mine," Rowan told the newcomers. "We do not walk in your moonlight world without invitation."

The tallest of the fair folk put up a hand. Silver hair floated about her thin shoulders, and her great oval eyes were silver as well, with hardly any white in them. She carried no weapon, but the other two had black stone swords held at the ready. "Peace, leader of the Mermaid's Children. Your father granted us the right to hunt in your lands, for your stepmother's sake."

"My father is dead," he reminded the fairy woman. "His wife returned to her own land."

She frowned in puzzlement, and touched the tip of her long, pointed ear. "Is this so? How oddly time passes in your world. I thought I talked to your father just a few days ago."

"Our years are your days," he reminded her.

"So someone once told me." She fluttered her long fingered hands, and a butterfly came to rest on her thumb. "Or perhaps I am remembering this conversation before we have it."

"Perhaps."

Rowan thought he heard beautiful music. The air in the clearing was scented with a concentration of all the flowers of spring. The day was ripe with promises of love.

It was the fairy spell that brought all these images to his senses. Rowan fought hard against it, though his blood flamed and pulsed with ever-growing need. Still, he thought he could feel the soft tendrils of the his promised bride's wine-red hair brush against his cheek. He felt her gaze caressing him, the blue color of her eyes darkened with desire. Her mouth opened to welcome his kiss.

The images were conjured up out of his own imagination and fairy magic, this he knew. The knowledge that it wasn't really real kept him from turning, from leaping through the protection of the salt circle and revealing the woman's presence as he fell on her to rut.

Though his limbs quivered faintly with hard-held craving, Rowan kept his wits, and his attention on the Hunters. He took a deep breath, then said, "If you hunt among my folk for bed partners to pleasure you, I will see you dead."

The fairy woman drew herself up proudly. She shone with impossible, haughty beauty. Rowan neither looked away nor ran to embrace her. It was hard not to move, but he knew his lust would not be satisfied by her immortal kind.

The fairy woman forgot her hauteur, and smiled enticingly. She held out her hand to him. "We dance in the moonlight with those mortals who come to us of their own free will."

Rowan shook his head, as much to clear it as in negation. He knew that her words were not completely true, for he could feel her trying to bend his will to hers even as she spoke of free choice.

"I will not be your mortal lover," he said. He gestured around the clearing. "You weave this net of lust around me to divert me from your true purpose in my lands."

Her smile was as sharp as a blade. Her words were piercing. "I set magic loose at our meeting," she admitted. "But it is your own loneliness that gives the spell the shape of mortal desire."

Her words sank deeply into him, though he denied their truth to himself. He had too many cares, too many people dependent on him, to allow himself such a selfish emotion as loneliness.

"What do you hunt, if not lovers?" he demanded.

"Nothing to do with mortal kind," the fairy leader answered. She glanced at the warriors who stood patiently beside her. "Our prey is a hawk. The great bird that soared, screeching through our sky last night."

Rowan lifted his head sharply. "You heard that? Saw the lights?"

The fairy fluttered her hands again, while her companions glanced at each other. The creatures were nervous, Rowan realized. Of course they would not tell him the whole truth; the fair folk never did.

"What was it?" he asked. "What sort of hawk, even a magical one, flies at night?"

"The bird belongs to us," the leader replied. "Our

mistress sends us to bring it to her. That is our hunt," she said with stern finality. She crossed her arms beneath her small breasts. Her expression was haughty, and utterly inhuman. "We seek what is ours. You will not hinder us."

If some magical creature had indeed escaped from their world into his, he wanted it gone. He wanted them gone. Enflamed by magic or not, his blood burned with growing lust. It made the effort to deal with the fairy hunters more difficult by the moment. He wanted to get on with his wedding and saving his people. Even more than the wedding, he wanted his wedding night. He didn't think he would be able to wait. The fairy magic had seen to that.

He forced his attention to remain on the immortal intruders for a while longer. "Hunt, then. Take from my lands only what is rightfully yours, and we have no quarrel."

The fairy nodded. "Agreed."

Rowan watched, with effort, but warily alert, as the Hunters moved back. It seemed as though they took but one step—then they were gone. Though the eerie sound of their fey laughter rang after them in the clearing.

Rowan took no mind of the noise. With the fair folk gone, he was alone with the red-haired mortal. She was his woman. He meant to have her.

3

She must have passed out again. She didn't know why she kept doing that, but she didn't like it one little bit. The world just kept coming up and hitting her in the face. The first time it had gone dark; this time everything had gone white. The effect had been the same. Except she was thoroughly annoyed when she came to this time.

Maddie got to her feet as Toby turned to her. "First off, wha—"

The look on his face told her he wasn't interested in talking. He tossed his sword aside. Maddie did not find his sudden lack of weaponry reassuring. She took a hasty step back, but he was very fast.

He swept down on her, all hard muscle and hot-blooded determination. Within moments he had one arm around her waist. She struggled, but there was no breaking his iron grip. He pulled her close. His other hand tangled in the hair at the nape of her neck. He pulled her head up, and his lips came down on hers just as she opened her mouth to scream. The sound was muffled by the sharp thrust of his tongue. His lips ground against hers with bruising possessiveness as he caught her even closer. She was aware of taut muscle beneath the rough wool and linen pressed against her skin. She was more aware of the big hand that pressed her to him, the heat that radiated from his palm, like a small sun sending out flares at the very base of her spine. His long fingers circled her waist in a powerful grip. Urgent need radiated from him, from his touch, from the way his mouth moved over hers as though he was drawing life from her.

She'd always wanted Toby to kiss her, but not like this. This was too much, too fast, too soon, too *sexual*. It was all wrong, and she was scared to death. Maddie was almost overcome by panic at being surrounded by such an overwhelming male presence.

She also knew what a Scotsman wore under his kilt.

She could feel his erection pressing hard against her thigh. Desperation forced her to drive her knee up hard with all the force she could manage into her assailant's groin.

Rowan howled with pain. Lust was forgotten. He thrust the woman away as he automatically bent to protect his crotch. As his head came down, a fist caught him hard under the chin.

He fell to his knees, with lights behind his eyes and agony in his privates. It didn't help his situation when he felt the tip of his own sword nudge him in the ribs just as he began to recover from the woman's attack.

"Keep your hands off me, Toby Coltrane."

Her words came out in an angry, breathless snarl. He heard the quaver of fear beneath. Rowan looked up a long way to meet her gaze, and saw the fear there as

well. He blamed her not one bit for her reaction to him.
And who the devil was Toby Coltrane?

It took him a few more moments to find his voice
around the ragged gasps of pain. "Give me the
sword, lass."

"Get real."

He was as real as he was ever going to be. The pain
certainly was real. The need to have her had been
real, even if not of his volition. The need was still there,
though shoved to the back of his mind by discomfort,
shame, and the immediacy of the situation. He didn't
think he was still being affected by the fair folk's spell,
though. There was something about the way the woman
stood bravely facing him that called to him. He still
wanted to claim her, and would, but his aching privates
warned him that it would not be in the near future.

He could tell by the slight quivering of her arms that
she was having trouble holding five feet of sharpened
steel steady. Rowan got slowly to his feet. If she'd had
sense she'd run him through, but he took the chance
that she would back away instead. She did. But the
claymore was still in her hands.

He hurt in the most vulnerable place a man could,
but he kept his attention on the woman.

"You did well," he told her, and briefly touched his
aching jaw. "Two blows instead of one are always better for felling a man."

"Unfortunately, you're still conscious."

"Aye."

"Where am I?" Her gaze darted nervously around
the clearing. "What are you doing here? How did either
of us get here? Why are you wearing a kilt? Why did
you kiss me?"

Maddie had no idea why she was standing here asking stupid questions. Especially the last one. There was a frightened voice in the back of her mind telling her she should run from this man. She'd been running *to* him before all this madness started, but now everything was different. There was something in the way he looked at her that shook her to the core. He didn't look angry. He looked determined. That was worse.

"What are you doing here?" she asked again, and hated the hysteria that went with the question. She had to stay calm, in control. Her mouth ached from his harsh kiss. Even though she'd stopped him, she was still trembling with reaction. She felt different, connected as she never had before, all because he'd kissed her. She didn't like it. "Where are we, Toby?"

His features went harder, it that was possible. "Will you stop calling me that, woman?"

"It's your name."

He bristled. "It is most certainly is not."

Maddie studied him closely. Maybe it had been two years since she'd been back to Montana, but this was the man she remembered. Only with a bad temper, an authentic costume, and an overactive libido. "If you're not Toby, who are you?"

"Rowan Murray." He gestured. The slight movement was imperious, definitive. His expression as possessive as his kiss had been. "We're in my lands. Near my stronghold of Cape Wrath."

This was the first useful information he'd given her. Maddie was so relieved to finally know where she was that she almost didn't notice him take a slow step to her left. The man who claimed not to be Toby Coltrane had cold eyes, cold as ice chips, narrowed and intently focused on her. She forced herself to concentrate on the information and not on being intimidated by the look in those eyes. If he was in pain, he hid it well. The sword was heavy, and the man—Rowan Murray—was way too calm. He hadn't been calm when he'd kissed her.

She certainly wasn't calm. She hefted the sword higher as he took another step. "Stop that." Maybe he wasn't Toby. Maybe she should run. "Which way's the nearest town?" There would be people there. A phone.

Rowan Murray's gaze shifted. Maddie didn't have time to turn. Rowan sprang forward. The sword was wrenched from her hands and she was knocked to the ground. Rowan loomed above her and raised the long sword over his head.

He was going to kill her. She knew it.

Then she saw the black-furred, snarling, fanged *thing* rushing toward her. Maddie screamed. Rowan stepped between her and the attacking animal. The sword flashed down—the sharp metal almost seemed to glow in a sudden burst of sunlight. There was a splash of red blood on black fur as the creature went down.

Maddie scrambled to her feet and fought the impulse to hide behind Rowan's back. She forced herself to look at the animal that had attacked her. It wasn't a bear or a wolf, but a bit like both. It had red eyes, faceted like an insect's.

"What is that?"

Rowan took care to clean his sword and sheath it safely away before he turned to the woman. When he grasped her arm, she was docile enough from shock not to try to pull away. The fair folk and their spell were gone. The beast they'd left behind out of sheer perversity was dead. There was no magic left in the clearing, just a tired man and frightened woman.

"Time we were on our way."

She looked at him. There were questions in her eyes, but for the moment she was too bewildered to voice them. He tightened his grip and tugged her forward. Time to go home and get married.

Maddie didn't know what to think. She looked over her shoulder at the dead beast as Rowan pushed her ahead of him. *It's a bear,* she decided. It couldn't be anything else. It was only her terror that had given the animal an unfamiliar shape. It refused to look like a bear to her tired senses, so she looked determinedly away. Only one thing that had happened in the last few minutes made any sense.

He'd saved her life.

She was still his prisoner. She suspected that one or both of them was insane, or at least hallucinating. He'd assaulted her—and she'd assaulted him back. But he'd saved her life. Without any fuss or bother. Without saying a word. He'd just slain what appeared to be a monster.

And now he was taking her who knew where. His grip was hard but not painful. She cast a furtive look at his face. The stoically calm Rowan Murray didn't look as if he'd just killed a mythical beastie. Or as if he'd ardently kissed her a few minutes before that. He was totally expressionless, as though his lean features were chiseled out of Scottish granite. Expressionless, but a hint of color streaked the Celtic fair skin that hinted at some strong emotion beneath his outward calm.

Suddenly she believed that he was not the man she'd

been going to Glasgow to meet. He looked just like him, but somehow wasn't him. There had to be some logical explanation to all of this. It probably involved her being in an intensive care unit after a plane crash. Or maybe she hadn't survived the crash and the after-life was an illogical, downright annoying place.

"This is all ridiculous," Maddie announced, and was ignored.

Rowan felt the woman's gaze on him, and wished she'd look away. He hoped she didn't ask him any more questions. There was nothing he could say by way of apology for his dishonorable behavior. He wanted to get her home, keep her safe, have his way with her by wedded right rather than uncontrollable rut. He wanted to forget about the doings of the last hour, or at least start over, and make things right. He just didn't want to talk about it.

He kept his attention on guiding her before him down the narrow, rocky path to the ford. He did not think about his sore jaw and aching privates, though every step jolted something that hurt.

4

Aidan waited at the ford, along with Rowan's horse. "Who's that?" Aidan asked.

"Where's Meg?" Rowan answered.

"Who's Meg?" the woman asked.

She sounded irritated. Rowan had some faint hope that she might be jealous at hearing him speak another woman's name, ridiculous as he knew the hope was. The last thing he needed or wanted was a jealous woman. She was confused and frightened by everything he did, and nothing more. She had every right to be both, even as he had every right to be curious at how and why she was in his lands and was now part of his life. Then he recalled that he didn't want this sunset-haired stranger or any other woman as part of his life, and his irritation returned.

He turned his temper on his brother. "And why did you not do as I told you?"

As usual, Aidan refused to be abashed. He laughed, and his merry-eyed attention was directed at the woman as he answered. "I tried and I tried. Argued and cajoled Walter, I did, but to no purpose. Walter refused to believe my errand. Said you wouldn't command any woman to a tryst. Said I only wanted Meg for myself."

"You do."

"Who's Meg?"

"Hush."

"Aye. But I would have brought her to you if I could." Aidan was grinning openly at the woman now, as though she should share in his teasing of Rowan. Aidan pointed toward the village. "Should I go back and try ag—?"

"Mind your tongue." Rowan took his mount's reins from his brother, then lifted his intended bride onto the horse's back.

As Rowan swung up behind her, Aidan asked, "How'd you lose the horse? And who is this wom—?"

"Your mother's folk were in the clearing."

Aidan nodded. "I thought there was a fey taste to the air today."

"You might have told me."

Aidan touched the tip of one ear. "I forget you're half-blind that way."

"Fortunately, only half."

"Which is more fairy sight than most mortals have, brother."

"Fairy sight? What's that?"

"Hush," Rowan told the curious woman.

"Stop telling me to hush."

"She's willful."

"Aye." Rowan answered Aidan as he wrapped his arms around her. She stiffened in his embrace. He kicked the horse into motion. "Your mother taught me well." He had to grant that the fairy wife had given him that much, though he granted it grudgingly.

Maddie really wished Rowan would stop touching her, even if it meant she'd probably fall off her precarious perch if he did. It wasn't that long a fall; the animal was really more of a sturdy mountain pony than a full-sized horse. Even a few bruises would be better than being surrounded by Rowan Murray's considerable, unfamiliar familiar presence.

She also wished someone would talk to her. She really wished she weren't right back where she'd started when she'd first met the barbarian horseman, captured and controlled and still in the dark—only more so. Rowan Murray's embrace when he'd forced her up on the horse the first time had been disturbing enough; it felt far more intimate now that she knew he wasn't Toby. And she was more confused than ever. She decided to concentrate on her confusion as Rowan and his cheerful companion rode toward the distant sound of the sea.

A few minutes later a walled settlement came into view, perched on a rocky cliffside that leaned out above the ocean. The stream they'd been following joined the sea at the base of the hill. The track crossed the stream there and wound up to the village gates. The water stretched away, gray and glassy, into forever from a cove dotted with numerous craggy islets. There were a few tiny, oddly shaped sailboats out on the water. A few more of the primitive boats were lined up on the shingle above the tide line. Nothing about the place looked right.

As they approached the ford the road widened enough for the other man to ride up beside them.

Maddie received a friendly smile when she looked his way.

"I'm Aidan. Your necklace has a pretty glow about it."

These people were crazy.

"Uh-huh."

And dangerous, she recalled. At least Rowan was. Rather than risk finding out that the equally oddly dressed and even more strangely spoken Aidan was a violent lunatic, Maddie managed to pull her lips into a semblance of a smile for the young man's benefit. He gave her a friendly nod, then rode on ahead.

She didn't think her necklace was glowing. It wasn't even her necklace. In fact, she'd almost forgotten she was wearing it. She could barely remember why she'd put it on. So much had happened in the last few hours that wearing an artifact that technically belonged to the British government was the least of her worries.

When she reached up to touch the chain, Rowan grabbed her hand before it reached her throat. He twined his fingers with hers and pushed her hand back down. Now she was holding hands with the man who'd kidnapped her. Kissed her. Saved her life. Wasn't this the man she wanted to do all those things, not counting the kidnapping part?

Maddie was almost dizzy with confusion, and awareness of the texture of Rowan's wide palm, of the contrast of his strong, callused fingers covering hers. She was not a small woman, but the disparity between them made her feel almost delicate, definitely female. The evident differences between her and Rowan Murray evoked a strong feeling in her. Strangely, it was not fear. Vulnerability, yes, but not fear. She shivered, and told herself it was from the cold wind that blew off the ocean as they approached the settlement. Only she wasn't cold at all. There was a warmth in her that was deep down and totally new.

Maddie fought her strange reactions and forced herself to study her surroundings. They'd crossed the stream and headed up the hillside. There were a few stone houses and thatched huts outside the walls of the fortress. Shaggy black cattle and some sheep grazed in pastures marked off by drystone walls. Chickens and geese scratched in house yards beside the garden plots they passed. People gathered around them as they approached the fortress gate. These people were dressed as crudely as her captor, ill-groomed folk in tartan, homespun, and leather. In short, the place did not look at all like a modern Scottish village. Not a shop in sight, not a car, not a post box or the ubiquitous blue of British Telecom phone booths. No power lines, or satellite dishes, or television antennas. No pubs.

Maddie craned her head around to glare at Rowan. "Where are we really?"

"Cape Wrath."

Maddie almost laughed. "I know for a fact that Cape Wrath has at least one espresso bar. Or Durness does. It's the nearest town. No one actually lives at Cape Wrath."

"This is my home."

"Fine. But it's not really Cape Wrath."

Who are you, really? Rowan wondered as his bride voiced her skepticism. She would learn that he never lied, but he saw no reason to point this out to her before she was ready to believe it. *Who are you other than mine? And what is espresso?*

The guards on the gate stepped aside to let them through. The crowd followed them into the courtyard. Rowan did not voice either assertions or his own questions about the stranger in his arms as he brought the horse to a halt before the chapel door. After he helped her to the ground he looked around at his watching people.

No, she was not his, he realized as he met many a curious look. Wanting her for his bed was just an illusion left imprinted on all his senses by the fairy magic. She'd been sent to him, yes, but for his people. He was to marry her to save his clan. His connection to her was only one of duty. He must be on guard to keep any selfish impulses to have the woman only for himself at bay. It was a mistake to care too much. That was another lesson his fairy stepmother had taught him.

Magic had clearly brought this woman here—some magic to do with last night's lights in the sky. The fair folk had hunted her, of that he was sure. She was clearly lost and had thought him to be someone she knew. Her odd clothing and confusing questions showed her to be from some strange land very different from his own. Perhaps she was some mortal woman stolen from her own kind by fairy magic. It could well be that she had escaped from the kingdom under the hills in a time and place different from her own, and took him for some ancestor or descendant of his own. She might not even remember the time spent among the fair folk; those who were taken often didn't. Or she might be one of them playing some joke on mortal kind.

They might want her back, she might want to return to them, but she was here now. His. Given to him to use as he needed. His to protect, not to cherish, to command, not to coddle. To breed with, if that would help his people, but not to love. For fairy love was as fleeting, as false, as fairy gold. His father had learned that to the cost of all the clan.

Rowan would not make the mistake of loving the savior of his people.

"Can you go into the church?" he asked as they stood before the door.

They were outside a low stone building. Maddie looked around for anything resembling a church. "I beg your pardon?" She decided to forget about the odd pronouncements of the grim Highlander beside her, and looked at the equally forbidding group gathered nearby. "Excuse me," she said, "but could I use a phone? Or call the police?" No one moved, or said a word. "I've been kidnapped," she went on. "Abducted by this man. I've been in a plane crash—I think. I'm not sure about that part. Would one of you please call the police? Or a doctor, 'cause I might have a concussion. At least, I seem to be hallucinating." She waved her hand in front of her. "Hello? Is anyone home?"

People continued to stare at her. Rowan Murray pulled her around to face him. He loomed, and glowered down at her. She was just under six feet tall, and she estimated that he was maybe an inch over six feet, so his having the ability to loom over her was more a psychological than a physical feat. She also began to suspect that he had an infinite variety of unreadable dour expressions.

"You are a very uncooperative hallucination," she told him.

"Can you go into the church?" he repeated.

"Sure. Where is it?"

His glower became thunderous. He opened his mouth, but before he could snarl anything rude two women pushed their way through the crowd to them. Aidan followed the women. Rowan turned his attention on them. So did Maddie, though she remained aware that Rowan's hand was firmly wrapped around her upper arm. There was no escaping the man, apparently.

One of the women was tall, with a willowy figure, and young, in her late teens, Maddie guessed. She had masses of shining black hair. The other was a few years older, also attractive, though shorter and more on the buxom side than her companion. Maddie thought she detected a family resemblance between them, Aidan, and Rowan.

The buxom woman planted herself in front of Rowan, her hands on her hips. She had quite a way to look up to meet his gaze, but she met it squarely. "What news do you bring from the White Lady?" she asked. "And what's this Aidan says about a wedding?" She glanced briefly at Maddie. "Who is this, cousin?"

"My name's Maddie," Maddie answered for herself. "I don't know anything about a wedding. I just know that I have to get out of here. Do you have a fax machine I can use?"

Rowan wondered why he hadn't bothered to ask the woman her name. It seemed wrong that someone else would know it before him. He frowned reprovingly at Maddie, as though it was her fault that he'd been ill-mannered. "She's to be my bride, Rosemary," Rowan said to his cousin. "I've just been trying to find out if she's mortal or fair folk so I can know whether we'll be married inside the church or out."

"Maybe I could call a cab?"

"She's mortal, though magic touched." Aidan said.

"So I thought, since she can grasp cold iron, but I don't think she's sure just what world she belongs in."

Maddie glared at her captor. "Of course I'm mortal. You, however, are nuts. Does a bus come through here?" she asked the woman. "A train?"

"Then we'll have the vows indoors."

"What vows?" Maddie asked.

Rosemary asked the question at the same time, then went on, "You're not marrying today, Rowan Murray. I'll not have it."

"Me either," Maddie concurred. If she married anyone it would be Toby Coltrane, not this look-alike barbarian. Who hadn't even asked.

"Hush, woman," Rowan ordered.

"Don't you tell me to hush. I don't even know you."

"That does not matter. You're to be my wife."

Maddie almost laughed, but was afraid she might get too hysterical to stop if she did. The situation might be out of control, but she wasn't going to be. "Why do you keep talking about marrying me?" she demanded. Nobody had ever talked about marrying her, at least not before now. Yesterday the idea of somebody wanting her had been appealing. Now it was annoying and frightening.

Rowan sighed. He looked at Rosemary, and his sister Micaela who stood at her side, at the grinning Aidan, and beyond them to the faces of his waiting clansfolk. He looked everywhere but at the woman who probably deserved an explanation. He was impatient to get this over with. He was annoyed that his commands as laird of the clan would be questioned. He felt uncomfortable about not giving this lost stranger any choice in the matter. He hoped that the sooner it was irrevocably settled, the sooner she could adjust to what must be.

"Meg said you sent for her," Micaela spoke up. "Or that Aidan claimed you did."

"I did."

"Why?"

"To marry her."

Micaela pointed at Maddie. "Aidan said you wanted to marry the lady in gray."

Rowan looked at Maddie and noticed the color of her odd, baggy clothes for the first time. Micaela was a gentle lamb, with an eye for the details of feminine fashion and a longing for a wedding of her own. Though this was a secret she didn't think he knew. "I will marry this woman," he answered Micaela.

"She should have flowers in her hair."

He sighed at her foolish notions. "Then fetch some quickly."

"What about Meg?"

This was going to take more explanation than he wanted to give, but he supposed he'd best get on with it if he didn't want to stand here all day. He told them as quickly as he could about his vow to the White Lady to wed the first woman he saw.

"Which was why you wanted Meg," both Aidan and Micaela said over the murmurs of the crowd when he was done speaking.

He nodded. "That's why I wanted Meg."

"Well, Meg doesn't want you," the pretty girl in question spoke up from the back of the group. "It's a good thing my father wouldn't let me go with Aidan."

Rowan blushed at such a firm rejection by a girl who should have been flattered to be his wife. "For shame," he told her. "I am your laird."

"And a fine one you are, but you were trying to cheat the White Lady. I'll have none of that."

"And so she shouldn't. For shame, Rowan Murray." Rosemary wagged an admonishing finger under his nose. "There will be no wedding," she went on.

"No," Micaela agreed.

Rowan drew himself up. "I'll not be thwarted in this. 'Tis for everyone's good."

"I'm with them," Maddie said. She smiled at the two women who'd objected to the man's strange plan. "Will you please let go of me?"

Rowan scowled at her. "No."

"I said please."

"You'll not leave my side until the vows are spoken, and not to go very far even then."

She shook her head. "I never said I'd marry anybody."

"I didn't ask."

The man was infuriating! "No, you didn't."

"I need not ask. You are the White Lady's answer to our problems."

Infuriating and stubborn. While he looked at her with set jaw and the ice back in his eyes, she tried to explain his mistake one more time. "I don't know who this White Lady is, but I didn't show up to fulfill her requirements. It was just a coincidence that I ran in to you, and a very weird one at that. I'm lost, or hallucinating. Either way, I have to find out what happened." She looked to Rosemary for help. "Can I go now? Is there somewhere around here where I could rent a car?"

"Where's the priest?" Rowan asked.

"Right behind you, lad," Father Andrew said from the chapel doorway. Rowan turned his head to look at the big man as the priest went on, "Have you her father's permission?"

"I'm not getting married. I think I'm going to try to wake up now."

"Have you a father?" Rowan asked her.

"Perhaps you didn't hear what I just said."

"Answer the question."

The coldness in his look sent a chill through her, but Maddie refused to be intimidated. "My father's in Montana. Why don't you call him and ask my opinion of marriage?" *Just don't get my mother*, she added to herself. *She'd tell you to go ahead with the ceremony for my own good.*

"It's not a high opinion, is it?"

"No."

Never mind what she'd confessed to her mother before getting on the plane. She wanted someone in her life all right, but she wasn't ready to think about any permanent relationship—with anyone but Toby, that is.

"Nor is mine." He put his hands on her shoulders and leaned closer. His voice was soft and menacing when he told her, "You'll do as I say, woman. You'll do it now, and you'll do it without fussing."

Close as they were, she could see the bruise on his jaw where she'd hit him. For all his barbaric posturing, he hadn't retaliated for the blows she'd dealt him. She gambled that he wouldn't now.

"No."

Rosemary forced her way between them, making Rowan take a step back. For the first time in hours

Maddie was free of his touch. It made her feel oddly vulnerable and alone among all these people.

"The lass is right," Rosemary told Rowan. "You can not be married."

Maddie sighed with relief. "Well, thank God someone sees it my—"

"First we must gather the clan and hold a feast," Rosemary insisted. "The omens must be read."

"The stars consulted," Micaela added.

"The proper spells read over the marriage bed," Rosemary went on. "Then we'll have the wedding."

Maddie's groan was lost in the agreeing shout that went up from the crowd.

5

"I love my kindred," Rowan said to the woman seated beside him. As she gave him a wary glance, he went on, "I'd love for them all to go to the devil for just one night and leave us in peace."

Her reaction was a blank stare. When he reached out to put his hand over hers she promptly folded her hands into a tight double fist in her lap. He accepted this rebuff by settling back in his chair. Rowan tried to ignore the woman and retreated into his more usual morose silence.

Maddie almost smiled at her captor's frustrated comment. She understood about large, interfering families; she came from one herself. If he hadn't been talking about spending the night with her, she might have made some equally sardonic, understanding reply. As it was, she really didn't have anything to be sardonic or understanding about. She thought she should treat the temptation to respond to the man on any level as some kind of aberration on her part. It was just because he looked so much like someone she loved and desired. That the aberration also probably took place on some basic, hormonal, female-response-to-dominant-male level was downright embarrassing.

Besides, it would be like teasing a tiger. He might be sleek and beautiful to look at, but you could get yourself killed mistaking a quiet beast for a kitty cat.

So she tried to stay as inconspicuous as her place beside him would allow. Being in the middle of a crowd made her feel only a little more secure. As Rowan pointed out, the crowd consisted of his extended family, and this strange, boisterous group was gathered in the cold, shabby hall for a wedding party. Though Maddie neither understood nor liked the reason for the gathering, she hoped it went on all night.

Though the people were strange, the setting was downright bizarre. The wide room took up the second floor of a stone tower. They'd entered via a ladder that led up to the outside door of the tower. The ladder had been pulled inside and a heavy door fastened in place as soon as all the Murrays were within. Maddie felt claustrophobic at being so closed in. Not only was she shut up with a bunch of crazy people, she knew there was no escaping once the log-sized pole was lowered into massive brackets that held it across the door. She'd been shaking with terror at this realization when Rowan led her off to sit beside him at one of the tables. It had taken her quite a while to compose herself enough to survey the room, if not the situation, calmly.

Only wall torches and a bonfire in a central hearth gave any light or warmth, and not much of either. The place was smoky, the low rafters covered in soot since the tiny windows up near the ceiling let in more air than drifted out. It looked as if a whole cow was being roasted over the fire. The smell was not particularly appetizing. A dignified man stood near the fire, his graying hair glimmering in the firelight as he sang. His rich baritone voice rose easily above conversation and the clatter of dishes. The whole setting made her feel as if she'd fallen into an illustration for a Walter Scott novel.

She had seen the ruins of several medieval Highland fortresses in the year she'd worked in Scotland, and had talked a lot with her archaeologist friends. She knew there were no intact castles like this one in Scotland. That this place, these people, existed made no sense. That she was sitting in a dark, smoky room with them made less sense. The airplane on the mountainside was impossible, and telling herself she was hallucinating was just a cowardly way of trying to cope with this altered reality. She was too uncomfortable for it not to be happening.

"I wish someone would explain it all to me," she said, unable to stifle her frustration no matter how much she wanted to be inconspicuous.

Rowan leaned forward and poured a cup full from the pitcher Rosemary had set before him a few moments before. He passed it to his bride. "This might help."

She sniffed the contents of the cup, gave him one of her skeptical looks, then downed the drink in one long gulp. Her eyes widened with pleasure. "Not bad."

"Rosemary brews the best mead in all Sutherland," he told her. "Or so she's happy to tell everyone."

Maddie set the cup down before her, and decided to try a conversation with Rowan Murray rather than to continue telling him she didn't want to marry him. "I shouldn't be in Sutherland," she explained. "We were heading for Glasgow, that's way south of here."

"So it is. We went to a fair in the village of Glasgow once. I thought little of the place."

She watched his reactions carefully as she went on. "I work on one of the North Sea oil rigs, but I was spending my vacation visiting friends on the Isle of Lewis. I'm a systems engineer. And her majesty's government isn't going to take kindly to your abducting an American citizen, you know."

The one thing he knew for certain was that Maddie had a lovely voice. It was deep and melodious. It made him wonder what the sound of her singing a babe to sleep would be like. He wondered what it would sound like late at night when she held him close and murmured love words into his ear. He thought that he must be careful not to become entranced by her voice, but as for what she'd just said, none of it made a bit of sense.

"I know where the North Sea lies," he told her, "and the Isle of Lewis, but no queen rules Scotland, nor ever has."

"What about Mary Stuart?" When he just stared at her in confusion, Maddie added, "You know, the one who got her head chopped off by the English?"

"I've heard the Sassenachs below the border are barbarians, but they've killed no queen of ours. The last I heard old William the Lion still sat his throne in the south." And as long as the old king stayed where he belonged, well below the Great Glen, that was fine with Rowan. His loyalty was more or less with the MacDonald who styled himself Lord of the Isles.

She sighed, and closed her eyes for a moment. "I've

studied Scottish history," she said when she looked at
him again. "William the Lion ruled from the late eleven
hundreds to the early twelve hundreds. Died in 1214, I
think."

"Will he?" The date of a king's passing was a useful
thing to know. Perhaps she would save his people with
foreknowledge and that was why she had been sent to
him. "Have you the Sight, then? Rosemary will be
pleased. She's always saying we need someone with a
stronger sense of foreknowledge in the family." Rowan
wasn't particularly pleased, though. He was sick of all
the dealings his clan had with magic.

Maddie considered the way Rowan answered her
comments and questions. The way he phrased things
disturbed her, and made her suspicious. "This is sometime *before* 1214?" she asked carefully.

"Aye."

"But—that can't be."

Her face was turned toward him, her expression
lost. He couldn't stop himself from cupping her soft
cheek in his hand. "Nothing makes sense," he told
her as reassuringly as he could. "Not to me, not to
you. We have our fate to face together and that's all
there is to it. Don't fret. If the fair folk took you
from your own time there's nothing that can be done
about it."

Her skin was ash white, and cold against his palm.
"Took me . . . from my own . . . time?"

Each word came out softer, until she only mouthed
the last one. Her eyes grew large and dark, then slowly
closed. Even before she had completely fainted, Rowan
snatched her up in his arms. He held her close, cradled
like a sick child against his chest, glared around him at

the questions and looks from his clansfolk, and carried her off to his bedchamber.

"I'll do no such thing."

"I said to get you gone, and I meant it."

"This is my room! That's my bed! She's my wife!"

"You have made two out of three correct assertions, which for a man is not bad at all. Go."

"This is not your wedding night."

"You stay out of this, Micaela."

"The lass is right. And your Maddie is ill."

"She's not ill, Rosemary. She just fainted. I can deal with her."

"I know how you plan to deal with her, and I'll not have it."

"*You'll* not—!"

"Not until you're properly wed."

Maddie heard the conversation, though it had a distant, unreal quality to it. It was like hearing a television playing in another room. *Some historical program is on, isn't it? One with weird fantasy elements and a hunky hero?*

While Maddie listened the man growled, then muttered some unintelligible words. A door slammed. The two women giggled. When a cool hand touched Maddie's forehead she opened her eyes and screamed.

She was out of bed and across the room a moment later. When she hit the wall and turned around she found both women facing her, with startled looks on their faces.

"I think she's a bit upset," the young one—Micaela—said to the older one.

"And so she should be," Rosemary answered. Maddie watched warily as Rosemary held a hand out toward her. "Come along, lass," she coaxed. "Let's get you to bed. A good night's sleep will do us all good."

"Sleep?" The very concept seemed alien. Memories of her last conversation with Rowan came back to her. "I'm already inside a nightmare." She glared at the women who were dressed in medieval garments in a room lit by candlelight. They looked perfectly natural. She was the one out of place. "Do you know what year this is? Do you know what's happened to me?"

As impossible as Rowan's explanation had been, she believed him. Somehow she had traveled through some sort of time/space anomaly/thing/warp something all the way back to ancient Scotland. Something had to be done about it, but for the life of her she didn't know what.

Rosemary took a step toward her. "I know you need to rest."

The women meant well, Maddie knew that. She'd probably scared them when she'd jumped out of bed like that. Maddie didn't mean to scare anybody. Whatever had happened, it wasn't Rosemary and Micaela's fault. She wasn't so sure about Rowan. Though he'd acted as surprised to see her as she had him when they met on the road, his behavior since had been completely suspect. He might not be responsible for her time traveling, but he certainly meant to take advantage of it. And why did he look like Toby? How did his physical appearance factor into this? It couldn't be just a coincidence, could it? Was he somehow responsible?

She had no intention of letting him take advantage

of the situation, no matter what his involvement. Rowan Murray was far too sure of himself, far too domineering, too full of masculine arrogance for her liking. He seemed to think she'd do whatever he wanted just because he ordered it.

"The world does not revolve around Rowan Murray," she told his female relatives.

Micaela gave her a soft smile. "It will for the woman who loves him."

Rosemary chuckled. "Micaela thinks love is everything."

"Boy, has she got a lot to learn," Maddie answered. Micaela bit her lower lip pensively, and Maddie smiled weakly and apologized for her comment. "Actually, my Mom always says that love's the answer to everything. Sometimes I think she's right, but mostly I just—"

"Run like the devil's on your tail at the thought of a man in your life," Rosemary finished for her. "But you're tired of running."

Maddie blinked. "How'd you know that?"

"She read it in the entrails of a chicken," Micaela answered.

"No, Micaela, it came to me out of the herb smoke when I chanted for marriage omens," Rosemary corrected her. "The chicken guts were useless, though the rest of it served well enough in the soup pot."

Micaela nodded. "That's right. Rosemary's getting quite good with love magic."

Rosemary waved away the praise. "I'll never be any White Lady, that's for certain."

Maddie glanced nervously between the pair. "Uh-huh."

"Enough of our babbling," Rosemary said. "It's late. We all need to get some rest."

Rosemary might not be too in touch with reality, but she was right. Maddie was exhausted. She vaguely remembered being in the hall before she woke up in bed. She must have fainted, and a flash of indignation shot through her at the realization that she'd let shock overcome her consciousness. Now that she was awake, she found she liked the idea of going back to sleep. Maddie let the woman take her hand. Let her lead her back to the box bed and tuck a warm woolen blanket around her.

Maddie waited until the women had gone before she considered getting undressed. She hated sleeping in her clothes, but she didn't see any other choice. The top of the sweatshirt seemed too tight around her throat when she was lying down. She reached up her hand to pull it down, and discovered that it wasn't the sweatshirt, but the necklace that was bunched up around her neck. She sat up and felt for the clasp, only to have her fingers burned the moment she tried to unfasten it.

"Ouch!" She rubbed her fingertips together, and blew on them. She could feel the chain against her throat, warm and slightly pulsing. The feeling was not unpleasant, but it certainly wasn't normal. It was almost like an electric current ran through the metal. Maddie cautiously touched the clasp again. The only way she could describe the sensation when she did was that she *felt* a warning. It wasn't something she could see or hear, but a very physical, tactile impression. The impression told her that she better not try to remove the necklace if she knew what was good for her. Like everything else today, it was totally weird.

"This is impossible," she complained. "This is an inanimate metal object." Perhaps there was some molecular change in the metal that occurred during the time warp. Or she was imagining things. She didn't know the cause. She just knew that the necklace wasn't coming off.

Maddie decided to try not to think about wearing a willful piece of jewelry. It was too much to try to comprehend in her exhausted state. So she lay back down and tried to get some sleep. Oddly enough, it wasn't hard for her to drift off at all. Something familiar tickled at her subconscious, making her feel warm and comfortable and safe. A faint scent lingered on the pillow and in the blanket. Just before she fell asleep she recognized that she was in Rowan Murray's bed, and the familiar scent belonged to no one but him.

Hunky hero he may be, she thought just before sleep completely overcame her. *But he still isn't Toby.*

6

"We've been through this before."

"Aye. But this time I'll have my way."

This time he'd managed to get her all the way into the little church.

She'd felt grubby when the women had woken her up sometime before the break of dawn. Her loathing of her filthy state played right into their hands. They coaxed her into a wooden tub of steaming water and then into fresh clothes loaned to her from Micaela. They'd fed her fresh-baked bread and the best oatmeal she'd ever tasted. When Rosemary asked her to attend morning services with her, Maddie was lulled into a false sense of camaraderie. She saw no harm in joining the woman in saying her prayers.

She'd forgotten about Rowan's wedding plans.

Until he grabbed her by the arm as she came in the door and marched her to the altar. All the Murrays were in the chapel waiting for her, of course. It was an ambush, a trap, and she walked right into it. The priest was in front of her, the Murray clan was behind her, and the adamant laird himself was at her side.

"You have to marry me," he said, as if reading her mind. "There's no way out."

She wished he hadn't put it that way. She considered kicking him in the balls again. However, she wasn't a violent person under normal circumstances. Being told by Rowan Murray that he intended to marry her had become a normal, if redundant, part of her life. So violence was out. Reason didn't work. Stubbornness wasn't any good; he was the most stubborn man she'd ever encountered. Maddie was willing to bet that the man would stand in front of the altar with her for as long as it took to get her to agree. Now, she was pretty stubborn herself, but she could tell from the firm set of his jaw and hard glint in his eyes that this man had her beat cold for sheer tenacity.

How ironic that she was being granted her wish to have a man in her life under completely unacceptable circumstances. Fate, and some sort of suspension of the laws of science, had conspired against her.

Still, she wasn't ready to give up yet. "I'm not marrying you. I don't even know you."

"I saved your life," he reminded her. "You owe me for that."

She winced from a twinge of guilt. "You're not playing fair."

"I canna afford to."

She didn't owe him marriage just because he'd saved her life. She also knew that no argument from her was going to do any good. She looked at the priest. He looked like a sympathetic man. Actually, he looked like a black bear in a cassock. He was short, wide, and very, very hairy. She wondered if there were birds nesting in his thick, tangled beard. "Will you talk to him?"

"Will you be wanting a short service or a long one?" the priest asked Rowan. "Will you say your vows before Mass, or after?"

"That's not what I meant!"

Rowan put his arm around Maddie's waist and led her away from the altar after she shouted at Father Andrew. They didn't go far, just into a shadowed corner presently unoccupied by any other Murray. He heard the murmuring behind him, and felt all the gazes on his back, but he kept his attention on Maddie. He kept his arm around her as well, though she tried to draw away. This had to be settled, and quickly. And his way.

"You need me," he told her. She opened her mouth to answer, but he hurried on before she could speak. "To survive. To adjust. I could let you walk out the gates of my stronghold, give you your freedom, but you'd be dead within hours."

Her eyes flashed with anger. "I think I can take care of myself."

Rowan almost laughed. For all her spirit, he strongly doubted her survival abilities. "You'd fall off a mountain, or be food for wild animals. Or you'd be worse than dead," he went on harshly. "Norse raiders come down from the Orkneys this time of year to collect slaves. They, or some man from another clan, will find you if you leave Cape Wrath. You're a fine-looking, strongly built woman. Many a man would gladly get sons on you without asking your leave in the matter. And work you to death in his fields while he was at it, or trade you for new cattle."

She looked as shocked at his words as he felt—she at the implications, he at having managed to string so many words together at one time. He wasn't done yet, for he knew this woman was going to take a powerful lot of convincing. He had plenty of practice with strong-willed women on his side. What he'd like just once would be a soft-willed, pliable female to do as he asked, not expect him to court her, leave him be when she wasn't seeing to his needs, and just generally make his lot easier.

"Or the fair folk we met out hunting yesterday may want you to serve them," he went on. "That's slavery as well. Worse slavery than among mortals, for fairies can drive you mad as well as drain the life out of you and make you love them while they're doing it."

Her thoughtful expression turned angry. "What are you talking about? We didn't meet any fairies yesterday. There's no such thing as fairies."

"Just because my spell cloaked you from their sight doesn't mean they weren't there."

"Fairies are cute little *imaginary* critters that flit around flowers in children's books. "

Her derision hurt. She clearly thought him mad. "I've heard the Sassenachs have little belief in the fair folk," he told her. "But it is not wise to mock them so close to their own lands."

"I'm not a Sassenach," she answered. "I know it's a Highland term for a Lowlander or anyone who lives south of the Great Glen. I'm not a Lowlander, I'm an American."

Curiosity got the better of Rowan's impatience. "You said you were from Lewis."

"I did not."

"You told me you were coming from there to Glasgow."

"I was. The plane crashed."

"Me, I think the fairies brought you."

"They did not—I mean, there's no such thing!"

He had no time to argue with her over that foolish notion. "If you'll not trust yourself to see the reality of what's happened to you, you're a fool. But a fool I'm determined to wed whether I want to or no. Now, say the vows with me, and all will be well."

Maddie really wished he weren't standing so close to her. She wished he'd take his hands off her. He made her feel vulnerable and out of control. The sensation didn't frighten her, not exactly, but it put her off balance as she fought to stay calm and reasonable and ignore the effects of his large, overwhelming presence. He had her wedged into a corner, and she couldn't see beyond him to the people she knew were in the church. He made her feel as if they were the only two people in the world, as though he were the only thing she needed to pay attention to. He concentrated solely on her and tried to force her to do the same with him.

He wanted her to think he was her only connection to this world, her only protection. That it had to be his way or not at all. The scary part was, she suspected he was right. He was the laird of this clan, a mighty warrior who had saved her life—if not from fairies, at least from a strange wild animal. These people would turn her out if he told them to. Or kill her. Or let him rape her if she argued about marriage much longer. Rosemary had claimed the omens were right as Maddie was pushed to the altar. They all obviously believed in omens, and might not take kindly to her continuing to ignore them.

She was a stranger who had nowhere to go. She knew history, but not how to survive in this primitive time. He offered her a place to stay, food and shelter, and the protection of his sword. These were not unimportant things to have in a time when a lone woman couldn't walk into a store or hotel and plunk down a credit card to acquire all the necessities of life. Rowan Murray offered her a means of survival.

All she had to do was share this stranger's bed and life.

"Sell myself into slavery to you," she said.

The icy expression returned to his eyes. "Put it that way if you want."

Rowan told himself that the woman didn't know him, that she had no reason to trust that he'd be a kind husband. He told himself that he had no reason to trust himself to be a kind husband, but her words still hurt. "I don't want to wed, either," he growled at her. "But that is how it will be."

He ran his hand up her back until his fingers tangled in her hair. He pulled her head up and forced a swift, hard kiss on her. He was breathless when he was done. He hadn't meant to kiss her, but having given in to the urge, he knew that at least it was not fairy magic that made him want her.

"I've a bargain for you," he told her. One he should have thought of sooner. He'd been so intent on obeying the White Lady's prophecy after meeting Maddie on the road, he'd forgotten all sense of cunning.

Maddie's head still spun from being kissed. The fact that it had gone on long enough and been intense enough for her to almost put her arms around him and let herself enjoy it left her very shaken. What would

Toby think? Would Toby kiss like that? Would she ever get the chance to find out?

It took some effort to make herself respond to Rowan's words rather than his actions. She had to think logically. She had to survive here long enough to get back to her time and find out just what she really wanted. Because despite his ability to kiss, Rowan Murray was not who she planned to spend the rest of her life with. "A bargain?"

"Aye. A home for you at Cape Wrath in return for a handfast wedding."

Maddie looked thoughtfully at him for a moment. He didn't think she realized that her expression was softer than it had been before he kissed her, more amenable. Rowan thought that perhaps he should have kissed her sooner. He would have kissed her and much more all last night if his cousin and sister hadn't interfered. He cursed the wasted time and wondered how long he'd have to wait today before getting his bride into bed.

Then she said, "Handfast. Handfasting? I know about handfasting."

He ran his thumb across her neatly dimpled chin. Did she have dimples anywhere else? "Do you?"

"It's an old Scottish custom. A couple agrees to a temporary marriage, a trial marriage of a year and a day."

"It will fulfill my needs," he told her.

Surely she could do whatever it was that needed to be done to save his people in that amount of time. He could manage a year with the woman, then have his freedom. There need be no attachment, no lifelong commitment. Knowing they would be quit of each other in a short time would keep both their emotions safe from a relationship that neither wanted. Handfasting could make for a bonnie time in bed without any guilt or shame or recriminations for the couple once they'd separated. Rowan thought he'd like a year of simply pleasuring himself, of giving in to his own desires without worrying about responsibility for once, of having companionship without having to worry about becoming obsessively attached. Maddie took to his kisses like a lusty woman. The temptation to lose his cares in a year's worth of sex with her was very strong. As long as he kept his lust in the bedroom and his mind on his people, all would be well.

Maddie considered his proposal, and gave a sardonic chuckle at the choices that faced her. It seemed to her that she'd gone from no alternative to at least some control over her fate. A year was still a long time. She supposed that if she went through with this she could use the time to figure out what had happened to her. She would find a way to go home, and long before this proffered year was up, even if she promised him a year. A vow made under duress couldn't be considered valid, could it?

Besides, it wasn't as if she had much choice. It looked as if she was getting married. To someone just like Toby Coltrane.

"Be careful what you asked for," she murmured. "You just might get it. All right," she added. "You're on. A handfast marriage it is."

"Fine." He guided her back toward the altar. "Let's get this over with."

Maddie had to admit that marrying a bare-kneed, kilt-wearing Highlander in a medieval stone church certainly sounded romantic. It wasn't. It was terrifying, especially since Rowan sounded so matter-of-fact and looked so grim as he set about informing the priest of their decision.

Even though she intended to walk out on this forced marriage, she found that she regretted this inauspicious beginning.

7

After the ceremony came a great deal of kissing. It seemed as if everyone in the Murray clan had a kiss for her, either on the cheek or on the lips. The kisses were often accompanied by a swift hug. Maddie felt engulfed, surrounded, very nearly drowned in the welcome of these burly men and hale women.

The only kiss that lacked any sincerity came from her bridegroom. When she'd still been resisting the marriage, Rowan had kissed her in a way that left her breathless, with the blood racing in her veins. She hadn't liked it, but that kiss had certainly been more interesting than the chaste peck on the lips she received the moment she promised to spend the next year as Mrs. Murray. It was though he didn't give a damn about her once he'd gotten his way.

"What's up with you?" she'd asked, but had gotten no answer but a grim-faced glare.

Rowan backed away while Maddie was showered with boisterous greetings. He watched in a state of shock while she was kissed and hugged by the elders.

Children presented her with flowers and shy smiles. Her arms were full of fresh-picked wildflowers by the time she made her way through the crowd to the church door. She answered those smiles with lively ones of her own. For a few moments she looked like a happy bride, with bright eyes, her pale, freckled skin flushed, her wild, shining hair crowned with blossoms.

Rowan found her beautiful, and it terrified him.

Rowan was at the doorway before Maddie. He took her arm before she could step through into the courtyard. Being physically connected to him again made her feel somewhat less lost in the crowd. This was a disturbing realization, one she pondered without trying to pull away as they stepped into daylight.

Once outside the church, Rowan didn't know what to expect. Perhaps he'd secretly hoped for some burst of magic that would make the Murrays the most powerful clan in the Highlands as soon as he said his wedding vows. Nothing happened, of course. It had taken a great deal of effort to get his way with the unwilling woman. His every thought had been on bending her to his will.

Now that he had her, he felt as if he'd walked into a trap.

She looked at him as though the very same thought was on her mind.

He had made the trap, and now they were both caught in it.

Maddie stood in the center of the courtyard at Rowan's side as the sun came out from behind a bank of clouds to light up the hall and outbuildings. She looked around. Inside she felt as bleak and desolate as the rugged Scottish mountains at her back. She was afraid, though she hated to acknowledge the fact. Everything was out of control.

No, she corrected herself, as her usual practicality struggled to assert itself. She was alive. She'd made a devil's bargain with the man beside her. Having made it, she would survive. She'd escape.

She made a critical visual inspection of the gray stone defensive walls, the square tower at the top of the cliff, and the buildings below it. She felt trapped here, but time and broken laws of nature were her main enemies. This fortress was also her haven in a hostile world as long as she did what Rowan Murray wanted. She resented that, but knew that he was also her guardian. She didn't like having to depend on anyone. She didn't like being blackmailed.

She said, "The place could use some work."

Rowan's habitual frown deepened. "Aye," he said, grudgingly.

"So could you." Rowan didn't answer this comment. "What next?" Maddie asked him after they'd stood in silence in the sunlight for a while.

While he regarded her in hostile silence, the inhabitants of Cape Wrath finished filing out of the little church. Some of the people stood in the courtyard and watched them. Most of the Murrays, having celebrated the wedding reception before the actual nuptials, went about their own business.

After an uncomfortable while under his unfriendly gaze, Maddie decided that her nominal husband wasn't going to answer her question. So she tugged her hand away from Rowan's grasp and began to walk toward the tower. The ladder was propped against the outer wall, the heavy door was open. The place didn't look inviting, but it seemed better to explore the fortress than linger in the warm sunlight with the taciturn man. It bothered her that though she disliked the way he looked at her, her other senses reacted disturbingly to his touch.

Rowan knew what he wanted to do. He wanted to take his bride to bed. That was the trap. He fought the urge with all his might.

He would not be like his father.

He would make a specific time and place for being with his woman and never deviate from a set routine.

So he told himself that it was midmorning, hardly a seemly time to retire to his bedchamber, even if it was his wedding day. Not even Rosemary would complain if he swept Maddie up in his arms and carried her off to have his fill of lovemaking. No one would complain, but everyone would know that he'd shirked his responsibilities for the sake of his own pleasure. Just as his father had done with his fairy wife. Rowan had vowed to never put his own desires ahead of the needs of his people. His clan might forgive him for indulging himself for one day, but he would not forgive himself.

Besides, he knew that one day wouldn't be enough to burn out desire if he gave in to the weakness that was bred into his bones. He'd have the woman, certainly, but necessary coupling for physical release and producing an heir was not the same as endless hours of love play. There was a proper time and place for conjugal duties, and that time was not now.

So he kept his lust in check and reluctantly let Maddie walk away. She went to the hall, no doubt to pursue some woman's work. And to avoid his company as well, he supposed. He hoped. It should be some comfort to him to know that she wouldn't welcome him in bed any more often than wifely duty required.

It should have comforted him, but it didn't. He knew that he secretly wanted a wife who'd love him, the way his mother had loved his father. But that love had brought out the man's weakness when his mother died, made him prey to the fairy woman's call. If he hadn't sought love to ease his grief, he wouldn't have lost himself.

Rowan vowed that tonight he'd set about making the stranger properly his wife without emotional entanglements for either of them. In the meantime, he had told Father Andrew two days ago that he'd spend today seeing to the account books with him. Since he had given his word to tally figures with the priest, that's what he would do, wedding day or no.

"This is ridiculous," Maddie said, and paced the length of the hall one more time.

She was full of wild nerves and pent-up energy, and she hated it. It was akin to the cravings that had sent her on the way to Glasgow, only worse. She could analyze it, but that didn't help much. Maddie recognized that this bubbling in her blood was all hormonal and out of her control. It was her body trying to control her actions—a biological clock or time bomb or something.

She hated being out of control.

While she wasn't as phlegmatic as her new husband, she wasn't given to fits of hysteria, either, even if that's what she really wanted to do. To just give in and let it rip, to scream and pound on things, then wrestle someone to the ground and have her way with him.

She wasn't going to do that, of course.

All right, she had good reasons to be hysterical, but she had already decided that she wasn't going to let a case of time traveling coupled with mating urges get to her. Having made this decision, she knew she could be rational about the situation. However, as the day wore one she became and more perturbed. She eventually had to admit that it wasn't time traveling that bothered her. It wasn't even the idea of having a husband. In theory she liked the idea of having a husband.

It was sex.

Oh, she could lie to herself, or come up with all sorts of rationales, but when it came down to it, she was scared to death of sex. Maybe she always had been. It was this conjugal rights issue that was unsettling her. She'd married Rowan Murray, made a promise to be his wife for a year and a day. To share his bed, his board, and his life. She had promised. He was going to expect her to fulfill her vows.

Having made them, she told herself she was prepared to fulfill them. She was a sensible, straightforward, honest person. She always tried to do what she said she'd do. She was terrified of going to bed with someone, especially a stranger who looked so much like the one man she thought she could love. Not only wasn't Rowan Murray anything like Toby, he was the enemy who'd backed her into a corner where she was forced to face her worst fears.

She stomped her foot emphatically. She didn't think of herself as the foot-stomping type, but under the circumstances the physical release of energy seemed to help. "I will not think of Rowan Murray as the enemy." People in the hall stopped what they were doing to openly stare at her as she spoke, but she ignored them.

Even if he is the enemy, she added to herself, *I have to find some way to get along with him.*

The fear had been with her for a long time, even if she hadn't realized until now that that's what her avoiding men was about. Rowan Murray hadn't caused the initial problem. She'd always been awkward and self-conscious and uncomfortable with her overendowed body. Her mother had always said she'd outgrow it if she'd just let herself. Maddie supposed she was a slow learner about some things, because twenty-eight seemed awful late to finally start coming out of adolescent shock.

She went back to pacing.

Despite the fire raging in the central hearth, the place was cold. The clothes she'd been given consisted of several layers of wool over a linen shift. This helped insulate her body from the frigid air, but her hands were cold as ice. She also noticed that she had them balled into tense fists at her side. She wished she had pockets to tuck them into, but since pockets hadn't been invented yet, she tucked her hands into her wide sleeves and held her arms close to her body as she walked. It made her feel like a nun.

Nothing new about that.

Feeling like a nun wasn't going to do her any good when Rowan Murray demanded his conjugal rights, though.

She stopped as a ripple of shock ran down her spine. A slow, wicked grin spread across her face.

If he wasn't the cause of the problem, maybe he was the cure.

"Conjugal rights work both ways," she said, and went in search of Rowan Murray before she lost her nerve.

8

"*What?*"

"Right now."

"In the daylight?"

"No, in your bedroom. Let's go."

Rowan looked from the long-fingered female hand resting on his arm to the priest sitting across the table. Far from being outraged at Maddie's having barged into his workroom and demanded that Rowan perform an act of sexual congress *right now,* Father Andrew was smirking. There would be no help from that quarter, obviously.

He looked back at Maddie. She was all bright-eyed and flushed of cheek. Her words to him had been rushed, emphatic, but he sensed that this demand was not easy for her to make. He didn't think it was lust that made her eyes blaze, but terror.

"You don't want me, woman."

"You want me," she countered.

"Aye," he agreed, though he blushed to say so before the priest. "That I do. In my own time and way," he added as he tried to control the eagerness that sprang to life within him.

She took a step back and looked him over with an eye as critical as any expert herdsman would a head of cattle at a sale. Having looked at her much the same way yesterday, Rowan balled his fists at his sides and endured her scrutiny, though it left him feeling more naked than if she'd actually stripped him bare.

"You're not ugly," was her final judgment.

Which was not the same as saying she craved to touch him and be touched by him. "It wouldn't matter how I look," he reminded her. "I'm still your husband."

She put her hands on her hips. "Which means you have the right to sleep with me any time your want, right?"

"That is indeed his right, my child," Father Andrew answered for Rowan.

Maddie looked at the priest. "Well, I think it ought to be my right to sleep with him anytime *I* want." She turned a glare on Rowan. "And I want to right now."

He understood immediately, and with relief, that she really wanted was to get the wedding night over with. She wanted to do her duty, not make love. He couldn't fault her for that. He could tell that her demand wasn't fueled by passion. She had none of the teasing, wanton light in her eyes, none of the provocative grace he'd seen many times in the fairy wife when she'd easily seduced his father away from important work. This mortal woman was practical. He approved.

Though his heart cried out that he wanted more than that, a life without love was for the best.

"All right, then." He grabbed her hand and led her out of the church.

Maddie regretted everything she'd said and done since she'd gotten out of bed this morning as Rowan led her across the courtyard. She especially regretted the way his expression had gone all hard and closed off when she'd told him he wasn't ugly. She didn't know why that had hurt him, but it had. It had actually been an understated way of saying he was the handsomest man this side of his look-alike back in her century, if completely impossible to deal with and rather rough around the edges.

The man must think he was a real dog, or something. Great, a husband with a self-image problem as bad as hers. Just what she needed, someone else's problems to deal with just when she'd discovered that she wanted to fix her own. He hadn't shown any sign of being the least bit vulnerable since she'd met him. Of course, neither had she. He'd given her the impression of being the confident master of his fate, and hers.

"Who knew?" she grumbled as he pushed her up the tower ladder before him and into the hall.

Besides, she was the one who was prostituting herself in return for security while she figured out how to get home.

Oh, Lord! that was exactly what she was doing, wasn't it?

She might suspect that Rowan didn't like himself very much, but she was none too proud of Madalyn McCullogh at the moment. What would her mother say if she saw her right now? Her father would be furious at her for agreeing to a shotgun wedding in the first place. Her brothers would offer to lynch Rowan, and her sisters—rabid though happily married feminists to a man, uh, woman—would actually do it.

And once Rowan was swinging from a tree, she'd be left alone to face the lectures, not to mention the disappointed looks from her parents. Her only consolation was that if this had to be happening, at least it was in a foreign land in a far-off century. Otherwise, she'd be in big trouble for getting involved in a marriage of convenience even if her mother had insisted she was getting a little long in the tooth.

She was in big trouble. This was a big mistake. Worse than that, it was wrong, immoral. It was too late to back out. This hit home when he dragged her up the stairs and the door slammed closed on his bedroom. *Oh, hell,* she thought. Then she reminded herself that she'd instigated the proceedings, she had no one to blame but herself, and it was time to get on with it. She was an experienced woman of the world. More or less. She'd just never had sex with anyone before. It wasn't as if she didn't know the mechanics.

She just had absolutely no idea what to do with the man now that she had him alone. Yesterday, when he'd been interested, her reaction had been to knee him in the groin. She'd followed this up by threatening to run him through. He'd still forced her to marry him. He'd still accompanied her to his bedroom.

"Where'd all these candles come from?" Rowan asked as he took in the sight of his bedchamber lit with a soft, golden glow.

His question jolted her out of her self-absorption. "I have no idea," Maddie replied. "I didn't tell anyone I was going to—well, you know." The castle women must have divined her intentions when she marched off to find Rowan.

"Probably some damned love spell," he grumbled.

A hot blush flooded her cheeks as she looked around the transformed chamber. Still, she couldn't help but smile at the notion of a love spell and at the misguided thoughtfulness of the clan women. The room looked very different in candlelight. The warm gold given off by the tiny flames masked the starkness of the stone walls, the spartan angles of the box bed. Candlelight even softened the hard-set planes of Rowan's long face.

He crossed to the table next to his bed and picked up a mixed bundle of bluebells and heather. "Wise-woman herbal rubbish," he muttered. "Micaela and Rosemary's doing, no doubt."

The unexpected aromas of beeswax and flowers permeated the room. That his sister and cousin had thought to make him a wedding bower brought a tender smile to his lips.

"Foolish women," he said. "To waste their time so."

"It's sweet."

He turned to face his wife. "Are you sweet?" After her glance slid past his to focus on the bed they were to share, he added, "Or just randy and ready to rut?"

Her gaze flashed angrily up. "Nice alliteration. But you don't have to be insulting."

"It was a simple enough question."

Maddie considered the situation for a moment. She considered whether or not she should get into an argument with Rowan Murray. Then she decided that conversation was just a way of putting off the inevitable. It would be better to get on with the dirty deed—to see if she could live with it, him, and herself.

"I think we should get undressed, is what I think."

"Aye." He reached for the buckle of the belt that held his kilt in place. "I ken you've the right of it."

His movements were casual and self-assured, and a faint smirk played around his lips. Suddenly she doubted her earlier assumption that Rowan Murray had insecurities. She remembered how he'd accosted her with intent to rape the day before. Maybe he'd had second thoughts when she fought back, but the intent had still been there. Maybe it still was.

Maddie could not make herself watch him get undressed. So she shed her overdress and then, after a brief, nervous hesitation, untied the drawstring that fastened her chemise together at the neck. Even though Micaela had loaned her the medieval clothing, she'd donned her modern underwear and bra when she dressed. She still had this final, flimsy barrier on when her new clothes were left lying on the floor.

She shook with nerves as she stepped away from her clothing. It took all her willpower to approach the bed. A brief glance showed her that Rowan was naked. Lean, long-limbed and rangy, fair-skinned with a light brown fuzz of hair on his chest and at his groin—she took in the details very quickly, but thoroughly. They sent a shiver of warm sensation through her.

She'd wondered what Toby would look like without any clothes on. Now she knew. Only she didn't know at all, of course. And it wouldn't be fair to Rowan to try to pretend he was someone else when they made love. She had always prided herself on being a realist, a pragmatist. She'd rely on that pragmatism to get her through this. Still, she felt a pang of sadness knowing that it wasn't Toby that she was about to give herself to.

She couldn't help but look again. Yes, he was definitely naked, and beginning to be aroused.

"Well?" he questioned. "What are you waiting for?"

Fair's fair, she thought, and took off her bra.

Rowan watched with growing hunger as Maddie took off her clothes. Yesterday he had touched her, been enflamed as he was given a tantalizing hint of the lushness beneath her clothing. He had weighed the fullness of her breasts in his hands, felt them pressed against his chest. She'd fought him, then, refused him, as well she should have. Now, his throat went dry at the sight of flesh bared willingly if reluctantly for his enjoyment. Desire far stronger than yesterday's fairy magic took hold of him.

He licked his lips and tried to find words, but words weren't necessary. Tender emotions weren't necessary. He kept both his tongue and his feelings in check. Only the deed between man and wife mattered at the moment. He stepped forward and touched her. She put her hands on his shoulders and lifted her mouth to accept his kiss.

Maddie closed her eyes as Rowan's hands circled her breasts. She wished she hadn't when all her senses immediately focused on the startling jolt of reaction as his thumbs brushed across nipples already taut from nerves and the room's chill air. When erotic heat instantly seared through her, she admitted to herself that the reaction was a response to Rowan Murray, and not the prevailing air currents. His strong, lean body attracted her, and she was glad to know it. It made her feel that much less like a whore when his mouth covered hers. This might not be so bad after all.

Rowan had barely begun to taste the delights of Maddie's soft lips when the door banged open.

"What the hell!"

Maddie shouted the words in a hoarse screech as she

whirled to face the unexpected intruder. She quickly scrambled to cover herself when she saw a pop-eyed Aidan standing in the doorway.

Rowan's response to the intrusion was to snatch the dagger from his abandoned belt.

"Peace," Aidan called out, decently covering his eyes with his hand, as Rowan stalked forward.

Rowan halted in front of the lad. "There had best be a good reason—"

"Iain's hurt, and all the cattle have been taken from the high pasture."

Such news was more than reason enough. Rowan hastened to his shirt and kilt. "Harboths?" he asked as he dressed. The question was a mere formality.

"The tracks lead toward Harboth land."

Maddie stepped in front of him as he started to leave the room. She'd pulled her shift back up to cover her magnificent breasts. "Where are you going?"

"To get my cattle back."

"But—" She waved toward the bed. Her cheeks were bright red. "What about—?"

Rowan's jaw tightened in annoyance. Was the woman going to be as bad as a fairy wife after all? Did she really have no sense of duty? Had her matter-of-fact approach been a trick? Of course it had, or she wouldn't have drawn him here in the middle of the day in the first place. He shouldn't have let himself be drawn, and that was a fact. He'd vowed he'd not be like his father, and then had taken the first opportunity and abandoned the care of his folk for the soft touch of a wanton woman. If it weren't for the possible loss of vital livestock, he should be glad that this interruption had called him back to his senses.

Without another word, he shouldered past Maddie and hurried off to do his duty to his people.

Maddie sat down on the edge of the bed after Rowan was gone. She burned with shame and the sense that she'd made a terrible mistake. It had taken all her courage to take the initiative, to fight her own fears, to refuse to take a passive role in this forced marriage.

"I'm glad you left," she muttered as she glared daggers at the blank face of the door. That she ached inside with the beginnings of arousal made her humiliation worse. "I didn't want you anyway. Not really. I don't need any man. I never have and I never will, no matter what my mama says."

The candles continued to give off their romantic glow; wildflowers scented the room. The setting only underscored the dreadful ignominy of the situation.

She had done her best, given it her best shot, and gotten walked out on. Typical.

Maybe he had good reasons. A cattle raid was more important than a roll in the hay. She understood that. It didn't make her feel any better.

But he could have said something. He could have bid her a fond good-bye, at least. Instead he just rushed off. It let her know just how unimportant she was to him now that she'd actually gone through with the wedding.

Maybe she'd gone through with the wedding, but now she knew there was no way she could ever go through with the wedding night.

"You had your chance," she said to the shadows. "And you blew it."

Maddie's words were as much to herself as to her absent husband.

9

"*Let's see if I've got this straight.* You're Rowan's first cousin on his mother's side, but you're both Murrays."

"Aye," Rosemary answered with a firm nod as she continued to spin a thick lump of carded wool onto a drop spindle, making coarse thread out of what looked like a lump of cotton candy on her lap. "We're kin on both sides, but more on his mother's."

Maddie was seated in the hall among a group of womenfolk. It had been nearly twenty-four hours since Rowan's departure to retrieve the stolen cattle. She was spending the time awaiting his return getting to know the people of Cape Wrath, starting with his immediate family. So far, it seemed as if everybody, in castle and croft, was his immediate family.

It was raining outside. The air was damp from water blown in through the tiny windows. Not only damp, but smoky from the hearth fire and the few torches set in metal brackets at distant intervals along the gray stone walls. The setting was crude and uncomfortable, but she had joined the womenfolk in making the best of it. And while she got to know them, Maddie considered how she was going to return to her own time.

First she needed to find out just what sort of technology was available to her. "Do you have a blacksmith?" she asked.

"Aye," Rosemary answered. She cast a significant look at the woman sitting next to Maddie.

"Angus is my man," Flora spoke up.

"But Angus is off chasing the raiders with Rowan right now."

"Stonemasons?"

"With Rowan."

"Carpenters? With Rowan," she added before Rosemary could.

Maddie sighed. It looked as if she was going to have to wait until the laird brought the Murray clan home before she could get any real work done. Of course, technology might not be the answer here. She had to figure out what had happened before she could build a time machine. It would help if she were a physicist rather than an engineer. She wanted to make notes, do some number crunching. She wished she had a laptop, or at least a calculator. She supposed she'd just have to remember that she didn't need a keyboard to write, get some paper from Father Andrew when he returned from the raid, and then get to work. In the meantime, she might as well get to know these people.

She looked at Micaela. The beautiful young woman was working on a piece of sewing. "You're Rowan's sister?"

"Aye," the girl replied as she glanced up briefly from her work. Micaela's eyes were as deep and green as the forests surrounding Cape Wrath. Her hair was a lustrous night black. Her face was fine-boned, her features delicate. She didn't look a thing like the lanky, brown-haired Rowan. "Half sister," she added, as though she'd read Maddie's thought.

"Aidan and Micaela are the fairy lady's get," Rosemary elaborated. She reached over an affectionately patted the girl's hand. "It explains why Micaela and Aidan are not always as attentive to this world as they should be."

"I don't pine for the land under the hill," Micaela said softly.

"We know what you pine for," Rosemary replied.

Micaela blushed while the women around the fire chuckled and exchanged knowing glances. It was enough to make Maddie assume that there was a young man in Micaela's life. She certainly understood a girl as pretty and sweet as Micaela having a boyfriend. She didn't understand about Rosemary's claim that a fairy had been Micaela's mother. She decided that it must be a figure of speech, just a way of saying the girl was unworldly.

She did asked, "You people don't really believe in fairies, do you?" Okay, so she'd time traveled, but there had to be a more logical, scientific explanation for what had happened than fairies or elves or whatever.

When they all laughed and exchanged knowing looks she wished she hadn't asked. Of course they believed. Not just in fairies, but in magic. That's all they talked about. She wasn't going to get into it right now. What Maddie was going to do was tend to her knitting, literally, and try to fit in. At least until Rowan Murray came back to disturb her illusion of peace.

All of the women around the fire were busy at some piece of craft work, including Maddie. She was taking knitting lessons from the young mother named Flora, the blacksmith's wife. Maddie had learned to knit from her grandmother during a cold Montana winter when she was a little kid, so this was more of a refresher course. The needles were whittled wood instead of plastic, the yarn was a heavy thread of undyed homespun wool rather than triple-ply acrylic, but the principles were the same.

"This is fun," she said to Flora, hoping to stave off any lecture on magical beings from Rosemary.

"You learn fast, my lady," the young woman answered. "You'll be making your man a knit shirt in no time."

Your man. The words stung. He wasn't hers. She didn't want him. He was just this—man.

A tall, lanky, attractive, virile, dangerous, impossible—man—whom she couldn't seem to get off her mind.

Rowan Murray was her problem. For better or worse.

At least for the next year and a day, minus one. Or until she could find a way out.

Rather than think about Rowan, she considered what Flora had called her. My lady. Rowan was the head of the clan. She was his wife.

"For a year and a day, minus one," she muttered.

"What's that, my lady?" Flora asked.

Maddie turned to the competent Rosemary for guidance. "Am I technically in charge of the castle while Rowan's gone?"

Rosemary laughed. "Aye, lass. The household's

yours to command whether Rowan's here or no. 'Tis your right, do you not know that?"

"I know that noblewomen ran castles, of course, but—"

"And a hard, unthankful task it is," Rosemary interrupted. "I've been taking care of things while we waited for the lad to settle on a wife. I'll hand over the keys to the storerooms anytime you'd like so I can get on with my magical studies. And perhaps other things," she added with a brief, dreamy smile.

Maddie was grateful that the other woman didn't seem jealous or upset about giving up her primary place in the clan hierarchy. "Actually," Maddie admitted, "I'm not much good at domestic stuff." She glanced at her knitting needles. "Okay, so I can do this, but that's about it in the domesticity department. Grandma taught me how to knit because I was hopeless in the kitchen. It kept me safely out of the way while Mom taught my sisters all the secrets to baking and stuff. Fortunately, Dad had more luck teaching me guy stuff. Not that my brothers didn't have to take turns doing housework and my sisters learned how to fix cars and all, but I was the only girl in the family who took to the . . ." Maddie's voice trailed off as the women's stares grew wider, their expressions more confused.

"Are you saying you canna cook?" Rosemary finally suggested after a long silence.

Maddie nodded. "I don't eat it if I can't microwave it. And my laundry never comes out soft and bright like in the commercials. I don't own anything I have to iron. I'm not sure I understand the principles of dusting or making a bed. I mean, you just have to do it again, right? It's not that I'm a slob, I have a house-keeping service come in when I'm not out working offshore. It's just that I'm good with my hands," she went on as all the women continued to stare at her. "I know how to make things work. For instance, I could replace all the plumbing in a house." She chuckled as she looked around. "If a house has plumbing, of course. I'd rather replace a toilet than clean it, if you know what I mean."

Of course they didn't. They just stared at her, owl-eyed and gaping in shock. She sighed.

"No, Rosemary," she said. "I can't cook."

"Well, I imagine we can remedy that."

Maddie recalled the time she'd set the Thanksgiving turkey on fire. "No, I don't think so."

"There's more to managing a household than overseeing the cooks," Micaela spoke up.

"I'm sure there is." Maddie looked pleadingly at Rosemary. "And I'm sure you're much better at it than I could ever be. I'll really appreciate it if you'd keep on doing whatever it is you do so well."

To Maddie's relief, she nodded. "Aye. I'd be proud to serve you any way I can, my lady."

Rosemary's busy fingers never stopped working the drop spindle as they talked. Making thread was tedious, necessary work. So much of the work these women did was tedious. All of it was necessary. Maddie admired them, knew that the community's survival depended on every member's hard work.

"Perhaps you're meant to be more like a pampered Sassenach lady who never does more than embroider and please her man."

"No," Maddie said. "I don't want to be pampered."

Micaela gave a romantic sigh. "I think it would be lovely to have nothing more to do than to please the man I love."

"What nonsense, girl," Rosemary scoffed. "Don't let Rowan hear you say so."

"Yeah," Maddie agreed with the first half of Rosemary's statement.

Rosemary turned a sardonic gaze on her. "Though a newly married woman should have a few foolish notions about pleasing her man."

Maddie was surprised that her tone was bitterly sardonic when she replied, "I'm not the one who went on a cattle roundup yesterday."

"He could have sent Walter in his place," Rosemary agreed.

"Especially after you took the time to make the setting feel so romantic."

Wait a minute, Maddie thought. *I sound like I regret Rowan's absence.* She didn't, of course, except for the matter of the unfinished business of consummating the marriage. Business that was going to remain unfinished. She told herself that the only reason she regretted Rowan's absence, or that of any of the Murrays, was because hunting cattle thieves was dangerous.

"No one's going to get hurt, are they?" she asked, and knew it was a stupid question. Highland history was full of the bloody deeds performed during such livestock raids.

"Not your Rowan," Rosemary reassured her. "He's a mighty warrior."

"All our men are," Flora said. "And the Harboths are cowards to a man."

"Not so," Micaela countered quickly. "Even the Harboths have one or two brave men."

"I can think of one or two," Rosemary agreed.

Micaela lifted her head proudly. Her eyes blazed with anger. "Even Rowan has said so. Besides, perhaps it was Sassenachs who stole the cattle," she suggested.

"You know well it was none other than the thieving Harboths," Flora insisted.

It looked as if Micaela and the other woman were about to get into a shouting match. Maddie decided to try to divert their attention. "I don't think that many Lowlanders—Sassenachs as you call them—come up this far north if they can help it. Maybe it was raiders from the Orkneys," she added for Micaela's sake. The girl seemed to admire the enemy Harboth clan.

"Aye, that could be so," Rosemary conceded.

"Are you from the Orkneys?" Flora asked.

Maddie was happy to change the subject. "No," she told the women. "Though I have been as far north as Fair Isle."

Further, actually, but she wasn't going to try to explain working on a North Sea oil rig to these women. They'd find a metal island serviced by dragonflylike helicopters as magical as they did the alleged fairies that lived in their hills.

"Perhaps you're from the Sassenach land below the Great Glen, my lady?" Flora suggested.

"No, she's from the fairy folk," Micaela answered.

"I am not. I'm—" Maddie began.

But she was cut off by Rosemary. "Where are you from, my lady? We've all wondered where Rowan found you and who your people might be."

These people believed in supernatural forces. And

Rowan had showed no surprise at the notion that she'd been brought back through time. In fact, he'd thought of it before she had. Maddie wasn't ready to talk about something she found incomprehensible.

"My family came from the Highlands," she told the curious women. "They moved to a faraway land over a century ago." That was all she could reasonably tell them.

Maddie put down her knitting and stood up. "You know, Rosemary, I think I might get into this lady-of-the-castle-thing after all. "I think it's about time I took a tour of Cape Wrath."

10

The one thing Rowan wanted to do but couldn't was kill Burke Harboth. It wasn't just that the lad was a Harboth that made him so annoying. No, it was something about the way he looked—the ripe barley color of the hair that hung in a thick braid down his back, the eyes as blue as a deep, cold loch; his wide, full lips. Only the strength evident in his square jaw and the width of his shoulders saved him from being as beautiful as a maiden.

It wasn't Burke's looks that stayed Rowan's hand, or the flag of truce the younger man carried. It was the fact that the words he'd shouted as he rode toward Rowan's band of warriors carried the ring of truth. There was another reason as well, but Rowan carefully refused to think about it.

"So," Rowan said, keeping his attention fully on the current problem, "if the Harboths didn't take my cattle, who did?"

Behind him someone muttered—it was Angus, he thought—"He's too pretty to trust."

"But the tracks don't lead toward Harboth land," Aidan pointed out.

"He's still a Harboth."

"Aye," Father Andrew agreed. "Cut him down and let's be on our way."

Rowan shot an angry glance at the priest. "Did you not speak to us about loving thy neighbor not a sennight ago?"

"Aye," Andrew replied. "But I was na thinking of the Harboths at the time."

"Nor should you have been," Rowan conceded.

"The brotherhood of man is all very well in the abstract," Burke Harboth spoke up, "but damned inconvenient in the particulars."

Burke Harboth had been sent away to Paris by his older brother to study at the university there. He hadn't come back a priest as many a father and brother in the district had fervently hoped. He'd hardly said an intelligible word since he got back, either. Somehow his newfound gift of speech made him even more attractive to the women, or so Rowan had heard. It just made the menfolk, at least those riding with Rowan, grumble angrily.

"I'm here to help you," Burke added.

Rowan silenced the complaints with a wave of his hand. He'd spent a hard, rain-soaked night sleeping on the ground, followed by the better part of a rain-soaked day in the saddle. He was tired of riding through drenched heather and churned-up mud left by the passing livestock. Dogged though he was in the pursuit of what was rightfully his, he wearied of the weather and the chase. He wanted to go home to his warm bed, though his mind was more on the unfinished business he'd left there than on resting. He had to admit that duty first or not, he'd far rather be riding his woman than his horse.

He glowered at the cocky lad before him. "Why would a Harboth offer to help us?"

"Why indeed?" Burke threw back his head and laughed, as if at some private joke. Rowan refrained from asking for an explanation.

"He wants his cattle back, and it's easier for us to do his work for him," Rowan said.

"It's a trap, Rowan," Walter advised. Angus, Andrew, and Aidan nodded their agreement while the rest muttered and glowered at the fair-faced, seemingly relaxed Harboth lad.

"The three men we found dead yesterday were Harboths," Rowan reminded them, adding, "Pity it wasn't the Murrays that killed them."

"I know you didn't have anything to do with my clansmen's death," Burke told him. "I've been following close enough to know everything you've done since leaving Cape Wrath. I was following after our own stolen cattle when I came across the trail of your beasts. You came across that trail as well."

"Someone's stealing from both of us," Rowan agreed.

"And letting us think we're stealing from each other. Gives them time to get away while we go after our usual enemies."

"Not a bad plan," Rowan said. "I hate thinking the Norsemen from Orkney have grown so clever, and so familiar with our ways."

"They've been raiding our coast for years—"

"Your coast!" Angus interrupted. "The shore

belongs to the Murrays, as well you know, you thieving Harboth!"

Men shouted. Swords were drawn. Someone began to chant a war song. And the rain just kept coming down. Rowan held up a hand to halt the clamor, and all the while, Burke Harboth looked on with eyes wide with amusement. His nonchalance alone was enough to make Rowan want to strike him.

Rowan wished the lad would go to the devil, but since the earth wasn't likely to open beneath him anytime soon, and Rowan grudgingly agreed with him, there was nothing to do but say, "Lead on, then, Burke Harboth. Just know that you'll be the first to die if this is a trap you're leading us to."

The men of the Murray clan protested, but Rowan had his way, and they set off through the wet heather with a Harboth riding in their midst.

"I'm sorry, I'm just not into all this New Age stuff." Maddie took her hand out of Rosemary's grasp, and almost unconsciously wiped her palm on the rough wool of her plaid skirt.

Rosemary gave her a puzzled look. "There's nothing new in the old wisdom. The lines in your hand tell your life story."

"No, they don't."

Micaela leaned forward. "As above, so below," she said.

"Huh?"

"As the universe, so too the soul."

"What?"

"The lass means that the grand scheme of things can

be discerned from studying what is around us," Rosemary explained. "Our fates are written in the stars, in many signs and portents, and in our palms. Magic is everywhere."

"That's what I was afraid she meant." Maddie tried smiling at the earnest young woman. "Mickey, honey, the world doesn't run on all that paranormal mumbo jumbo. There are rules to the universe, sure, but they're the rules of science. You know, like Einstein said, God doesn't play dice with the universe. . . . Of course, from what I've been reading on Chaos Theory lately, it seems like maybe God not only plays dice but that they're loaded." *Or I wouldn't have ended up several centuries from where I'm supposed to be,* she added to herself.

"There are logical rules to the way the world is set up. We humans just haven't discovered them all yet."

Rosemary beamed. "Precisely. That's why we study magic."

"No," Maddie countered. "That's why we study science."

The women looked at her with a benign patience that was beginning to get on her nerves. She sighed. She didn't know why she was bothering. This was the thirteenth century, for heaven's sake! Of course, just because it was the past it didn't mean people had to remain ignorant and superstitious. The Scots she knew in her own time were a hardheaded, practical lot, some of the finest scientists and engineers in the world. She was of Scottish descent herself, and she didn't have an unrealistic bone in her body.

Maddie looked up from where she sat between the women on a bench in the courtyard. As she glanced up, the sun came out from behind a patch of clouds. The heavy rain of the last few days was finally giving way to sunny weather. She wondered when the men would get home. She wondered if they'd run into trouble. Not that it mattered on a personal level, of course, if Rowan Murray was safe and well. What mattered was that these were dangerous times, and the more armed men a stronghold had, the safer it was for the noncombatants.

What also had to matter, she thought, must be the attitude of the people who dwelled inside the thick walls of Cape Wrath. She was afraid that these people might be more likely to rely on some ridiculous spell or chant or something than on more realistic resources. That could not be good for the survival of the population. Something really ought to be done about their attitudes.

Before she could launch into a lecture on the folly of their erroneous beliefs, Rosemary said, "I can't help it if you don't like what the lines in your hand show to be true."

Maddie fervently wished she hadn't let Rosemary have a look at her palm. At first she hadn't even realized that the woman had fortune-telling in mind, since Rosemary's request came after Maddie complained that she was getting calluses from trying to learn how to spin wool.

She'd been surprised when Rosemary said, "You'll have a long, adventurous life. Your love will have a rocky start, but you'll be giving our Rowan at least four strapping sons."

She didn't want to have an adventurous life. Nor did she have any intention of given Rowan Murray sons.

Besides, not only was the prediction unscientific, she had no intention of staying around long enough to give anyone four strapping anythings.

"I shall enjoy having four nephews," Micaela said.

"I'm not having any—"

"Did you see any daughters, Rosemary?" Micaela forged on over Maddie's protest.

"Two."

"No!" Maddie was on her feet before she realized that she'd shouted. When she whirled around to face them, she saw that the women were laughing at her.

"Lady Maddie doesn't believe in our ignorant superstitions," Rosemary said, eyes twinkling with merriment.

"No, of course not," Micaela agreed.

"That must be why she just jumped like someone had stuck her with a pin."

Maddie began to laugh herself. "All right, you got me," she acknowledged. She pointed at Rosemary. "I don't believe in palm reading, but it's unnerving to be told I'm going to have six babies."

"That's because you hunger to hold a child of your own," Rosemary said.

"No way. I'm too old to start having babies." Besides, she didn't have a husband, not really. Never mind the longings that had plagued her before she ended up in the past, her arrangement with Rowan wasn't going to do anything to fulfill them. All she had here was an agreement to live with a man for a year and a day. It wasn't the same as having the love and commitment she knew was necessary for raising a child. Besides, she didn't intend to let Rowan Murray close enough for the subject, or anything else, to come up.

"I don't have time start a family," she reminded the staring women.

"Rowan will have some say in that," Rosemary answered.

"And you only need one time to make a baby," Micaela added, and blushed.

Which was another good reason not to go to bed with Rowan Murray. Maddie didn't know anything about birth control—at least, she hadn't had any hands-on experience with the subject. Besides, she doubted if a Highland laird, probably used to having his way with every woman in the countryside, would graciously consent to slipping into a condom even if she had any on her.

I'm not going to think about that right now, she decided, even though she couldn't stop herself from conjuring up an image of how he looked completely unclothed.

"You're blushing, Lady Maddie," Micaela said.

"She does that quite a bit. No doubt thinking of our Rowan," Rosemary added with a canny nod.

"I admit it," Maddie answered. She crossed her arms under her breasts. She turned away. "But not for the reasons you think."

Rosemary stood and put a hand on her shoulder. "Was he rough with you, then? Hasty? Or do you fear he would have been if Aidan hadn't gotten past us before you had time to have your way with the man?"

Maddie cringed at Rosemary's well-meant questions. Everyone at Cape Wrath knew far too much about everyone else's business. She did answer, "I don't expect anything from the man."

"Well, you should."

"I think," Maddie said, "that I want to go for a walk."

"You always go for a walk when you don't want to talk," Micaela spoke up. "You've walked a great deal since Rowan left."

"Usually after someone's mentioned his name," Rosemary added.

Not only did everybody know what everyone else did, they were far too discerning about motivations. If there was one thing Maddie liked to avoid, it was analyzing her own emotions. If there was one thing she was sure of, it was that emotions just got in the way of clear thought. It was giving in to emotions that got her into this mess. If she hadn't given in to her longings, she wouldn't have gotten on that plane.

She fervently wished Rosemary, Micaela, and the rest of the Cape Wrath women would stop going on at her about Rowan. It just made her think about him more, and thinking about him was the last thing she needed. What she needed was some peace and quiet and a certain reserved respect for her privacy.

She rounded on the women. "When do the Scots become a dour and reserved people, anyway?"

Rosemary rubbed her chin thoughtfully. "Rowan's a dour lad." She brightened. "Is that what you like about him, then? Because he can be endlessly moody."

"More's the pity," Micaela said. "Though if that's what you like—"

"I'm going for a walk," Maddie said again.

This time she didn't hesitate to move away, though the women continued to talk about her relationship with her so-called husband as she made for the castle gate.

At the castle gate, however, a guard called out, and then a group of plaid-clad riders and men on foot came pouring noisily into the courtyard. At the head of this rag-tag band, of course, was her so-called husband.

11

He was frowning mightily, and he looked tired, but for some reason Maddie felt a flutter of something she could only define as pleasure at seeing him. Then he looked at her and her pulse jumped and she couldn't explain her reaction to his fierce gaze at all. It wasn't fear, though maybe it should have been, because he looked anything but friendly. Of course, she'd never been afraid of a man in her life, and she didn't intend to start now.

It was some sort of visceral excitement that was akin to fear but rich with other textures, she had to concede that. Sort of like a, what was that French word, *frisson?*

"Oh, Lord," she muttered. "Whoever thought I'd start thinking about a man in French?"

She'd be wearing lacy underwear next.

Why? she wondered as she did her best to stay out of the way of the sudden tumult in the courtyard. Just because a muscular male on a big horse gave her a sharp look? Toby had looked down at her from a horse a few times, and the thought of lacy underwear had never once crossed her mind.

"And he's not Toby," she grudgingly reminded herself as Rowan, a great deal of hard-muscled thigh showing, swung down off his horse.

She considered going into the tower or the chapel to get away from all the noise and bother as much as Rowan Murray. Shouting women and children came rushing up to the returned warriors. People, horses, and cattle milled around, churning up even more mud in the already sloppy, slippery courtyard. Rowan momentarily disappeared from her view in this chaos. Maddie turned and began to walk away.

Only to react instantly when Rowan rapped out, "Give me some help here, woman."

It only occurred to Maddie that perhaps he hadn't been addressing her when she was helping him hold up a wounded man he'd eased down from one of the horses. They shared a glance as she wondered just how she'd gotten through the crowd so quickly to reach Rowan's side. Then she looked at the man they held between them. He was young, blond, totally unfamiliar to her. Maddie had a good memory for faces, and she definitely didn't recall seeing this one either at the banquet or at the wedding.

"Who is he?" she asked as she helped Rowan guide the young man through the crowd that had closed back around them.

Her answer came when Micaela pushed through to them and cried, "Burke! What's happened to him, Rowan? You've killed him, haven't you?"

"I don't carry dead men into my house," Rowan gruffly told his sister. They slowly moved on toward the entrance ladder to the tower. "Not that a living Harboth's any more welcome than a carcass."

Maddie looked from Micaela's anxious face to the semiconscious man slung between her and Rowan. *Oh, that Harboth,* she thought. No one had actually come out and told her that Micaela was interested in one of the enemy, but the hints had been broad enough.

"Is he your prisoner, then?" Micaela demanded. "Will you torture him to death for stealing cattle?"

"He would be, and I would—if he'd stolen the livestock. He's my guest, girl, now hush your wailing and hold the ladder steady. And keep away from him," he ordered.

"He'll need his wounds tended," Micaela protested. "Or do you hope he'll die without nursing?"

"What happens to him is no business of yours. My wife will nurse him," he added.

Me? Maddie thought, but she didn't say anything. She had enough to worry about just helping Rowan get the man up the ladder. "He's heavy," she pointed out, and glanced at the watching crowd over her shoulder. "Why didn't you get one of your strapping clansmen to help you?"

"You're strapping," was his answer.

All right, so she wasn't delicate and feminine. She didn't need to be reminded. She didn't even know why she was bothered rather than complimented that a medieval male assumed she was strong and competent—just like all the modern males who'd treated her as one of the boys all her life. She sighed.

"Besides, you gave me help when others wouldn't," he added as they hauled Burke Harboth through the doorway.

"You need a stairway, you know," Maddie said, rather than respond to the flash of gratitude that passed across Rowan's face.

"This way," he said, and they stumbled into the smoky hall.

"And a chimney," she went on. "And plumbing."

"Stairs make it too easy for raiders," Rowan replied. "Can't pull stairs up after you if the walls are breached."

"I suppose not." She gave him a quizzical look. "Do the walls get breached often?"

"Never. No use taking chances, though." Not knowing what the other things she wanted were, he didn't comment on whether they were needed or not. "We'll put him here," he directed after he kicked a dog away from a choice spot near the hearth.

"The wound's not bad," he added after they'd settled Burke on the floor and Maddie had not bent solicitously over his ailing form. After a strained silence, he said, "He'll not need much nursing."

"That's nice."

The woman still made no move. Rowan puzzled over her uncharitable behavior. "Have you a feud with the Harboths as well?"

"No."

"Well, then. Do your duty."

The man on the floor looked up at them, and said, "I'm going to be fine." They both ignored him.

Maddie crossed her arms under her very ample bosom. Rowan tried not to think about her bosom. He'd been thinking about it far too much since leaving Cape Wrath.

She gave him a crooked, sideways smile. "Honey, I

don't know nothing about birthing no babies—or anything else connected with first aid. I suggest you call this kid's HMO—or Micaela, whichever one is first on your speed dialer. Bye."

He grabbed her arm as she started to walk away. "What language are you speaking, woman?"

"Damned if I know," she answered. "We're probably, improbably on my part, speaking Gaelic."

"I am, at least."

Maddie didn't know why she was behaving so badly. She did know that she wanted to get away from the situation. Probably because Rowan expected her to do something for which she was totally unqualified. She could barely dose herself when she had a cold, let alone nurse a wounded man.

And she was so tired of being out of her depth and out of control.

"I want to go home," she said. "Where we speak English and sick people go to hospitals."

"It's barely a cut," the man on the floor said.

"Well, you canna go back to where you came from."

She put her hands on her hips. "Just watch me."

"I was not offering a challenge, woman, but speaking the truth."

"More like a bruise, really."

"Don't you 'woman' me."

Rowan took a step closer to her. There was a dangerous glint in his eye. "Are you not one?"

"Not the way you mean it."

"I've seen your body, lass, and you're no a man." As she blushed he snagged an arm around her waist, and pulled her to him. Maddie found herself trapped not just by his embrace, but also by the look in his eye.

"I'll be going now," Burke Harboth said. "You two just go on with what—"

"Burke!"

His sister's shout pulled Rowan's attention away from the woman in his arms. Though he kept an arm around Maddie's waist, he turned his attention to Micaela.

"Go away," he ordered the girl who was already kneeling solicitously at Burke Harboth's side.

She ignored him, and gently stroked the young man's fair face. "Are you hurting badly, lad?"

Burke weakly lifted a hand to her cheek. "The pain's terrible."

"What can I do for you?"

"Just the sight of you helps."

"I'm here for you. I'll take care of you as long as it takes to get you well." Micaela gave Rowan a swift, determined, look. "You'll be safe here."

Burke gave a sickly cough. "It could take weeks."

"Weeks," Micaela repeated.

"He'll be gone tomorrow," Rowan declared after he heard the lovesick dreaminess in his sister's voice. "I shouldn't have brought you into my house, Burke Harboth. And get your head out of my sister's lap."

"I didn't put it there."

"I'll put it on a pike outside my gate if you push me to it, lad."

"He's a sick man," Micaela said. "Leave him to me and tend to your own business. Bedding your wife might help your temper," she added with a toss of her head.

"Mind your tongue."

"Yeah," Maddie agreed with him.

Rowan became aware that his fingers were curled around Maddie's waist. He became aware that he'd been breathing in the scent of her and welcoming the warmth of her body against his own. He'd pulled her into his embrace without even quite knowing he'd done it. That he had such an automatic reaction to the woman disturbed him. Had he not spent the time away from Cape Wrath calculating every degree of intimacy he would allow himself with his wife? That she was already in his arms greatly disturbed him. He dropped his hand to his side, and carefully stepped away from temptation. "Maddie will tend Burke," he told his sister.

"She hasn't the healer's skills," Micaela said before Maddie could protest again. "She told me so herself just yesterday."

"Oh, leave the girl be," Rosemary said as she came up to them.

Rowan looked around, and saw that the hall had filled with people since Maddie had helped him bring the Harboth lad inside. He wondered why he hadn't noticed, and blamed his distraction on too closely concentrating on the woman he'd married. The few inches that separated himself and Maddie was too great a distance. He didn't give in to the urge to step back, though.

Maddie hugged herself to keep a sudden shiver at bay. The temperature in the room seemed to get colder when Rowan moved away from her. Or maybe it was just the look he'd given her, as though something was her fault and that something had nothing to do with Burke Harboth.

"You're insufferable," she told him.

"That I am," he acknowledged, then turned to his cousin. "You sort out who nurses who . . ."

Rosemary gave a brisk nod. "And so I will." She waved a hand toward Burke. "Micaela, mind the lad's wounds."

"I intend to." Micaela stroked the young man's brow as Burke gave an exaggerated groan. "I'll fetch you some wine, Burke, then we'll get you settled on a warm, soft pallet."

Burke gave the girl a weak, but devastatingly charming, smile. "You're too good to me."

Maddie hid a laugh behind her hand when a frustrated growl escaped from Rowan at the sight of his sister fraternizing with the enemy and the enemy laying it on thick. She still got an icy look from him, despite the fact that she didn't make a sound. A very brief look, as though the very sight of her annoyed him. Her own good humor disappeared in a flash of temper. The man obviously couldn't take a joke, or share one, and blamed her for daring to see any humor in the situation.

Before she could complain about his rudeness, he said, "I'm going to see to settling the animals. There's horses and cattle that need more looking after than the men who rode in."

Rosemary grabbed Maddie's arm as Rowan started toward the door. "Your man's weary, and that makes him more vexing than usual. See to his comfort like a good wife while I tend to the rest of the household."

He did indeed look tired, Maddie had to agree. Maybe his bad attitude had nothing to do with her. She tried to tell herself it wasn't any of her business. She didn't succeed. She marched determinedly after

Rowan, and caught up to him before he reached the door.

"You do look like you could use some rest."

He whirled to face her. "I have work to do." She looked solicitous, and her words seemed harmless. He knew the road that could ruin his clan too well. He would not be tempted.

She put her hands on her hips. "Fine. Go catch a cold or get some stress-related injury." She turned away. "See if I care."

Rowan grunted, almost apologized, but caught himself in time. "Have a hot supper waiting," he ordered. "Then I'll take you to my room and tup you."

"Fat chance on both counts," he heard her reply as he reached the door.

Her words sounded strange to his ears, but he had no doubt about what they meant. "We'll see about that," he called back, then hurried outside.

Maddie returned to Rosemary's side after Rowan was gone. "That man is a pain in the butt."

"Aye, always has been. He has no balance in his stars."

"Right." Maddie didn't want to discuss pseudoscience with the other woman. She did lean close and whisper, "Uh, what does 'tup' mean?"

Rosemary's answering laugh was bawdy, and not at all reassuring.

Maddie sighed, as nerves and heat curled deep in her stomach. "That's what I was afraid of."

12

The grooms told him to mind his own business and let them mind theirs as they went about taking care of the tired horses. The herdsmen were no less adamant, and their dogs barked impudently at him, as though to chase him off. The smith was already heating up the forge to mend dented weapons. Father Andrew knelt before the chapel altar, praying for the souls he'd helped dispatch to Hades. Aidan had settled himself in the kitchen and was already giving more than enough orders for the roasting of meat for a victory celebration despite the bad-tempered glowers of the cook. The stronghold of Cape Wrath seemed to be working in good order. Rowan felt almost as if his people conspired against him to get him back into the hall. So he went to the village to quiz the fishermen, or would have if the boats hadn't been out in the bay. He did find a workman on a village roof, and helped him to mend the thatch.

All in all he felt his time had been wasted when he finally made his way up the ladder to the hall at sunset.

He'd proved to himself that he could control his lust, now he had every intention of satisfying it.

"Here," was the greeting he received when he came through the doorway. Rosemary handed him a steaming pail of water. "Clean yourself up," she commanded.

Rowan glowered suspiciously. "Why?"

"You stink of cow manure, horse, and your own sweat."

"Hmmph. Where's Mad—Micaela?" he said, changing the question in midsentence. He was determined not to seem too eager. Besides, it was important to know what his sister was doing with the Harboth lad.

"Don't you worry, Rowan. He's weak as a kitten. I've told her we'll send her back to the fair folk if she dares to even give him a peck on the cheek."

"I shouldn't have brought him here." He shook his head. "It seemed better to send him home mended rather than wounded. I didn't want to give Allen Harboth cause to complain after his little brother helped rescue our cattle as well as his."

"Are you sending the cattle home to the Harboths?"

"Most of it."

"And you'll send the lad home to Allen as well? He's not your prisoner?"

Rowan bridled. "I've said as much already."

"So you have. Well, I suppose Micaela might as well spend some time with him under my managing eye instead of sneaking off to meet him in the heather—which I've no proof she's ever done," Rosemary added hastily.

"Keep close watch on her."

"I always watch what's going on in the heather with the Harboths. Now, you get yourself washed. There's clean clothes laid out for you."

"What? Why would I need a new shirt so soon? Has the season changed while I wasn't looking?"

She laughed, and slapped his arm. "Go on, lad. Do as I say and stop your fussing."

Rowan rubbed his jaw. He was wearing several days' worth of beard stubble, which was more than he liked. Most Highlanders grew thick, warm beards, but Rowan preferred his face bare. He weighed the bucket in his hand. Being clean wouldn't be a burden to him, though he hated the thought that he might be suspected of primping for his wife.

"Where is my wife?" he asked before he turned toward the stairs.

Rosemary gestured into the depths of the hall. "Standing over Flora at the loom," Rosemary said. "Studying how it's done, she said."

He gave a grudging nod of satisfaction. It was good to know that Maddie took an interest in the household. His stepmother had been useless about such things and had led the mortal Murray women into all sorts of foolish notions.

"Did I tell you she built us something she calls a spinning wheel while you were gone?"

Rowan eyed his cousin suspiciously. Perhaps Maddie had notions as mad as any of the fair folk. She must have dwelt among them, after all. "Spinning wheel? What's that?"

"A device for spinning wool, of course. And easier to use than a drop spindle, I can tell you that. She says it will improve production, quality, and process. I've no idea what she means, but I do know the work's not so tiring as I'm used to."

Rowan didn't know whether to be pleased or

annoyed, or simply to ignore the whole issue of women's work as none of his affair. "Oh."

Rosemary patted him understandingly on the arm. "Get cleaned up. You'll feel better. I'll send your wife and your dinner to your chamber."

He couldn't deny that he wanted both. So he nodded, and took his bucket of warm water off to his room.

"What are you doing here?"

Maddie stumbled to a halt just inside the bedroom, almost dropping the tray in her hands. That would have meant spilling the dishes of fried bannocks and stewed beef. She was too hungry to lose her dinner even if dropping it and running was tempting. Someone closed the door behind her while she caught her balance. She registered the sound as Rowan, wearing only a thigh-length yellow shirt, looked up.

"Where else should I be? Put my supper down here."

He pointed to a low table by the bed where a basin of water already sat. He held something that looked like a small knife in one hand. She noticed that his cheeks were smooth, and a bit pink from scraping, and realized that it was a razor.

"You ought to try using some soap with that."

"Soap's dear."

"Taciturn *and* parsimonious. How stereotypical. And you're not even a Presbyterian yet. You could give Scotsmen a bad name, you know."

She was blathering. She knew it. He said it. "Stop your blathering."

"Bugger off," she replied. She was going to get Rosemary for conspiring to get her alone with her husband, but she took her annoyance out on Rowan for now.

If Maddie hadn't been distracted with an idea for the loom, she might have suspected Rosemary was up to something. Instead, blissfully involved in developing an improved design, she had accepted Rosemary's suggestion to take her meal and escape the noisy, smoky hall. Lost in her own world, she had totally forgotten about Rowan's return. She'd forgotten about his plans for "tupping"—or she'd hidden from thinking about them by getting involved in practical, controllable, work-related speculations.

"I'm really getting into textile manufacture, you know," she said, and was aware of just how inane and incongruous her words were. She almost didn't blame him for looking annoyed, and she hurried to put the tray where he'd told her to under his frowning gaze. "Really," she went on. "There are so many relatively easy ways to improve—"

"You talk too much."

"Aye," she agreed, then smiled at her use of the word. Well, why not? She thought. She'd been living in Scotland long enough—even without the time travel— to pick up some of the vernacular. She'd long ago learned how to swear in British, including quite a few words for sex—she'd worked on an oil rig, after all, not the most genteel environment in the world. "Tup" was not one of them. It was one bit of slang she had no interest in learning how to put into a sentence. Or doing, for that matter.

But there was no reason to be rude and uncivilized.

There were other subjects besides sex. Other distractions. And speaking of distractions, she really wished his shirt covered a bit more of his well-muscled legs.

She motioned at the food. She tried not to look at him. "Have some dinner."

Rowan put down his razor, then splashed water on his warm cheeks. Whether they were heated from recent shaving or from awareness of the furtive but interested way she studied him, he wasn't sure. He took refuge in the thought of the meal. He took a bannock from the tray, sat down on the bed and proceeded to polish off the warm cake while he made an open study of his wife. He had to admit that though his thoughts had been too much on her while following cattle thieves over the rocky coastline, it was her form more than her face that he recalled. He remembered freckles and thick copper-bright hair, but not much else. He knew many a Highland woman with freckles and coppery hair. They were as common as tides and stormy sunsets. Perhaps that was a blessing, he supposed—if she looked no better or worse than any other woman, it would be easier to fight an attraction to her. She was far from ugly, pretty even, healthy-looking, with good teeth and clear blue eyes. Good teeth counted for a lot in a young woman. Her tongue was too lively, of course, but he was used to that. He might have wanted an obedient wife, but fate and the White Lady had given him one with more common characteristics.

He knew already that her body was not common at all; her curves and softness were uniquely her own. Her kisses tasted like no one but Maddie. He'd spent his nights and his waking hours longing to cup her breasts and her buttocks in his hands, to know the flavor of her mouth again, to find the soft heat between her legs and bury himself in it.

Now he fought hard to keep from translating that longing into action too quickly, to keep control of the night. Maddie, meanwhile, settled on the room's only chair and ate, with her eyes averted from him now that she had looked her fill at his thighs. He supposed that her refraining from hungrily throwing herself into his embrace was a good thing, but he was already half-hard just from the look that had been in her eyes.

So he pulled off his shirt and sat naked on the bed. He patted the place beside him. "Come here."

Maddie dropped the empty bowl and jumped to her feet. Her gaze flashed to Rowan, and away immediately. The man was naked! In his own bedroom. What was she doing here? Trapped by her own hunger, hunger she didn't want to try to define too closely, and Rosemary's plotting, that's what she was doing here. She risked another quick look at the man as she backed toward the door. He was more than just a naked man, he was an aroused naked man. A fine-looking aroused naked man.

"Oh, hell."

"Come here," he repeated.

She ran for the door.

The next thing she knew she was flat on her back on the bed, and Rowan was poised above her, his weight pinning her down, his hands on either side of her head.

He put his lips close to her ear. "When I say come here, I dinna mean get you gone."

She was panting, vaguely aware that there had been a brief struggle that she had lost. "Get your hands off me!"

"They're not on you."

Before she could argue the point, his mouth covered hers. Her mouth was already open to speak, and he took advantage of this, his tongue delving into her mouth. The sensation of having his tongue stroke against hers was shocking, but not unpleasant. For a moment she closed her eyes, pretended it was Toby, and just let herself be kissed. He looked like Toby, and his rangy, muscular body felt like Toby's must. Maybe she could make love to him if she made herself think—

She couldn't do that to Toby.

She couldn't do it to Rowan, either.

She especially couldn't do it to herself.

Kissing might feel good, but there wasn't any love here. Without love it wasn't right. Not for her.

But it still made her limbs feel all warm and heavy, made her insides tingle and ready to melt. Her body was telling her just to lie here and enjoy it. Her body was increasingly aware of the heat generated in the spots where their flesh touched. He was naked, her chemise was open, and her skirt was pulled up around her hips, so their flesh touched in several important spots.

His mouth moved to her breast. She heard herself moan. Her fingers began to caress the taut muscles of his back. It was like touching velvet over heated steel. A fire began to kindle deep inside a part of her that had never been touched.

Good was too petty a way to describe this delicious ache. It wasn't just delicious, it threatened to grow into an urgent, burning need.

There wasn't going to be any burning going on here tonight. There shouldn't be. No matter how good it felt, it was wrong. She was still lucid enough to know right from wrong—which was somewhat regrettable, under the circumstances. Still, she made herself take her hands off Rowan's back, and sink her nails deep into the soft skin on either side of his throat.

He howled. She pushed.

Rowan sat up and shouted, "What the devil are you doing, woman?" He swiped a hand across the scratches. "I'm bleeding!"

Maddie scrambled into a kneeling a position. He was bleeding. "Sorry. I didn't mean to hurt you."

He held out bloody fingers. His eyes held fire and ice at once. So did his voice. "Is that so?" He grabbed her by the shoulders. "If you wanted to say no, you could have just said no."

"I'm saying no."

"You can't say no, you're my wife."

"You just said—"

He kissed her again. It was demanding and passionate and sent a wave of utter panic through her. She pushed at him, but there was no breaking the grip he had on her shoulder. So she flailed her hands out, groping for something, anything, as he pressed her backward across the side of the bed.

Eventually she grasped the edge of the water basin.

13

"She said no, didn't she?"

Rowan was wet, his head hurt, he wasn't quite sure where he was, and he was lying flat on his back, naked but for the clothes piled on top of him. The one thing he was sure of was that the voice belonged to Rosemary, and she sounded amused.

He sat up very slowly, pulled his saffron shirt on over his pounding head, then looked up to see his cousin smiling down at him from over the bright wick of a tiny oil lamp. Even that small light seemed overly bright at the moment. It occurred to him that perhaps he'd had too much mead, which wasn't his usual habit but was not an unreasonable assumption.

"She said no," Rosemary repeated, and it wasn't a question.

Then it all came back to him. He'd been acting like a mad stag in rut, and now he was on the floor outside his bedroom.

"Aye," he agreed, as he rubbed the rising lump on his head. "She said no. Why is it," Rowan wondered as his cousin stepped back to give him room to don his clothes, "that the woman can't make up her mind whether she wants me or not?"

"Well, that's easy enough to answer."

Maybe for a woman it was; it was a puzzlement to him. He glowered at Rosemary. "All I want's a woman who'll spread her legs when I need it, and leave me in peace when I don't."

Rosemary cuffed him on the shoulder. "Mind your tongue, Rowan Murray. And stop expecting so little from life while you're at it."

He didn't know whether to rub the spot where his cousin had struck him or the throbbing knot on his head from his wife. "You're a pack of violent harpies."

She smiled benignly. "So we are. It's good to see Lady Maddie has the spirit of a Murray woman even if she was born to the McCulloghs." Rosemary patted the spot where she'd struck him. "She's a good lass. Talks too much, but kindly. And she keeps herself busy about the holding. She's a doer and a fixer even if she hasn't any household skills. I like her, Rowan."

Rowan didn't know whether he liked his wife or not. He knew he liked the sight, touch, taste, and feel of her. He barely knew her name, only had guesswork as to how she'd ended up on the road back from the White Lady. She certainly hadn't been waiting for him through any choice of her own.

"You and she are still strangers," Rosemary interpreted his thoughts. "I wouldn't want to be under any stranger the first time I made love to a man."

"She's my wife."

"Aye. So?"

"I'm her husband."

"You've said the same thing two ways, lad, but I still don't take your meaning."

"She agreed to be my lover," he said, "for a year and a day." He touched his aching head. "She's trying to renounce the bargain. I'll not have it." For the sake of his pride as well as the welfare of his people, he couldn't let the woman lock him out of his own room. He would be laughed at by kith, kin, and countryside if the tale got out that his woman wouldn't have him, and he couldn't abide that.

Rosemary hit him again.

"What?"

"That's pride I see glowering out of your eyes, lad, and I won't have it."

"You won't—"

"You listen to me, Rowan Murray." She wagged a finger under his nose. "The White Lady sent her to you, did she not? For the sake of all the clan?" He nodded. She gave him a smug smile. "Then you're fated to be lovers."

He was on one side of a closed door, his putative wife on the other. He had a headache. "She's here to help the clan. Love is not necessary for marriage."

"Oh, don't be ridiculous. You sound like some Sassenach noble who makes a marriage for sake of dowry and breeding stock."

"It could be that the Sassenachs have the right of it."

"You're just soured on the subject because you're still jealous of the fairy wife."

"Jealous? I was never jealous. I never wanted her—"

"Of course you didn't. You wanted your father's attention. You were a growing lad then. You deserved more of him than you got after he brought the lady of the fair folk home while you were still grieving for your mother."

Though Rowan's heart tightened with pain at her words, he answered, "The clan deserved more attention, not me."

"He made you grow up too soon, and I fault the man for that. But he knew how to love, he was happy."

"Too happy."

She shook her head. "Lost himself, perhaps, irresponsible, I'll grant, but it's not possible to be too happy."

"And none of this has anything to do with my own marriage."

Rosemary took him by the upper arm and gave him a good shake. "Think of your wife, lad, and not the good she's supposed to bring to the clan. If you're so dead set on doing your duty, do it to her."

He gestured toward the door. "I just tried."

"It's not just sex that makes a marriage, you fool."

He was not a fool. Sometimes he thought he was the only member of the clan who wasn't. He also knew that despite her dabbling in things best left to the likes of the White Lady, Rosemary was no fool, either.

She was so earnestly well intentioned that he couldn't even be angry with her for long. He ducked his head, and ended up smiling at her. "Don't be so harsh with me, Rosemary. Just tell me what you mean." The hour was late, and he was more tired than he'd thought. He stifled a yawn.

Rosemary brushed her hand across his cheek. "Be gentle with the girl. Get to know her. Court her."

He sneered. "Och!"

"You heard me."

"It was what I was afraid you were going to say."

She put a hand on her hip. "You know I'm right."

"I know no such thing."

"Bring her flowers. Hold her hand. Ask her how she feels. Find out what she dreams of. Be there for her when she shows she's afraid of the world she's a stranger in. Make her feel welcome and wanted and needed."

Rowan shook his head impatiently. "You talk like a woman."

"I am a woman. I know what women need. Aidan told me he told you the same thing while you were riding after the raiders."

"Aidan thinks like one of the fair folk."

"He knows what women want. And has had far more success with tumbling pretty girls than you've ever had."

"I've no time for courtship."

"You have a year and a day—less the time since the wedding. Court her." She pointed toward the door. "Go on," Rosemary commanded, then disappeared back down the stairs to the hall, taking the light with her.

Rowan was left in the shadows, to look at the door, a fierce frown on his face. He had every intention of going back into his own bedroom as Rosemary wanted, but it wasn't courtship that he had on his mind.

Maddie heard the voices outside the door, but even with her ear pressed to the thick wood, she couldn't make out a word they said. It was Rowan and Rosemary, she thought, talking about her, she supposed. She fingered the necklace that refused to come off, and worried about what Rowan planned.

Maybe she shouldn't have hit him on the head.

She hadn't exactly been thinking straight at the time. She hadn't been thinking straight since before she got on the airplane in Stornoway, and meeting Rowan Murray had only made things worse.

She leaned her head against the door as unwanted memories stirred of the way he'd felt, of the way he'd made her feel before the panic set in. Maybe if she'd met him in another place, another time—

She had, she reminded herself. There was a man just like Rowan Murray waiting in her own time. The right man for her. "Accept no substitutes," she told herself.

For some reason she'd lost track of her need to return home in the last couple of days. Having just rolled around on the bed for a while with her so-called husband, Maddie was achingly aware that she had better get her mind back on her original objective.

She glanced back at the bed. "I don't intend to repeat the experience any time soon," she vowed, though she wondered how she was going to continue to stop Rowan if having sex with her was really what he wanted. He was stronger than she was, after all, and legally within his rights, as he'd pointed out before she'd conked him on the head. She had agreed to their marital arrangement, even though it was under duress. Besides, parts of the rolling-around-on-the-bed scenario hadn't been that unpleasant. It would have helped if he hadn't come on quite so strong, so fast.

"A girl needs a little foreplay," she muttered. "It says so in all those women's magazines Mama's sent me over the years."

While she talked to herself she stepped back from the door, but not fast enough to avoid getting hit in the forehead as it was forcefully opened.

"Ow!" she shouted as she went down. She glared up at Rowan from the floor. "You did that on purpose!"

"I wish I had."

Rowan regretted the words immediately. "Are you hurt?" he asked as he reached down and hauled Maddie to her feet.

She rubbed her forehead. "I'm fine."

He leaned close, keeping hold of her wrist to stop her from backing away. "You'll have a headache."

"I suppose so." She wouldn't look him in the eye, but after a moment she cleared her throat. "How's your head?"

"It'll do." The throbbing pain had settled down somewhat.

"I'm . . . I'm sorry I hit you."

Now here was a new twist. He'd never yet met a Murray woman who apologized for an act of violence. His anger faded at Maddie's words, and Rosemary's lecture reverberated in his head. In some ways his cousin had the right of it, though he hated to admit it. There was wisdom in getting to know the woman, as long as he didn't let himself get too attached in the process.

He released his hold on Maddie. It was his turn to clear his throat, turn his head, and mumble, "Sorry I frightened you."

She quickly retreated across the room, sat on the bed, then jumped off of it as though she'd it had burned her. "Uh—"

"Go to sleep," Rowan told her. "I intend to." He

made sure the door was securely closed behind him, then rolled himself in his plaid and settled down in front of it, with his back to his wide, warm bed and the woman he should be sharing it with. She wasn't going anywhere tonight, and neither was he. Everyone but Rosemary would assume they'd passed the night in love play and would wish them well in the morning. He'd rather face the lie than rowdy laughter at both their expense.

Tomorrow, when neither of them suffered from an aching head, he'd see what he could do about setting to rights this foolish muddle that was supposed to be a marriage.

14

Maddie didn't mind that Rowan snored. It wasn't one of those window-rattling, thunderous sorts of snores. It was a rather comforting sound, really, a domestic touch that came out of the darkness occasionally during the long, sleepless night.

She hadn't been able to sleep because he'd apologized, not because she was afraid he was going to jump up and ravish her. In part it bothered her—ludicrously, she knew—that given the choice between a difficult ravishment and a good night's rest, he'd chosen to go to sleep. It bothered her that she wasn't the sort of woman who inspired uncontrollable lust. Then, of course, she already knew that, and she should have been glad of it. She didn't really want Rowan to jump her bones—she just sort of wished he'd put a little more effort into it. Which was a very foolish attitude to entertain, even if only in brief, intermittent, sleep-deprived spurts. Her mixed emotions both annoyed and confused her. It didn't help that he'd apologized.

It was hard to hate someone who apologized. She'd

had to spend a lot of those sleepless hours reminding herself that abusive males frequently apologized for their behavior. Then she spent even more time wondering if she'd been abused. Okay, she'd said no and he hadn't wanted to take that for an answer, but was that abusive behavior under the medieval circumstances? And he hadn't apologized for the assault, but for frightening her.

So she rolled around on the straw-filled mattress a lot, and didn't doze off until near dawn. It did not help her mood when Rowan shook her shoulder just as she was getting comfortable.

"Time to fetch me my porridge, woman," he announced, sounding far too alert and cheerful for Maddie, who was not a morning person even in the best of circumstances.

Rowan had dreamed about Maddie and the things they hadn't done all through the night. It wasn't the first time he'd had such a dream, but last night was the first time when he'd been in the same room with her. He'd woken up a few times, considered joining her in the bed and turning dream into reality. Each time the slight pain in his scalp, and Rosemary's warning voice in his memory, kept him from giving in to the impulse.

Now an ache in his belly and the call of the day's duties kept him from greeting her with a kiss and a quick tumble. "Well?" he demanded as she regarded him out of barely open eyes.

"Well, what?"

"Are you wife enough to at least see to my meal?"

Maddie sat up and scrubbed her hands over her face. "You," she told Rowan Murray, "are a churlish, surly lout. And those are your better qualities."

She sounded so miserable that he couldn't take offense. "Didn't sleep, did you?" He couldn't stop the slight smile. "Thinking of me, lass?"

He was surprised at his words. He was not a man with a talent for teasing, not like Aidan. Rowan didn't approve of his brother's teasing ways. He was a serious man with serious concerns and no gift for banter. The urge to tease Maddie was a sudden and strange thing. He even suspected that he'd done it before, at the wedding feast, and hadn't even noticed at the time. He didn't know what to do about this inexplicable reaction to the woman, other than turn from her curious look and walk away.

Maddie scratched her head as Rowan left the room. Had that actually been a smile, or something very close to one? She must be dreaming, hallucinating. The man couldn't be capable of smiling. "It was a trick of the light," she decided, and, since she was too tired to deal with the medieval world right now, she pulled the covers back over her head and went to sleep.

It was only the dread of cold haggis for breakfast that woke her a few minutes later. Rosemary had served her the leftovers of the stuff one morning when she'd come down to the hall late. Dealing with a concoction that involved oatmeal and a sheep's stomach was difficult enough when it was fresh and warm. Maddie gulped back nausea at the memory as she hurried to get dressed. She had something much more appetizing in mind.

Rowan was seated at the main table with his mouth full of porridge when Maddie came down the stairs.

For a moment a faint hope flared in him that she'd join him. Instead she walked right on past without giving him a look. Perhaps she wasn't hungry, he thought as he watched her go to the door. Or more likely she just didn't want to share his company. Annoyed at the thought, he left his meal and followed her outside.

As he suspected, she headed for the kitchen hut. He hurried after her. He grabbed her by the arm before she reached the kitchen door.

She spun angrily to face him. "What?"

"Rest easy, lass, I'm not going to try to kiss you. I'm here to offer a warning. It's not safe for a woman to step into that building." Was that a hint of disappointment he saw in her eyes when he said he wasn't going to kiss her? The woman was maddening. Did she want him or didn't she? It was probably his imagination, and he knew well how to keep that in check.

Maddie glanced from Rowan to the hut. She nodded. "Oh, right. Malcolm."

"Aye, Malcolm. You'd best stay away from Malcolm's fief."

Even Rosemary, who planned the meals, rationed out the stores, kept the inventory of foodstuffs, and saw to serving what emerged from the kitchen, kept a respectful distance from the cook's domain.

"He's a terror, all right." Maddie grinned. "Don't worry, I'm not interested in his job. I don't cook."

Rowan frowned. "You dinna?"

"Nope."

"Rosemary said you're not the domestic sort."

She waited for him to complain, to say something disparaging about her lack of femininity. When he didn't, she asked, "Well?"

"Well, what?"

He was not the most forthcoming man Maddie had ever met. "Well, are you going to say something about how every woman should know how to cook and clean house and all that other domestic junk?"

"No. Are you going to leave Malcolm in peace? Or do I have to stand at your back with my claymore in my hands while you invade his den?"

Maddie was confused by his answer and amused by his question. She couldn't help but smile as she looked him over. His long hair was windblown, and there was a glint in his ice blue eyes that might be answering amusement. "You're not wearing your claymore."

He patted the long dagger at his waist. "My dirk, then."

She pointed toward the kitchen building. "I've been told there's smoked salmon in there. Sounds delicious, doesn't it?"

"Aye. Better than porridge."

"That's what I think. You up for an assault?"

Rowan rubbed his thumb along his jaw. After a few moments he said, "Aye. Lead on, Lady Maddie."

She chuckled. "Lady Maddie. That sounds silly."

His perpetual frown returned. "You've a right to the title while we're wed."

While. She felt a brief prick of annoyance, or maybe it was regret, at the impermanence of the situation. Or maybe it was just hunger. It wasn't as if she wanted the situation to be permanent. She tossed her head. "If you're going to call me a lady, Lady Madalyn sounds fancier. I'd rather just be called Maddie, though."

"Maddie's a pretty name." Rowan was startled that the words had come out so easily, just a truth spoken without thought. He wondered what was the matter with him. He was not given to flattery, but he found himself wanting to tell her that he liked the way her hair caught fire in the sunlight, that he—

Och, he'd seen how foolish it was to say such things to one female, how her vanity had grown with each flowery word that had poured from his father's lips. It would not do to spoil his own woman with such foolishness, despite Rosemary's admonitions.

She blushed at his words, looked down, then up through long lashes. "Thank you."

Rowan fought against finding her reaction charming. "It is no more than the truth. Do you want that salmon or not?"

Maddie tried very hard not to be flustered just because someone who wasn't her parent had said that something about her was pretty. She was relieved to latch on to Rowan's practical question after his flattering words. She took a deep breath and made herself look him squarely in the face. His expression had hardened back into his usual dour countenance. Good. She could deal with dour.

"Let's go get that salmon." She marched confidently off, with the lord of Cape Wrath at her back.

The kitchen was smokier than the hall, with a fire blazing the length of long central hearth. Maddie got a quick view of grates and spits and oversized cooking utensils all suspended over the blaze. Unidentifiable things hung from the sooty rafters, and jars and dishes and boxes were stacked on the floor and worktables. It was not like any kitchen she'd ever imagined.

A large-bellied, half-naked, red-bearded man stood over a gigantic boiling pot at one end of the hearth. He turned angrily on them the instant they stepped into the room. "What are you two doing here?" he shouted at them. "Be gone!"

Maddie fleetingly wondered what her mother, sisters, aunts, and cousins would do to organize this disastrous-looking kitchen, but couldn't come up with a clue. Her natural response was to wonder how to go about building the man a proper stove and getting some ventilation into the place. Unlike the drafty hall where people lived and slept, it was damned hot in here where all they did was cook. Maybe she could figure out some way of connecting the two to tap into the energy wasted in this environment.

"Welcome to hell," she muttered and stepped up to the cook. "Good morning, Malcolm, you old devil."

He must have found her cheerfulness disconcerting. For an instant the patented Murray glower that twisted his face relaxed. He took a step back. "I don't allow women in my kitchen."

"My mother doesn't allow men in hers. I think you're both terribly sexist. I also think you're lucky I'm the one who married your laird and not her." She gestured toward Rowan. "We came for breakfast."

His glower came back, full force. "I sent porridge to the hall hours ago. Leave me to get on with my work."

"Don't you take that tone with me."

"Aye," Rowan spoke up. "You'll show respect to my lady."

"Did I invite you in here, Rowan Murray?" was Malcolm's surly reply. "You mind training the fighters and overseeing the village, and leave me to my work. You're altogether too much of a busybody, and everyone knows it."

"I do my duty."

"You do too much, and you can do it elsewhere."

Maddie crossed her arms, looked from one man to the other. "You can discuss this later. Where's the salmon?"

"The what?" Malcolm demanded angrily.

"It's a fish. Sort of pink. My favorite food in the whole world." She looked around. "Where is it?"

"What makes you think I'll give it to you?"

"Not the milk of human kindness, that's for certain." Malcolm gave an unfriendly laugh. Maddie decided to try this lady of the clan thing to see if it worked. "That's an order, cook." She hated going through all this nonsense because of something so simple as wanting a decent meal. "I mean it," she added as Malcolm's face went red with anger.

"You'll not have it," was his stubborn reply.

"My lady gave you an order," Rowan told the cook. "You'll do as you're told."

Malcolm drew himself up to his full height, his belly stuck belligerently out before him. "I'll not waste the best food in the castle on a woman's whim. I'm saving the smoked salmon for the Lord of the Isles."

Rowan was appalled at his next words, but he couldn't stop them. "You'll give my wife what she asks for, and the devil with the Lord of the Isles!"

He couldn't believe that he was indeed indulging a woman's whim, but she smiled at him when he gave the order. That smile brightened his day, blinded him for an instant to what he was doing. He knew Malcolm was right about Maddie's taste for salmon—it was a foolish, selfish whim. Porridge was good enough for the household; they should save their best for the upcoming visit from the clan's overlord. Here he was spoiling the woman instead. He was as bad as his father, but having said it, having promised her his help, it was too late to back down now. "Do it," he said. Then he turned around and walked out of the kitchen, but not before giving Maddie a hard look on the way out.

What's wrong with him? Maddie wondered, but she didn't waste time pondering Rowan's odd behavior. She commandeered enough salmon and fresh bread for both of them and hurried to catch up with Rowan.

She found him sitting on a bench by the curtain wall, shoulders slumped and apparently studying his feet. She settled beside him, made a quick pair of sandwiches and held one out to him. "I'm a firm believer in sharing the booty. Come on, you're too skinny," she added when he hesitated. He was all rangy, spare muscle, actually. "Come on," she coaxed, "waste not, want not and all that. I could never eat all this myself."

That got him. The man had a deeply frugal soul. He took the sandwich and began to eat. A grudging, angry silence emanated from him, but Maddie waited until she'd polished off her own meal before she said, "So what do you perceive I did wrong?"

"You're a woman," he answered after a further few minutes of silence in which she didn't go away. "You cannot help being sly, lazy, dissolute, perfidious, and greedy. I should keep a more careful watch against your wiles."

Wiles? What wiles? She'd never used a wile in her life—she wouldn't know a wile if it bit her on the butt! And speaking of pains in the butt, Rowan Murray deserved a good trouncing.

Maddie managed to hide her anger, and kept her

voice calm. "Oh, I see. Do you think this about all women, or just me?"

"Some women are better than others."

"Uh-huh. Is Rosemary one of the good ones?"

"Aye."

"Micaela?"

"Aye, for the most part."

"Flora? Meg? All the other Murray women?"

"They're good women."

"But I'm not."

Rowan wished he'd never answered her at all. He wished she hadn't spoken her last words as a statement of his beliefs when he wasn't sure what he thought at all. "I have work to do."

He started to get up, but she grabbed a handful of his kilt in her fist and hauled him back down. "No one calls me a slut and walks away."

He turned to her in shock. "I called you no such thing!"

She was crying.

She hadn't sounded like a weeping woman when she'd been questioning him. It twisted his insides to see a woman crying because of his words. It made him ache to take her in his arms, to comfort her and swear that he was the worst fool that had ever lived.

Before he could do anything, she shifted her grip to his shirt and hauled his closer, until their faces were inches apart. "I have had it with you. At no point have I taken advantage of you. You're the one who dragged me here. You're the one who forced me to marry you. This is your game, not mine. I'm sick of playing it. Your attitude sucks, your opinions are dead wrong and of no importance, and I'm out of here."

Her words were furious, but he was too close not to see the deep pain he'd put in her eyes. Rowan was so shocked, chagrined, and confused by everything that had happened in the last few minutes he didn't react as quickly as he should when she got up and walked away.

In fact, Maddie was through the fortress gate before it sank in that she meant to leave Cape Wrath, and him, altogether.

"No, wait!" he shouted, and ran after her.

15

I've had it with all the Murrays, Maddie thought as she ran blindly toward the sea. The castle was behind her, and the village. If there were people around, she didn't see them. She didn't care. She didn't know where she was going, she just wanted to get to the water's edge. She'd grown up among the valleys and cliffs of the Rockies, but her heart belonged to the sea, especially the great, rolling, gray North Atlantic. It was the place she went to for comfort for her aching, lonely, deeply wounded soul.

"I've had it with Murrays," she said as a she reached the black shingle where a few fishing boats were beached. She halted at the spot just where the shore ended, looked down at the foamy edge of a wave that stopped not an inch from her feet, then glanced up at a loud call from a stand of nearby boulders that leaned out over the bay. It was steep place, fit more for puffin and gull nests than for people, but a group of children had climbed to the very top. They were waving, and calling to her.

Maddie scrubbed tears off her cheeks, and half-heartily waved back. *Not all Murrays are bastards,* she reminded herself. *Just one.* The kids were kind of cute. She'd become fond of the women as well. Nobody was to blame for how she was feeling but the laird of the clan. The same laird who'd forced her into his family but suspected her of every nasty bit of behavior humans were capable of.

"He forgot to mention murder, pillage, and cheating on my income tax," she muttered as she stepped back to avoid spray that splashed in from a particularly powerful wave.

"What's income tax?"

Maddie whirled around at the sound of the voice, lost her balance, and would have fallen back into the water if Rowan hadn't made a swift grab for her.

"Get your hands off me!" she shouted, and pushed hard against his chest. He didn't budge. The man was as immovable as Scottish granite.

Rowan wasn't sure what he should do with Maddie now that he'd caught up with her. Throwing her over his shoulder and dragging her back to the privacy of his room came to mind. "I'm not letting you go," he told her. "Not now. Not for a year and a day. You're my wife."

Her eyes blazed while the wind whipped at her coppery hair and the sea roared at her back. "You don't give a damn about me."

"I care about what's mine."

"About your clan, you mean."

She struggled to break out of his grip while Rowan struggled to find the words that would calm her. Nothing he'd said so far was of any use. He'd be angry himself if someone he'd been forced to marry spoke only of clan loyalty when something more personal was needed. "You're part of my clan," was all he could manage. He knew that wasn't enough.

"You don't trust me. You don't like me."

"You don't understand."

"You don't ever explain."

"I just spent half the morning talking to you."

"Well, excuse me for daring to interrupt your solitary thoughts."

He hadn't meant to sound so annoyed about a bit of conversation. He hadn't minded talking. Why did people always think he didn't want to have conversations? "It was no burden talking to you, woman. You didn't like my explanations."

"There was nothing to like."

"Aye, I'll grant you that."

Tears welled in Maddie's eyes again. "What do you want from me?"

If he weren't convinced she'd run if he loosened his hold even a little, Rowan would have reached up and wiped the tears away. His next impulse was to hold her close and comfort her, tell her it wasn't what he wanted but what fate had dictated for them. Instead of doing either of these things, he admitted, "I don't know what I want." Not for himself. "But for the clan—"

Terrified screams from the children on the cliff halted his words. He whirled about just in time to see a small body hit the water.

Maddie swore. "Can he swim?" Even as she called out the question, the children on the rocks were yelling that Iain was going to drown, that he couldn't swim a stroke.

She would have jumped into the surf, but Rowan held her back. "Stay here!" Not wanting to be weighed down by the heavy wool, he stripped off his kilt, tossed it to his wife and plunged into the freezing water.

Maddie didn't know whether to wait on the shore or jump in after him. She was a strong swimmer, with plenty of lifesaving training—you didn't live for a year on a platform over the raging North Sea and not learn how to survive as long as possible in the cold, stormy water. She was torn, but hesitated when she saw that Rowan could swim like a seal. He cut through the water, reaching the child quickly with swift, clean strokes. It bothered her that the kid didn't move when he grabbed the small body and made his way back toward the shore. She feared hypothermia had already set in despite the relatively balmy temperature of the summer sea.

"It's maybe forty-five degrees if we're lucky," she muttered. She paced up and down the shingle, her gaze never leaving the figure of Rowan Murray as he swam back toward shore. "Maybe the boy passed out when he hit the water," she guessed as she worried about the child. "Maybe his lungs are already full of saltwater. Maybe—" She barely noticed the arrival of the other children who'd been playing on the cliff or of villagers alerted to the accident by the children's cries.

A crowd was gathered around her by the time Rowan stumbled out of the water, Iain's small body cradled in his arms. The crowd parted as Maddie hurried forward. The first thing she did was wrap the cold body in Rowan's warm plaid as he settled Iain onto dry land.

"How's he doing?" she demanded as they knelt on

either side of the unmoving boy. Iain's skin was blue with cold, and lack of oxygen, too, she suspected. She grasped the boy's wrist.

Terror gripped her stomach as Rowan shouted. "Fetch Father Andrew!"

"I've got a pulse!"

A woman cried out. Someone else demanded, "Is the lad dead?"

"He drowned," Rowan confirmed. "I dinna get to him quick enough."

Maddie moved to kneel by Iain's head. She gave Rowan a quick, commanding look. "Press on his chest after I breathe."

"What are you talking about?"

She ignored his outraged question, took a gulp of air, put her mouth over Iain's and exhaled as hard as she could. She shot Rowan a look as she took in another lungful. He looked appalled, but he grasped her meaning, and pressed down on Iain's chest. She bent forward to breathe out again. Rowan pressed down.

Within a few seconds Iain coughed and took in a great gasp of air on his own. Maddie sat back on her heels. Iain sat up and began to cry. A man ran forward and snatched the coughing boy up into his arms.

"It's a miracle!" Father Andrew cried.

"Magic!" Maddie heard Rosemary chime in.

"Girl Scout merit badge," Maddie said, but no one was listening to her. Mouth-to-mouth was the only first aid technique she hadn't flunked.

No one but Rowan paid her any mind; he was smiling at her. Her cheeks went hot with pleasure at the intensity of that smile. Now she knew why he didn't do it too often, because when he let that smile loose it was devastating. It almost made her forget she'd hated his guts not ten minutes ago. Almost. She looked away. She tried to get back her righteous anger, but it was too late, the adrenaline rush from the crisis had burned out her bad mood. She couldn't help but be happy—but she told herself it was because the kid was okay, not because Rowan Murray was smiling at her.

She did let him help her to her feet. His hands were cold. She turned to him in alarm. There he stood, soaking wet, wearing nothing but a short saffron shirt and a wide, boyish grin. "Get those clothes off," she demanded. "You're freezing!"

"If that's what you want, lass."

He was still grinning when he stripped off the shirt and stood before her, completely naked. The villagers stopped fussing over poor wee Iain long enough to look at her staring at not-so-wee Rowan. For a man who'd never displayed a sense of humor before, he seemed to take an inordinate amount of amusement in exhibiting himself to her.

It was Rosemary who laughed first. Someone made a lewd comment. Maddie squeaked in shock at another earthy suggestion, from Father Andrew, of all people. Then, with gales of ribald laughter ringing in her ears, Maddie turned around and stormed off toward the castle.

"That was unconscionable."

"I only did as you wanted."

"I was concerned for you. You could have frozen in that wet shirt."

"I'm grateful."

"That was no way of showing it."

"Well, I'm not used to showing it in public."

"Will you stop!"

Her cheeks were as bright red as her flaming hair. Rowan didn't know what devil had gotten into him an hour ago, but it still rode him as he joined Maddie on the bench they'd vacated earlier in the day. He felt giddy, wild, happy. The sun was still warm, the breeze soft. He stretched out his legs before him, and gazed at his wife's tense profile.

"The lad's alive," he said. "Your doing. You're here to save the clan. I believe it, now." He put his hand on her shoulder.

She slipped away, moved further down the length of the seat they shared. "Good for you."

He'd found her on the bench when he'd returned from making sure Iain was settled in his own warm bed. She looked so lost and lonely he didn't have the heart to point out to her that he'd just seen to one of the functions that should have been hers. It occurred to him that he shouldn't expect her to perform traditional duties, but to leave her free to save his people in her own way.

"Have I told you we're all thankful for your saving the lad's life?"

Maddie was so shocked at his gentle tone that she looked at him for the first time since he sat down beside her. He was bare-chested but for a fold of kilt thrown over his left shoulder. To avoid looking at is chest, she looked at his face. Rowan looked younger, somehow, lighter, if that made any sense. As though he were an approachable human being instead of a duty-driven tyrant. That bothered her. She wasn't in any mood to deal with him as a human being—a practical-joking human being at that.

"I didn't save him," she said. "We did. You're the one who got him out of the water."

"You brought him back to life."

"He wasn't dead. His lungs were just full of water," she explained as Rowan gave her a curious look. "We got air to him and then he started breathing on his own. No magic, just commonsense first aid."

Rowan was intrigued. "No magic?"

"There's no such thing as magic."

She sounded so adamantly opposed to the simple fact of life Rowan decided not to try to persuade her differently. Why fight more than necessary? "Can you teach me this, what did you call it, first aid?"

"Mouth-to-mouth? Sure." Maddie blushed as she saw his icy eyes suddenly take on warmth at her words. He reached for her. She stood. "I'm not talking about kissing."

Humor as well as desire lit his expression. "But you're thinking about it."

"Because you are."

"More than thinking. I'm going to do it." He stood, snagged her around the waist. He pulled her against his bare chest. "You were concerned that I wasn't warm enough a few minutes ago." Her eyes went wide as he leaned closer, but she didn't try to pull away. That was a good sign. Her lips were soft to the touch as he covered her mouth with his. Desire began to replace playful giddiness as he teased her lips with his tongue. He was ready to deepen the kiss, taste the sweetness of her mouth, then an errant thought intruded and he pulled abruptly away.

Maddie staggered back as Rowan released her. He was glaring again. "What?"

"Did you not tell me yesterday that you know nothing of healing?"

Maddie ran a hand across her mouth. "Well, yeah, I guess. But I—"He grabbed her shoulders and shook her. "You lied to me."

"Stop that!" He did, but only long enough to grab her wrist and angrily haul her toward the tower entrance. "What are you doing? Where are we going?"

"You're going to tend the sick," he informed her. "And you're going to do it right now."

16

Burke Harboth had been given a thick pallet in a curtained-off section of the hall. The area seemed far too private to Rowan, especially as he found his sister seated next to the Harboth lad as Rowan stalked over. It didn't help his angry mood to see her solicitously combing Burke's thick blond hair.

"Micaela, get away from there," he ordered as he dragged Maddie forward. "You don't know where it's been." Micaela sprang indignantly to her feet as Rowan pushed Maddie to her knees. "I've brought you a new nurse, Harboth." He looked at his sister. "Where's your chaperone?"

"Rosemary ran off when we heard about Iain."

"How is the lad?" Burke asked.

Rowan ignored the question. He took Micaela by the hand. "Come with me." He glared down at his wife. "You tend him."

"But . . ." Maddie, Micaela, and Burke all said at once.

Rowan paid no attention to any of them. He marched Micaela away in implacable silence.

Maddie stayed on her knees for a few moments, recovering from the shock. Finally she looked at Burke. "What was that all about?"

Burke laughed. She watched her hand as he took it in his own and began to gently stroke her fingers. "Apparently the laird of the Murrays would rather have me court his wife than his sister."

"Oh." She snatched her hand back to her side. "Stop that."

Burke propped himself up on his elbows. "You look like you need courting, my lady."

Maddie grimaced. "Do I?"

"Aye. But since my heart belongs to Micaela Murray, perhaps I should call in my brother to woo you—for the saints know Rowan Murray hasn't the wit or will to make a woman happy."

"Amen to that," Maddie grumbled. Then she stood up quickly. "I'm not interested in anybody courting me, anyway."

He smiled, showing roguish dimples. "All women are."

She shrugged. "Well, maybe. A little. This is hardly the place or time for it."

"Place and time don't matter—it's the man, my lady."

Maddie crossed her arms, and changed the subject. "How are you feeling?"

"I'm fine." He sat up and brushed a thick lock of blond hair out of his face. "How's the lad?"

"Iain's fine."

He stood up, and Maddie saw that he was very tall, though slender. She already knew he was heavy. He straightened his kilt. "Have you seen my sword belt, my lady?"

"No. Are you sure you're all right?" she asked as he rolled his shoulders and winced.

"Well enough to return to my own clan," he answered.

"Since Rowan won't let Micaela near you anymore?"

He grinned at her question. Micaela pushed back the curtain before he could answer.

"My brother's a fool," Micaela declared. She gave Maddie a passing glance. "Though I doubt you think so."

"You're not getting any argument from me." While she spoke, Micaela and Burke clasped hands and gazed into each others' eyes. Maddie could practically see the pheromones sizzling through the air between them. She shook her head. "Why don't you take a walk or something? It'd probably do Burke some good to sit in the sunshine." They stepped closer to each other. She put a hand on Micaela's shoulder. "Get out of the house, Mickey. You two could use the fresh air. The sun doesn't shine that often around here. Go on, take advantage of it."

Micaela put her arm around Burke's waist, and he put his around her shoulders. Maddie didn't think they needed to be quite that close as she watched them walk away, but she couldn't help but be amused by their obvious devotion. Amused, but a bit melancholy as well. She wondered what it would be like to have someone devoted to her. Then she suddenly recalled the moment Rowan had started to kiss her in the courtyard.

"That wasn't devotion," she told herself.

She wasn't even sure it was lust. He'd probably thought it was his duty to kiss her just then. Maybe he considered it some sort of reward for her helping to rescue Iain. Lord knew he'd been easily enough distracted just as she was getting interested in the proceedings.

"Oh, the devil with Rowan Murray," she said, and marched after the young couple toward the door. "I'm going to get to work on that chimney design."

"Don't you ever do as you're told?"

Maddie turned from one scowling man to the other. "Not usually, no," she answered Rowan, and smiled sweetly as she said it.

"Why aren't you in the hall?" He wiped a bead of sweat off his forehead, then glanced back down the hill he'd just climbed. It was warm, even for a high summer day. The wind was picking up, though, and there were clouds piling up over the mountains. Soon there would be cool rain to break the heat, and he'd no doubt spend the night out in foul weather once again.

In the meantime, the day was getting on, and too much of it had been taken up with dealing with his errant wife. He wasn't even sure why he'd gone looking for her by Burke Harboth's bedside. He did know he was justifiably annoyed to not have found her there. "Why didn't I find you nursing Burke?"

"Because he doesn't need nursing."

"You should be with him." He waggled a finger under her nose.

"Why?"

"What if he'd run off with you?"

"Is that why you came looking for me? Afraid I ran

off with a rival?" She stroked her chin. "He is awful handsome. And nice."

"He's a murdering Harboth. I wouldn't put it past him to steal away—"

"Micaela," she cut him off. "Not that he'd have to steal her. She'd run off voluntarily."

"She'd do no such thing. She's a good girl. Never you mind Micaela's doings, it's you I've come to chastise."

Maddie lifted a sardonic brow. "Oh, really?" Her words dripped sarcasm.

"You're to obey me. Get you home."

"I'd love to, but unfortunately I'm stuck in medieval Scotland."

"Home to my house."

"No."

"Maddie—"

"I have better things to do than obey you, oh laird and lord of the land." She grinned, looking mightily pleased with herself. "I think I'm getting good at this alliteration thing, don't you think?"

"No, I do not." Rowan studied the stubborn expression on her face, the tense set of her body, and realized that his responding with equal stubbornness would get them nowhere. He wasn't about to toss her over his shoulder for the long trek back to the hall, however. Nor was he quite up to being reasonable yet. Perhaps he had feared for her safety as he searched barn and byre and fields for some sign of her whereabouts.

All he knew was that one moment he'd been discussing hunting some unknown beast that was frightening the shepherds up in the hills, and the next moment an insistent urge to see his wife overcame him.

Whatever the cause of the sudden need to see her, he was relieved to have found her at last, even if she wasn't where she was supposed to be. He wasn't about to give in and mildly go away until he'd had his fill of her irritating but interesting presence.

"Why aren't you in the hall?" he asked.

"Because she's plaguing me," the other man answered. "Take her back to the hall and let me get on with my work."

"Walter's being very helpful," Maddie told Rowan. She took a seat on one side of the break that had been made by the cattle raiders in the drystone fence. She waved toward the artfully layered rocks and the pile of stones on the ground. "He's been explaining how the fence is fitted together without any mortar."

"I haven't been explaining. She's been pestering."

"I've been asking very pertinent questions."

"Where's Harboth?" Rowan asked.

For no reason she could think of, Maddie fluttered her eyelashes coyly at Rowan. It made his scowl deepen. "You know, you frown so much your face could freeze that way and no one would notice."

For a moment a glint of humor warmed his icy ices. Not long enough to do any real good, though. "Where's my sister?" he demanded.

"With Burke."

He grabbed her arms. "Alone?"

She shook him off. "Stop that."

"Rowan, will you talk to this woman?" the other annoyed Murray demanded.

"I am speaking to her, Walter."

"Make her stop bothering me," Walter insisted. "This is men's work."

Rowan gave Walter a quelling look, then returned his attention to Maddie. Lord, but her eyes had a passionate blaze when she was angry. She'd been angry all day from one thing and another, just as he had been. Did she find him attractive when he was angry? he wondered, inane and useless though he knew the thought to be. The woman gave him good cause to turn his temper on her, yet he found himself attracted to her even as they fought. It made no sense. There were more important things at stake than getting her riled just because he liked the flash of her eyes and the glow in her freckled cheeks.

"Are my sister and Burke Harboth together?"

"I suppose so. Why don't you leave them alone?" she questioned. "They are in love, you know." She gave a bitter laugh. "Oh, that's right, he's a Hatfield and she's a McCoy."

"You're mad, woman. He's a Harboth and she's a Murray."

"Same thing," she shot back. "Wrong century." When he continued to stare at her in confusion, she added. "You know, feuding families brought together by love."

"What!" Rowan's face went red with fury. "I'll not have it!"

Maddie couldn't stop her laughter. "How are you going to stop it?"

"I'll kill him!"

Rowan whirled to hurry away. Walter stepped in front of him before he could take a step. "You're not killing Harboth until you do something about your wife."

"You're not killing Burke at all," Maddie spoke up.

"You're going to let him marry Micaela and end the feud."

He whirled on her. "What?"

She dusted her hands together. "There. I've just solved your problems, saved the clan, whatever." She glanced up at the sky. "Can I go home now?"

Nothing happened, of course, except that the men looked at her as if she were insane. Maybe she was. It was ridiculous to have even a tiny bit of hope that there might indeed be a supernatural explanation for her being in the past. For a moment there, though, she'd tried to believe that she was here to save Rowan's clan. She'd tried to do it his way, but she wasn't up to believing in magic. Magic didn't exist. People had to find their own solutions. And she was still stuck in the Middle Ages.

And she had every intention of making the Middle Ages a more comfortable place for everyone involved if she was going to have to live in them.

She looked back at Walter. "We're going to build a fireplace in the hall. I need your expertise with stone working."

Walter drew himself up indignantly. "Mind women's work, Lady Maddie, and leave men to theirs."

"There's no such thing as women's work!" she answered. "Well, maybe breast-feeding, but we can do that while we're building walls. Can you?"

Walter went so red in the face that Rowan was afraid he was going to have a seizure. "You're as bad— no, worse—than every other woman at Cape Wrath! Is it any wonder the clan's the laughingstock of the Highlands! First a fairy woman turns all the others into a pack of witches, and now—you!" the older man shouted. He turned to Rowan. "Do something about her."

"Aye," Rowan agreed. "I will." He took Maddie by the arm. "We're going back to the hall. And you, Walter," he commanded, "will give her a fireplace if she wants one."

Walter gave a braying, angry laugh. "You sound like your father, lad, giving in to your woman's every whim."

The words stung, but Rowan didn't back down. "No," he answered. "A fireplace is a good, practical thing. They've had such things in the Lowlands for a hundred years. Time to learn how to warm our backsides like the Sassenachs, I say."

"Yeah," Maddie said, nodding firmly.

"It's not spoiling a woman to make a few improvements to my hall."

"It'll be good for everybody," Maddie assured him. "I've got a nice, simple corner design in mind."

Walter gave her a furious glance and sputtered, but he just gave Rowan a dour nod and went back to work as though they weren't there.

Rowan gave her a stern look. She was used to his stern looks by now; this one didn't bother her, since he'd actually agreed with her for once. She just hoped he wasn't going to throw it up to her like he had over her choice of breakfast. She was so pleased with Rowan's actions that she let him help her off her perch and guide her down the hill as if she somehow needed help. It was a funny thing, really, how feminine it made her feel to have his hand cupping her elbow and his somewhat larger presence so close behind her. Under other circumstances, having him so near had felt threatening, but this time it didn't. It filled her with a syrupy warmth that had nothing to do with the feeble late afternoon sunlight.

She was still enjoying as well as puzzling over this strange reaction when they entered the courtyard and came face-to-face with Burke and Micaela near the gate. Rowan instantly stepped away from her. She noticed that Burke and Micaela were holding hands. They held their ground as Rowan stalked up to them. His hand was on his dagger, while the younger man was unarmed. Burke didn't seem to notice. Maddie couldn't help but admire the Harboth kid's nonchalant bravado. She thought he was crazy, but she understood the romantic appeal he projected. She understood it, but looking from one man to the other, she found she preferred the serious, protective determination exuded by Rowan. It was just so much more—grown-up. Even if she didn't necessarily agree with his attitude, she appreciated it.

"Keep away from my sister," Rowan demanded. He didn't draw his dagger, but he didn't take his hand off the hilt.

"I'm a guest in your house, Murray," Burke answered calmly. "I'd not try to despoil her under your roof, man."

"Nor would I let him if he tried," Micaela declared.

"You'd rather meet in some secluded glade and tumble in the heather?" Rowan questioned suspiciously.

"Something like that," Burke agreed.

"But not until we're wed," Micaela insisted.

"You'll not be married," Rowan told them. "No Harboth cur is wedding a Murray lass." He pointed toward the gate. "You're healthy enough. Get out."

Burke and Micaela looked at each other. "I told you he'd say that," Burke said.

She nodded, sighed. "Aye. I know."

"Come with me."

Rowan's fist clenched around the dagger hilt.

Micaela shook her head. Tears spilled over and ran down her cheeks. Burke's fingers brushed them gently away. "I'll not disobey my laird," she told him.

"And rightly so," Burke capitulated. He sighed. "I love you, lass."

"And I you."

"Get out," Rowan repeated.

"I'll go, Murray."

Rowan called for a groom to fetch Burke's horse and his own. "And one for my wife, while you're at it," he added.

"What?" Maddie asked as Rowan came back to her. "Where are you going?" She looked at him in alarm. "Where am I going? What about my fireplace?"

"We'll build your fireplace when we get back." He took her arm again and didn't let her get away. She was anything but reassured by his touch this time. "Tonight," he said, leaning close to whisper in her ear, "we're going to spend some time together. Alone."

17

"I don't know if you've noticed this, but it's raining." Rowan didn't answer, but he did reach over and drape the hood of the cape he'd provided for her over her head. "I didn't say I minded," Maddie informed him coolly, and got down off her mount.

Rowan dismounted and led his horse through the door of the abandoned house. Maddie hesitated for a moment at the entrance. She looked around for somewhere else to stable the animals, though she could barely see for the rain and deep twilight. They were in a clearing halfway up the side of a mountain. There had once been other buildings here besides the small stone hut, though she could make out signs of fire. There was nothing standing that was intact but the house. *Norse raiders?* she wondered. Or had the place been attacked by one or both sides in the Murray-Harboth feud? Whatever happened here had been some time ago.

She wondered if anyone would come back to repair the damage and get on with their lives. It seemed to her that there was a desperate air of barely surviving hanging over the countryside. A fanciful notion, and she didn't approve of fanciful notions. It was one that was bolstered by evidence of want at Cape Wrath and other tumbledown places like this ruin that they'd passed. It bothered her to see this beautiful land damaged, worried her that the people were in turmoil.

In the meantime, she and Rowan would just have to share the shelter with the horses. She sighed at the joys of primitive living and led her horse inside. It turned out that the building was designed to house humans and beasts, the stable area divided by a low wall from the living area. The living area was nothing more than a small, dirt-floored room. She took her horse into the stable.

Inside, Rowan had already seen to his animal and was bent over a hearth circle, striking a flint to steel. He had a fire going by the time she was done.

"What are you using for fuel?" she asked when she joined him in the human half of the room.

"Found some dried cow dung in the stable."

"Charming."

Maddie looked around, not that there was much to see by the small glow shed by the fire. They were sitting on a dirt floor, with a thatch roof not that far over their heads. The sights and scents were earthy, but not unpleasant. She was as comfortable as she would have been in the hall at Cape Wrath, and without the crowd. The steady beat of the rain was actually soothing. She was a bit tired from the ride, but not unduly, and the ride itself had been nice. She liked being out in the open, away from the confines of the castle and other people's expectations. If it weren't for the realization that she was alone with the man she'd decided it was best to avoid,

Maddie might have said something about how she was happy to be here.

Instead, she asked, "Why did you bring me here?"

Rowan had not exactly been forthcoming about his intentions on the ride. In fact, the only thing he'd said had been to Burke Harboth before they parted ways at a crossroads, and that had been something along the lines of, "Stay away from my sister." Then silence had descended again until they'd reached this abandoned dwelling.

There had been a time when she'd actually enjoyed silence. She had never been much of a talker; she took silent walks in vastly lonely places and kept her thoughts to herself. Lately, however, ever since she'd ended up in this place, it seemed as if all she'd done was talk. In a way, this urge to communicate, to make contact, had begun to stir in her own time. She had this overwhelming need to reach out and touch and to be touched.

And here she was with the quietest man in the Highlands. She strongly suspected that he had something totally different from verbal communication in mind. Something more tactile was probably in Rowan's plan for the evening. Was sex a form of communication? She didn't know. She wasn't sure she was ready to find out.

She wasn't prepared to remain in isolation even with a companion across the fire from her. When she looked back at him, she found him watching her. She didn't know if the warmth in his eyes came from some emotion or the glow of the fire. *He has nice eyes,* she thought. When she looked into his eyes it was easy to forget that he looked like Toby Coltrane. The odd thing was, she was forgetting what Toby looked like. That made no sense, she supposed, or was some sort of paradox. It was just that Rowan was so distinctly himself, despite the superficial resemblance to another man she wasn't even sure she loved anymore. If she didn't love Toby—

Fortunately Rowan chose to break his silence, and into her confused thoughts. "Come here."

Maddie jumped. "I am here."

He patted the ground beside him, then held up the bag of provisions he'd brought. "If you want your supper, lass, you'll eat it by my side."

She disliked the reminder of just how dependent she was. She also wanted to eat. "How do you know I won't march out and hunt up some nice wild vegetables to eat?"

"Will you?" He looked at her intently. "Can you?"

Maddie glanced out the door. There was nothing but night and rain and wild things out there. "Maybe I'm willing to try."

He laughed. "If the answer to a question is no, say so." He patted the ground again.

Maddie did consider fleeing. "Are there still wolves in the Highlands in this century?" She'd already seen a bear, or something. "What was that thing you killed, anyway? Something that went extinct before my time?"

"If you want answers, do as I tell you." He glanced inside the bag. "There's bannocks and a bit of a honeycomb in here."

She had a weakness for honey, and she did want answers. Maddie moved around the fire to sit next to Rowan, close enough that their thighs touched. She felt the warmth of his bare skin through the layers of linen and wool she wore. The surprising thing was that she wasn't tempted to scoot away from the contact. She told herself it was because the damp night was chilly despite the fire, that she needed all the shared heat she could get.

"Well, I'm here," she said, and held out a hand. "You said something about honey?"

Maddie reflected that her simple words might have sounded like a provocative invitation to another man. Not Rowan. He gave a nod and unpacked their dinner. She sighed with relief, but at the same time she felt a small bit of disappointment that he hadn't taken her words wrong. She tried to bury her confusion as she ate her meal and stared into the small fire.

"What's the matter?" he said after a few minutes, interrupting her thoughts.

"With what?" Maddie glanced sideways at Rowan as she licked honey off her fingers.

"You've got a frown as dark as you accuse me of having marring your face. Is the meal not to your liking? Or is it the company?"

He sounded glum. Now, this was not a rare occurrence, but for the first time she thought her answer might cheer him up, and it mattered to her. Why it mattered to her, she couldn't say.

"It's not you," she said, with more conviction than she felt. "Or the food. It's me."

"What's wrong with you?"

"I don't know." She gestured toward the door and the downpour beyond. "Maybe it's the weather."

She didn't expect for her comment to draw the reaction it got. Rowan drew closer, and settled an arm around her shoulders. "I'm here to keep you warm."

"I've got the fire for that," she said, but she didn't try to scoot away. There was a certain comfort factor in the arm that circled her.

"That won't last long, and I'll still be here." He spoke softly, his lips close to her ear. For a moment Maddie found it difficult to breathe. She stared at the flames and was very aware of Rowan's presence. "Do you want your questions answered yet?" His breath brushed her cheek as he spoke.

"Questions? Wh-what questions?"

"About wolves, and the beastie?"

She'd forgotten the queries she made about the local wildlife before she got involved in thinking about her own weird emotions. Now she recalled the odd animal, its size and smell and the strange eyes like no mammal should have. She shuddered at the memory, and knew he noticed because his embrace tightened. She craned her head to look into his face. "Does the beastie have a name?"

"The Questing Beast. The fairies send them to hunt special prey."

"That's folklore. What was it really? Don't you know?"

"I know exactly what it was. I've killed them before, and I'll no doubt kill them again. Perhaps that's what's plaguing the shepherds who sent for me, though no one's seen the thing for certain."

She had to admit that it made sense for a primitive people to attach supernatural attributes to something they didn't understand. She just didn't like thinking of Rowan and his clever relatives as being so ignorant. All right, so this was the thirteenth century, but that didn't mean the natives had to remain superstitious.

"The Loch Ness monster doesn't exist, you know."

"That's no affair of mine," he replied. "Loch Ness is a good ways from my holding. Besides, what does the Urquhart clan's curse have to do with the Murrays? We're plagued enough by fair folk of our own."

"That wasn't my point."

Rowan wasn't much interested in debating the woman's strange beliefs with her. "It's not wise to talk about the fair folk," he warned. "It draws their attention."

Her answer was a deep sigh he could feel all along the length of his body. He liked holding her near, communicating without the medium of words. Words were malleable things, hard to grasp, harder to let go. Actions had true honesty; the language of the body didn't lie. He could feel her tension, her frustration, perhaps a bit of growing trust from the way her head rested in the crook of his arm.

He liked the way she felt, a warm, soft bundle of female curves. He had thought he was attracted to a more delicate sort of woman, but found that he liked Maddie's robust figure just fine. There was more of her to hold onto than some little, fragile thing. He rubbed his cheek against the springy thickness of her hair and drank in the scent of her. She smelled of rainwater and heather soap, of smoke and of herself. If he kissed her she would taste of honey.

He didn't want to talk. He wanted to have her on her back and have sex with her. Then he wanted them to bundle up together in his plaid and her cloak and get a good night's sleep, for there was a hard quarry to pursue tomorrow. He'd brought Maddie with him for the express purpose of finally making her his wife in more than name. The problem was how to begin. He couldn't just force his will on her. She'd just find something to hit him over the head with if he tried, he was firmly convinced of that. Besides, he didn't want her unwilling.

Rosemary had said to court her. He'd decided that it wasn't such a bad notion. He granted that she deserved more than gruff orders. She was growing on him, was his handfasted wife. He liked her fire, and her looks, and even her stubbornness. He liked being with her, and wanted her to like being with him. She deserved more than he could give her, but he would try to open up as much as his guarded heart could bear. He wanted to give her more, to give in to the urge to properly love her. He sighed, and set about doing the best he could with what little he had to offer.

Maddie liked words. Rowan thought it would be easier to try to impress her with gifts of silk and dainty sweetmeats than to give her the conversation she seemed to crave, even though he was a poor man. Earlier in the day it had not seemed so hard to talk to her. She had drawn words out of him of curiosity and of anger—Maddie had a gift for making him feel both. Right now he wanted to fill the darkness with kisses, to hear no sound but mutual sighs of pleasure. Before that could happen, he would have to try to set his tongue free as he had a few hours before.

She helped him when she said, "Dung's not a bad idea."

"What?"

"Dung," she repeated. "As a fuel source. I've been thinking about alternate fuel sources."

"What are those? No, I think I take your meaning,"

he went on before she could. "Alternate fuel source—things that burn besides firewood."

The proud grin she gave him at his answer warmed him. It made him want to coax more from her, to see her looking at him with pride and joy, curiosity and concern. It made him want her to want to take an interest in *him*. He knew he felt an interest in her, not just in the way a man should be interested in a woman, but an interest in the great knowledge she'd brought with her from her world.

"Bingo," she said to his interpretation of her words. "I mean, aye. Fuel for the new fireplaces, and the forge, and the pottery kiln, and a greenhouse if I can figure out a way to build one."

"What kiln? What's a greenhouse?"

"And we need a grain mill," she went on without answering his questions. "Do you know that those stone querns the women use to make flour are far too inefficient for the amount of food they produce? And that coarse flour might be high-fiber, but it's terrible on people's teeth." She looked at him, earnest expression illuminated by the firelight. "All this stuff is fixable, doable, but I don't want to cut down every tree on the mountain to improve the quality of life for a few people. We have to share this ecosystem, you know."

"I wouldna let you cut down my forest even if you wanted to," he told her.

She smiled. It brightened the whole room. Or at least it dazzled him. This was a new experience, and he wanted her to keep looking at him like that for days and days. Instead she said, "It would be nice if we had a few more pigs."

Curiosity changed the spell her smile had started, but didn't dissipate it. "Pigs? Why?"

"Actually, there are coal deposits not that far from here, but I refuse to be responsible for introducing fossil fuels to the world even if I do work for a petroleum company in my own time." She stroked a hand across her jaw. "If I'm going to start the Industrial Revolution, I'm going to do it right."

Rowan grasped her hand with his free one. "Maddie, love," he urged patiently. "Why do you want more pigs?"

Rowan Murray was stroking her fingers, and he had just called her love. These facts were not lost on Maddie. She chose to try to ignore them, and gave the man a simple explanation about synthesizing methane from animal waste, that of pigs in particular, and how it could be used for fuel.

When she was done, he said, "I see." He also kept touching her. He'd touched her the whole time she'd been talking—held her fingers, stroked her temple, touched her throat. It had been very distracting, but she'd managed to remain lucid. He also seemed to understand what she was talking about. It was so nice to have someone understand what she was talking about. Even better, he seemed genuinely interested.

Rowan was fascinated. "This is a fine magic," he told her.

"It's chemistry."

"Call it what you will, it's the best use for magic I've ever heard."

He considered the implications of the things Maddie spoke of for a few silent moments. He liked that she was eager to teach what she knew, to be up and doing.

Taking pig waste and making it into something useful seemed as practical as taking a piece of iron and turning it into a sword. Rowan liked being presented with practical strategies and solutions. Lord knows he'd had his fill of frivolous magic and moonlit illusion that faded in the light of day.

He kissed her temple. The gentle, brief touch of his lips sent an electric current all through her. She'd never felt anything like it before. *Chemistry in action?* she wondered.

She was distracted from this new sensation when Rowan asked, "Are pigs all we need?"

"That's one thing we can use." She answered. She gazed thoughtfully into the glowing embers of the fire. Rowan's presence surrounded her, the rain lulled her. She relaxed against him. "With a little work there's plenty of accessible energy."

He shifted position so that she leaned back against his chest, with his arms around her waist, supporting and enfolding her. She could feel the rise and fall of his chest as he breathed. That, too, was soothing.

"What sort of energy?" he asked.

She yawned, then answered. "If there's one thing Scotland's full of, it's weather. We could use water and wind for power."

"Windmills and water wheels?"

"You've heard of them?"

"Oh, aye. My great-uncle went on Crusade. He came back with many tales of devices used in foreign parts. Drew pictures of them to show how they were built."

"He never built any?"

Rowan shook his head. "My grandfather wanted nothing to do with Sassenach ways. My father—"

It was painful to hear the way his voice trailed off with angry resentment at the mention of his father. It was enough to make her want to hold him and comfort him. She didn't know what the elder Murray had done, but she was certain Rowan didn't need to live with the pain that obviously haunted him. She'd never wanted to comfort anyone before, but the urge to help Rowan was very strong. She didn't know how—she didn't know if he'd accept compassion, or interpret it as pity. She wondered if it was wise to talk to him about it. She also knew wisdom had nothing to do with breaching emotional distance.

She cleared her throat, then said, "Was your father . . . mean to you?"

Rowan couldn't stop the low, bitter laugh. "No. He was a good man. Everyone loved him."

She hesitated, but couldn't keep from asking, "Everyone except you? Or do you think he didn't love you?"

"Love is not an issue."

"Love is always an issue. It's important."

"Not always. It's not the most important thing. Love gets in the way."

"In the way of what?"

"Of duty, responsibility. You wouldn't understand."

"Why not?"

"You're a woman."

"What's that got to do with it?"

"Women only think of love."

"No, we don't. And you haven't answered my question."

"It's none of your business." The bitterness was knife-edged. There was the hint of threat in his tone.

Maddie thought about it. One moment she'd been enjoying this man's company, the conversation, the intimacy. She'd thought he'd been enjoying it as well. The instant they'd veered into personal territory, he'd closed up again, rebuffed her, insulted her, let her know that she wasn't welcome, that her opinions weren't important. She hurt, and she didn't like it. It filled her with a deep, malignant anger.

She finally said, with the same sharp tone he'd used. "I see. We aren't friends, we aren't lovers, we're just husband and wife. No emotion either of us feels is the other person's concern." She pulled away from him. She got to her feet and drew her cloak tightly around her. "Good night," she told him as she turned away. "I think I'll sleep with the horses."

18

He shouldn't have let her go. Rowan knew that even as he watched Maddie walk out of the tiny circle of firelight.

That was his first thought as he came fully awake at dawn. It wasn't the only time he'd thought it in the long hours, but for the first time he allowed himself a resigned sigh as he sat up by the cold hearth. He should have called her back or gone after her. Perhaps what he should have done was follow his first instinct and taken her. It would have proved to her once and for all that she was his wife.

Or perhaps he should have answered her questions, he thought as he ran his hands through his tangled hair. It wasn't as if his opinion of his father was secret. Every member of the Murray clan knew how he felt. Mostly they didn't ask him questions, though. Oh, Rosemary railed on about what he should do from time to time, but that wasn't the same as trying to probe the depths of his soul. That sort of thing was for a confessor. Fortunately, Father Andrew wasn't the probing sort.

It appeared that Maddie was. Perhaps wives were supposed to be. He didn't know. He'd never been married before. He'd heard other men complain about their nagging womenfolk, but some had smiled fondly even as they complained. He barely remembered his mother. He knew how his father had mourned her loss. He only knew that the fairy wife had never seemed to bring anything but joy to his father. He thought that was just a part of her magic.

She'd also brought nothing but neglect to the people and property of Cape Wrath. No, Rowan admitted, his father had been the neglectful one, the besotted, foolish one. It wasn't the fairy's fault to follow her own frivolous nature. Human concerns were not hers. His father had been entirely responsible. Rowan had been told often that he was very like his father. That was why he knew he had to guard his heart from following the same besotted course. He struggled hard not to let emotions rule him. He felt himself losing that battle since he'd found Maddie standing in the road waiting for him whether she knew she was waiting for her husband or not.

Of course, Maddie wasn't a fairy princess, but that wasn't the point. His determination not to follow his father's course was the point. It had stopped raining, and thin trails of fog brushed across the ground outside. Oh, Maddie was touched by magic, he admitted, but she wasn't happy about it, didn't even want to acknowledge it. She wasn't a delicate, ethereal, whimsical creature made for dancing in moonlit glades. She couldn't run lightly across the wisps of mist outside or dance on the raindrops gathered on the treetops. She was a big girl, with big feet and a brash tongue and firm notions. Firm breasts, as well; and wonderfully curving hips; big, bright eyes; and bright red hair. She was very much a creature of the daylight, probably far too practical to go frolicking in the moonlight. She was full of practical notions, for all that they required large leaps of thought to follow. He liked it that she made him think.

He wasn't so sure that he liked that she made him feel, as well. Feelings were dangerous, too easy to lose control of. He shouldn't have frightened her away just as they were getting to know each other. She threatened his control. Being a woman, she wouldn't see showing emotions as a threat. Women liked to talk about their feelings, to pry into other people's. She'd only been following her nature to ask.

He should have followed his, and her, into the stable and brought her back to sleep beside him. Well, he hadn't. He'd spent the night in a fevered doze while his dreams and thoughts ran wild with visions of what might have been. He only hoped that she'd been just as miserable, just as restless and needy. With a feral smile, he got up to go see.

Maddie felt as if she'd spent the night sleeping on a dirt floor in a stable. "Probably," she muttered as she shook out her rumpled clothing, "because I did."

"You talk too much."

Since she doubted either of the horses had acquired a voice during the night, she could only assume the husky voice behind her belonged to Rowan.

"You sound like you've got a cold," she said. She didn't turn around. She concentrated on running her fingers through her hair, then plaiting it into a thick braid. She heard him come up behind her as she worked, close enough so that she could feel his body heat, but she still didn't turn around.

He put a hand on her hip. "I'm not cold."

She moved away, and finally turned to face him. Rowan didn't look as if he'd slept any better than she had. "If I had to time travel," she addressed the unknown agent that had brought her to the past, "couldn't I have ended up in the lap of luxury in Renaissance Venice? Or maybe a Turkish or Moorish palace where they had running water and hot baths? No." She gestured around the primitive surroundings. "Do I end up somewhere where I could be an exotic, pampered beauty? No. I end up as one of my own starving peasant ancestors. There is no fairness to this."

Rowan put his hands on his lean hips, and gave her one of his narrow-eyed, icy looks. "What makes you think life should be fair?"

"Why shouldn't it be?" she shot back.

"Make the best of what you've got."

She nodded. "Oh, I agree with that. Having been given peanuts, I might as well make peanut butter and cooking oil and crush the shells for fertilizer. I'll make do, I'm just tired and whiny. It was a rough night."

A sudden grin transformed his face. Lord, but he was handsome when he let himself be! "You missed my company in the night."

It wasn't a question. Maddie snorted. "You wish." No way was she going to let him know he was right. Sleep had come in fits and starts, mixed with speculation and questions. And anger, lots of anger. Some of it had been directed at Rowan Murray, some at herself, and most of it at the fate that had been thrown her way. She'd even cried a bit, which was not like her at all. She'd been tempted a few times to march into where Rowan was sleeping and demand a hug. That wasn't like her at all, either, but she couldn't deny that she was feeling pretty vulnerable and emotionally needy.

It wasn't just emotional need, either. She'd craved Rowan's physical presence as well. She'd craved his touch. She still did, even though she'd automatically moved away when he put his hand on her just now.

She was terribly confused.

It had just sort of happened.

She wanted him. Physically and emotionally wanted him.

That night when she'd beaned him with the basin she'd been certain that she'd never want him touching her. Now she couldn't think of anything else. Not that much time had passed, not that much had happened, but something was different. Was she reacting to his having saved that little boy's life? Okay, that had been a fine act of heroism, very manly and all that. Rowan was all sinewy muscles and sweat and steely-eyed determination to do what a man had to do. In theory these were not bad qualities. Except possibly the sweat, but even it had a certain masculine appeal under the right circumstances. Rowan Murray was all man.

The problem was, she wasn't much of a woman. She didn't know how to be a woman. She suspected that he could teach her. But how could a man teach a female how to be womanly? All she knew was that she felt more like she thought a woman was supposed to feel when he looked at her—all warm and alive and aware, all the way down to some part of her that had never been touched. It was ironic that Mr. Stern and Stoic was the one who made her feel all Soft and Squishy.

Besides, he wasn't exactly Mr. Perfect. Hell, she didn't even think Toby Coltrane was Mr. Perfect anymore. She didn't know what she thought. Except that she wanted something to eat and a bath. And maybe a kiss. No, she wasn't going to think about that.

"Maybe there is no Mr. Perfect," she muttered, and sidled past Rowan to go to the door. There was a light fog covering the ground, but the sky overhead was mostly clear. The day promised to be warm and somewhat sunny. Maddie took deep breaths of the clear mountain air, appreciating it until her stomach began to rumble. When Rowan followed her outside, she looked back at him and asked, "Where's the nearest lake?"

He looked at her suspiciously. "Why?"

"I'm going to go fishing and take a swim."

Rowan frowned. "I didn't come up into the hills to take a holiday. I've got work to do."

"Well, then, go do it. *I* want to go for a swim."

Rowan considered her intentions. He liked fish, and he didn't doubt she'd find a way to catch some. If she was going for a swim, she'd have to shed her clothes to do it. He'd like to see her shed her clothes. "Aye," he agreed. "We'll do what you want, just this once. Come on, help me saddle the horses."

While Rowan gathered firewood, Maddie stood in the water and tickled fish. Once she'd lulled them into her grasp, she tossed them out of the water. She let Rowan take care of cleaning and cooking. So far she'd coaxed four trout from the stream that flowed out of the small mountain lake he'd brought her to.

They shared a fairly comfortable silence until they settled down to eat. Then Maddie looked around, sighed, and said, "It's really beautiful here. So peaceful."

Rowan chewed thoughtfully, and followed Maddie's gaze as he picked bones out of his teeth. "Beauty? 'Tis just rocks and trees and water, the same as always."

Maddie laughed. "It may be just home to you, but a few hundred years from now this is going to be a tourist's idea of paradise—Northern Grandeur variety. Tourism," she explained as he gave her a puzzled look, "is something I think the Vikings probably invented. You know, going off on summer cruises to faraway lands, and doing a little shopping before heading home to the fjords for the winter."

Rowan grunted. She was joking, he could tell by her tone, but he had no idea what the joke was. He answered, "There's many Norsemen that settle in the lands they invade."

She shrugged. "That's true. I've got a clan Anderson in my Scottish background. The point is, darlin', this place is beautiful and I'm enjoying the beauty of the day." She wiped her fingers on damp leaves, then stood up and stretched.

Rowan watched her, though not as openly as he had when she'd stripped down to her underdress, pulled it up around her knees and waded into the stream to fish. He rubbed a hand thoughtfully along his jaw. It was rough with a day's growth of beard. Unlike most men, he liked his face smooth and hairless, though a beard was less trouble than having to take a razor everywhere he went.

"This tourism," he asked as he considered her, "does it have something to do with looking at things?"

She smiled at him. It was a smile so bright he felt as though he'd been hit by a brilliant shaft of sunlight. "Yes, it does."

She was wearing little more than her underdress. Her luscious body was wonderfully outlined by the thin linen. He recalled the sight of her breasts very nearly spilling out over the top of her shift when she'd been bent over the water. Now *that* had been a beautiful sight. It was a pity she kept her breasts covered in an odd, twin-pouched sort of band of cloth, or he would have had a proper view of them then.

He got to his feet. "There are some things in the Highlands worth looking at." He stepped closer to her. "I'm looking at one of them now."

Maddie had no idea what Rowan was talking about, but there was a disturbing glint in the man's eyes. Actually, it wasn't disturbing, it was more compelling. It was like he was *really* looking at her, as opposed to *merely* looking at her. She wasn't sure what the difference was, but it sent a warm shiver all the way through her.

She pointed at herself. "You talking about me?"

"Aye."

"You feeling all right?"

Her brows were drawn down suspiciously, her generous mouth thinned in puzzlement. She'd looked at him like this before, but this time he found it adorable. He didn't know why. "You're a difficult woman," he said. "Can you not recognize a compliment when you hear one?"

"I didn't know you knew how to make them."

"I don't."

"But—" Maddie shook her head in frustration. "I'm going for a swim," she announced. She moved toward the lake, kind of hoping that Rowan would grab her and start some kissy-face stuff on her way past, but he didn't.

Rowan didn't know why he let her go—maybe he wanted her to come to him, to offer herself as she had on their wedding day. He wanted her to let him know what she wanted instead of letting him guess. He thought he should just grab her, but Rosemary's admonition to court his wife held him back. That is, until she paused by the edge of the loch, glanced provocatively back at him, and pulled off her shift.

She had dived into the cold water by the time he got there, but Rowan did take the hint. He stripped off his kilt and plunged in after her. The water was freezing, nearly as cold as the sea the day before, but as on the day before, he was powerfully motivated to ignore any discomfort. There was someone he was determined to get to, another rescue of a sort to perform. If he was trying to save a life, it was his own, by grasping hold of something, someone he suddenly realized he wanted very much.

She was a good swimmer, was his Maddie, as good as he was, and it turned into a chase. One that he won when he hid himself in some rushes growing near the shore and waited for her to come by. She laughed when he grabbed her around the waist and tossed her up on the shore; that was a good sign. Rowan followed after, and she watched him come out of the water as she lay on the grass propped up on her elbows. He liked how she looked, wearing nothing but bands of cloth around her breasts and loins and the necklace that she never seemed to take off. The wet cloth was very nearly transparent. In a few moments he intended to have her bare but for the necklace. He had it in mind to count the freckles that covered her from head to toe one by one, count them and kiss them and lick all the cool water from her fine, fresh skin.

He glanced for a moment at the nearby heap of his discarded clothing, but abandoned the idea of using his dagger to divest Maddie of what little modesty she had left. He wasn't interested in frightening the woman to satisfy his impatience.

Maddie watched the naked man approach in a combination of panic and anticipation. She couldn't look away, she couldn't stop the bold, inviting smile that pulled at her lips. She had no control over the heat growing deep inside her, over the pleasant, aching heaviness of her breasts. She felt totally out of control, and for once she didn't mind.

Rowan Murray, his skin sleek with water, his hair slicked back away from his long, strong face, was suddenly the center of her world. When he smiled as he knelt beside her, she gasped with delight. It took her breath away, and a moment later he gave it back when he kissed her. Her lips clung to his and drank him in, opened beneath the gentle urging of his tongue and let him explore with a growing sense of wonder and longing.

The kiss went on and on, her eyes closed, her head somehow coming to rest on the strong support of his arm. Maddie lost track of where she was and just about everything else until a strong tug on one of her bra straps brought her back to some awareness of the world.

"What the—oh. Let me."

Her bra was a practical, functional garment made of cotton, elastic, and plastic boning, with wide straps that fastened with a row of four metal hooks and eyes. It took a lot of engineering to comfortably support her size D cups. While a medieval male had no practice at undressing a twentieth-century woman, it took her only a few seconds to liberate herself from the brassiere.

Rowan watched how she took off the offending rag so he would know how to rid her of the thing in the future. "Good," he whispered huskily when she was free of it, and buried his face in the deep cleft between her breasts.

Maddie felt his lips on the side of her breast, then the long, slow, slide of his tongue as his mouth traveled up to settle over one hard nipple. She threw back her head, eyes closed, totally immersed in sensation. While his mouth claimed her breast, his hands stroked over the rest of her, caressing, exploring, teasing, even.

It was nice. So nice that she forgot to be frightened, forgot to feel awkward and ungainly. She liked the way she felt when he touched her, loved the way he felt when she touched him. He was all hard muscle, and she liked his masculine scent and fuzzy chest. The scratch of his unshaved cheeks against her softer skin was pure sensuality, like the slightly rough texture of a cat's tongue, only sexier. If all this touching and tasting and sharing was what sex was all about she didn't know why she'd always found the prospect of it so daunting. It was intimate, it was sharing, it was the ultimate in vulnerability—and it was *nice*.

She touched him, a lot, in all sorts of places. She couldn't manage to do it with her eyes open—she wasn't ready for that just yet—but she liked finding out about his body in a purely tactile way. She liked the firm ripple of muscle beneath his skin. She liked all the different textures that made up Rowan Murray, from silky smooth to hard and rough. She liked the taste of him, as well, when she ventured to kiss him, on the mouth and throat and his small, hard nipples.

All the time she tentatively explored Rowan, Rowan kept kissing her. He kissed her mouth, her face, throat, breasts, belly, thighs. He kissed her in places she hadn't been absolutely sure she had until his lips found them and left her squirming and arching and begging for more. She wasn't sure where her underwear had gotten to, and she certainly didn't mind its absence. What she liked was how she felt as she opened herself to Rowan's exploring fingers and mouth. She whimpered when he pulled away, then he kissed her mouth again and she tasted herself as their tongues played urgently over each other.

While they kissed, his fingers slid over her shoulders, her throat, between her breasts, and back up. They tangled in the chain around her throat.

Maddie screamed.

She arched away from the hands on her throat, and kept screaming as she curled around herself, blind with agony and fear.

There was nothing Rowan could do.

He heard the shuffling movements and the wet snuffling of the Questing Beast coming from the trees even over Maddie's cry of pain. He dove for his claymore while he fought both his need and his urge to help the woman writhing in pain on the ground. He wanted to help her, but first he had to protect her from the monster that had come hunting them.

He cursed his carelessness, and he cursed his shunning of responsibility for the sake of pleasure. If he'd remembered that he'd come to the hills to hunt this thing, it wouldn't have found them first, found him unprepared.

Naked, half-rattled by desire, he put himself between Maddie and the beast, and raised his sword.

19

"Do you want to tell me just what the hell happened?"

Rowan pointed at the dead animal as Maddie scrambled to her feet. He tossed her clothes to her. "Hurry. The fair folk sent the beast. You passed out while I fought it."

Maddie put a hand to her aching neck. "Fair folk, my butt. What did you do to me?"

"They're looking for you." He grabbed her arm. She shook it off. "Get dressed, woman! We have to ride!"

Maddie noticed that he had his kilt back on. She didn't know how long she'd been out. Long enough for him to dispatch another one of those strange animals, she saw, and roll himself back into his Highland garb. She did know that she wasn't going to stand here bucknaked while she argued with him. So she turned her back on him and got dressed. Her throat felt burned, her head ached. Worst of all was the humiliation of knowing Rowan hadn't wanted her, he'd just wanted to make a point.

When she was done she turned back and found that he was already on his horse. He looked around as if he was anxious about something. "Come on. We must go."

She knew he was capable of practical jokes. She hadn't thought he'd hurt her, though. "What did you do?" she demanded. "Hit me on the head? Choke me with the necklace?"

He looked outraged. "I just saved your life." He glared down at her. "Do I have to tie you to the horse, Maddie?"

"I'm not going anywhere with you, you scumbag. All right, I hit you on the head, I kneed you in the groin, and you wanted to get even." She braced her legs apart and pointed an accusing finger at him. "I did what I did because I said no and you wouldn't stop." She pointed at the ground, to the trampled spot in the heather where they'd lain together. "What we were doing was consensual. I thought it was. I thought you wanted me, but you were just setting me up. You had no business doing anything like—" She stopped talking and began to back quickly away when Rowan got down off his mount and stalked purposefully toward her. "What are you doing?"

He spoke slowly, and very firmly. "Be silent." He grabbed her by the shoulders and his icy gaze bored into hers. "You are being hunted."

"What?"

"The fair folk want you back. You belong to me."

"I do not!"

"Silence." He looked around as if he really believed there was someone hunting them.

"Stop trying to frighten me. Stop trying to make

me think you're protecting me from imaginary little men."

"They aren't little, they aren't all manlike. There are monsters among them, Maddie. They'll not have you."

His words sent a shiver through her. She fought the sudden fear. She fought believing him. This was just some sort of cruel joke. When he touched a finger to her necklace, she asked, "How did you know it would do that? Why did you hurt me?" Much to her annoyance, she heard the hurt in her voice. She was fighting tears, as well. She hated that he'd brought out this sort of wimpy behavior in her. "Let go of me."

He didn't. He pulled her over to her horse and forced her to mount. He swung up onto his horse, but grabbed her reins before she could try to ride away from him.

"Where are we going?" she demanded as they sped further from the lake.

He didn't answer for a long time. When he finally looked back at her, all he said was, "The White Lady."

"How could she think I tried to hurt her?"

"Did you?"

Rowan stopped pacing back and forth in front of the White Lady. He gaped at the woman's cool question. He'd dragged Maddie here for shelter and to seek counsel from the person who'd brought them together. She'd greeted them with a calm nod as he'd pushed Maddie through the doorway and hurried to close it behind her. He'd meant to tell the White Lady of the danger they'd faced earlier in the day when the Questing Beast attacked and he sensed the presence of fair folk hunters coming toward them. Instead he'd blurted out the grievance he'd nursed through the whole ride and the climb up the narrow path to the little house. He was as shocked at his own words as he was by the White Lady's response. All he could do was sputter like a fish gasping in the air.

While he was speechless, Maddie said, "That's the only logical explanation."

Rowan couldn't bring himself to look into his wife's accusing face; just the sound of her words was hard enough to take. He spoke to the White Lady instead, though the words were meant for Maddie. "She doesn't trust me."

Did she not hear the plea for trust that he hated to have to voice? And why did it matter to him that she trust him? He didn't know the why, just that it did.

"Why should I?" Maddie didn't know why she addressed her comments to this stranger, but it seemed easier than actually talking to her alleged husband.

She didn't want to talk to Rowan, she wanted to get away from him. While they'd ridden at a mad gallop across the rocky countryside she'd come to the conclusion that she wanted to be away from the whole mad, overimaginative world. She had to get her mind off Rowan Murray and back on finding a way home.

She ran a finger along the circle of slightly burned skin beneath the ever-present necklace. "He did something to this. It was in retaliation for—" She felt her skin blaze with a furious blush. "Well, never mind why he did it."

"I did nothing."

The White Lady was seated across her hearth from

them. A pot boiled on the fire, filling the house with the aroma of something pleasant. She calmly folded her hands in her lap, looked from Maddie to Rowan, then said, "Why don't you explain to her why she can trust you, laird of the Mermaid's Children?"

"Mermaid's Children?" Maddie asked, with a skeptical, exasperated glance at Rowan. "You people don't believe in mermaids, too, do you?"

"It's just symbolism," the White Lady explained with a wave of one elegant hand that drew Maddie's attention back to her. The beautiful, white-haired woman smiled reassuringly, "We wise folk are supposed to talk like that."

"Oh." Maddie sighed in relief. Maybe she'd finally found someone with a realistic outlook on the world. "Symbolism I can deal with."

Rowan looked at the White Lady in confusion. "What do you mean, symbolism? The Murrays are descended from a vain selkie that left the sea to wed a warrior who offered her a silver mirror and comb in exchange for her magical sealskin."

"Right," was Maddie's tart reply. "He believes in fairies, too," she told the other woman.

The White Lady's pale brows rose. "Does he?"

"Of course I do."

"He uses it as an excuse for all sorts of nonsense."

"I see." The White Lady looked at Maddie sympathetically. She moved over and patted the space on the bench beside her.

"And magic," Maddie said as she moved to sit next to the White Lady.

"Magic. I see." The White Lady touched her on the knee. "You find magic disturbing, don't you?"

"Of course not!" Maddie declared, too quickly. "I just find it . . . ridiculous."

"How can you let her talk like that?" Rowan demanded of the wisewoman. "How can you let her belittle all you are in your own house?"

The White Lady gave him a stern look, but her tone was mild. "We're discussing Maddie's beliefs, Rowan, not mine or yours. I'm being polite to my guest."

Rowan had never known the White Lady to be polite to anyone before. Her way was to command, not accommodate. He didn't know what had gotten into her now. He thought it better to keep quiet about it rather than have her temper turned on him when he had deep problems he needed her help with. He decided to sit down opposite the women and nurse his grievances with both Maddie and himself while they talked for a while.

When the White Lady—Maddie knew she was the White Lady only because that was who Rowan had said he was taking her to and the woman was a platinum blonde—called her by name, Maddie was puzzled. There hadn't been any formal introductions when they'd come in; Rowan and she had just started pouring out their complaints to the house's occupant.

"You know my name?" Maddie asked the other woman after Rowan sat down. "You know about me?" It seemed ridiculous that the White Lady would have heard about her arrival and incarceration at Cape Wrath all the way out here on this isolated crag.

"Of course she knows about you. She brought you here with her magic," Rowan said.

"I did no such thing," the White Lady countered.

She took Maddie's hands. Rowan did not think

Maddie noticed that what the wisewoman was doing was studying her palms. She would see the gesture as one of comfort and of reassurance. Perhaps it was meant to be those things as well, but Maddie was maddening in her deliberate blindness to the true nature of the world.

"These are strong hands," the White Lady said after a few moments. "Strong but gentle. Fit for hard, skilled work as well as cradling a bairn."

Maddie blushed, inordinately pleased by the woman's words, though she didn't know why she should be. "I'm an engineer," she answered. "I like to build things."

The woman looked up at her, a sharp glance through pale lashes. "And you'd like to have children as well."

"Well—yeah. I guess."

The White Lady shook her head. "Such diffidence hiding such longing. Though not hiding it very well."

"Wait a minute," Maddie protested. "I don't want to be rude, but I don't think my emotional state is really any of your business."

"Your wishes and dreams are very important. They've shaped where you are now."

Maddie blinked to keep back unwanted tears, but they spilled over anyway. Her voice was tight with both pain and bitterness when she answered, "Stuck in the past with a man who hates me?" She wiped her cheeks. "That's just bad luck and physics."

Rowan clenched his fists and hid his pain in silence. How could she think he hated her?

The White Lady gave him a hard look. "What have you done to show her otherwise?"

He shifted uncomfortably. "I married the lass."

"Not because you wanted her."

He stood up. "Because you told me to."

Maddie stood as well. "What?" She pointed at the White Lady. "You're the one. The prophecy person."

The White Lady looked calmly up at them, her hands folded in her lap. "That I am, lass. Prophecy and portents, spells and potions, those are the things I trade in."

Maddie felt a dull ache in the pit of her stomach. She sighed. "And for a moment there I thought I'd found somebody sensible."

"Ah, but you're a relentlessly practical one," the White Lady told her. She leaned forward a bit. "Tell me, did you not once wish, speaking only to the deep dark waves, to find a way to remain in the Highlands forever?"

Maddie shrugged. "Well, yeah, but that was when I'd only been in Scotland for a couple of weeks and hadn't gotten fed up with the food and weather yet." She narrowed her eyes at the other woman. "Wait a minute. You're just guessing I said that, right?"

The White Lady ignored her skepticism to ask another question. "And did you not ask for someone just like the man you wanted who didn't want you?"

"Just like?" Rowan asked. "Better is what she's got."

"Do you think so, Rowan Murray?" The White Lady asked.

"I do."

"Did you make the wish?" The White Lady asked her.

Maddie blushed. She couldn't bear to look at either of them. She scuffed her foot across the dirt floor. "Maybe," she admitted.

"She thought I was someone named Toby at first," Rowan told the White Lady. "So it sounds to me like she got her wishes but doesn't want to pay the price."

"Perhaps she doesn't know that magic has laws, just the same as her science."

"Magic isn't real," Maddie asserted. She looked angrily between the two Highlanders. "Wishes don't really come true. All right, I made them, but I'm too practical to—"

"They came true whether you expected them to or not," The White Lady said. "The question is, who answered your pleas and what do you owe them?"

"I thought you sent her to save my clan," Rowan added.

The White Lady shook her head. "I did not bring her here. I only knew that the first woman you met on the way home was the one you needed."

"Is she?"

"Answer that yourself, Rowan Murray."

Maddie touched the chain on her throat. "The question is, how do I get this thing off before it electrocutes me?" She glared at Rowan. "I don't want to take any more chances of his playing practical jokes with it."

Rowan answered her glare with one of his own. "I would never harm you, woman. It is the fair folk," he insisted. "They are hunting you."

Maddie knew the way to madness lay in agreeing with him, but she decided to go along with his delusions for the moment. He really did believe in magic, so maybe she if she listened to him with an open mind she could figure out what was really going on by applying a logical interpretation.

"All right," she said. "Let's say these fairies are hunting me. Why?"

Rowan rubbed his jaw thoughtfully. He glanced at the White Lady, but she seemed more interested in stirring her supper pot than the conversation. Then he looked at the entwined chains of gold and copper that circled Maddie's throat. "Perhaps they want that back. Did you steal it from them?"

"No, I did not steal it from them," was her indignant reply.

"How did you get it?" The White Lady asked. "Is it yours?"

"Well, no, it's not exactly mine. It was—well, maybe it is stolen, in a way." While the others looked at her, Maddie sat down and attempted to explain. "It came from an archaeology dig. That's when scientists, historians, find old . . . things, places. Like burial sites and such."

"Treasure hunting?" Rowan asked. "Grave robbing?"

"No! It's a way to study history."

"Was the necklace found in a grave?" he asked.

"Yes," she conceded.

"A fairy grave?"

She bit back her skepticism and asked, "Are there such things as fairy graves?"

He touched the dagger on his belt. "Oh, aye, even the immortals can die under the right circumstances."

"Their bodies can, at least," the White Lady clarified.

"That's good enough for me," Rowan said.

"About this grave," the White Lady said to Maddie. "Could it have been a fairy grave?"

Maddie thought back to the details of the dig she'd been working on during her vacation. "It was a strange site," she admitted. "At least that's what the archaeologists said. They were puzzled by a lot of the grave goods and the positioning of the cairn and the fact that the grave hadn't seemed to have been disturbed, but that there wasn't any skeletal remains in it." She swallowed hard, and forced herself to add, "Does that sound like a fairy grave to you?"

The White Lady nodded. "Oh, aye, most certainly."

"Right."

"And the necklace, were you the one who took it from the grave?"

Maddie shook her head. "Dr. Ishida found it."

"Hmm. Were you the first person to wear it?"

"No. Every woman at the dig tried it on. Kevin insisted. He was kind of obsessed about it, actually."

"The curse or blessing was working through him. It should have taken effect on the first one to put it on." The White Lady came nearer to Maddie, and peered closely at the necklace, though she didn't touch it. "This obviously was made to respond to a woman's touch. These were Scotswomen who wore it before you?"

Maddie thought about it for a moment. "No, actually, it was an international group, mostly German and Japanese, overseen by Dr. Patel from the University of Glasgow. She was born in Scotland, but I think her parents came from Pakistan."

The White Lady touched a strand of Maddie's red hair and traced a line of freckles across her nose. "You have the look of Scotland about you, though I sense you were born far away."

"My family came from Scotland originally."

The White Lady nodded. "So you had the wishes, the will, and the right blood to activate the spell."

"I don't know anything about spells, I just know it's dangerous," Maddie said. She looked accusingly at Rowan. "I want it off."

The White Lady stepped back and folded her arms. "Then take it off."

"I can't."

The White Lady looked at Rowan. "Take it off."

Maddie jumped backward, with her hands at her throat. "No way!"

"I can't take it off," Rowan said to the White Lady. "I tried when she was unconscious."

"You did what?" both Maddie and the White Lady demanded. Maddie was surprised to hear the White Lady sound as appalled as she did.

"I thought the fair folk were hunting her, tracking the necklace," Rowan told them. "I was going to toss the necklace in the loch after I killed the Questing Beast, but it wouldna come off."

"And a good thing you didn't succeed, laddie," the White Lady declared. "That would have gotten you both killed."

He held out his palms, and Maddie saw the burns on them for the first time. "So I suspected," he said.

Maddie looked from his hands to his face. She was startled both by his injuries and by his look of concern. She didn't know what to think about what he'd done. Had he tried to hurt her? Was she actually sure of what had happened back at the lake? She remembered soaring pleasure that had been on the verge of taking her out of herself, of blending her soul with his.

Then horrible pain had plunged her down into darkness. Had she misread the situation? Had something else set off the necklace? Had her own insecurities transmuted actual events into a false sense of betrayal?

She didn't know.

"That's why I brought Maddie here," Rowan went on. "It needs your magic to keep the fair folk from taking my wife from me."

"It needs magic," the White Lady told them, "but not mine." She looked at Maddie. "Do you want it off?"

"Yes."

"And you, Rowan, you want her to be free of it?"

"Aye."

"It is good you both want it off, for it will kill her if not returned to its true owner."

Maddie didn't believe in curses, but she knew the necklace somehow carried some sort of strong electrical charge. "I don't want to go through what I felt earlier ever again."

"It will be worse next time," The White Lady said.

Maddie nodded. "It has gotten worse every time it's been touched. At first it was just a tingle, now it's hundred thousand volts."

"Then it has to come off," Rowan said.

The White Lady smiled. "Indeed."

"You'll help."

"Not I. Rowan, take off Maddie's necklace."

"I already told you I cannot."

"Ah, but only you can."

He glowered. "How?"

"Yeah," Maddie said. "How?"

"It looks to have a simple clasp. He has only to undo it."

Rowan stepped in front of the wisewoman. "Is there a trick to it, then?"

"Aye," she agreed. "It is a matter of trust, of strength of will, and the deeper thing between a man and a woman. If you share these things, then the necklace will come safely off." She picked up a basket and went to the door. "I'm going to pick herbs in the moonlight," she told them. "I'll expect you to have the necklace off by the time I return," she told Rowan. "Or for the Murrays to build me a new house if you have not."

20

"Did she mean what I think she meant?"

"About love?" Rowan answered.

Maddie shook her head. "No, about the place blowing up if the necklace isn't taken off correctly?"

"Aye, I think she meant that as well."

Maddie had been paying more attention to the White Lady's words than to Rowan's; now a startled shiver ran up her spine. At the same time a tightness clutched at her heart. "Did you just say love?"

"Aye."

Maddie looked at the blank face of the door that had closed behind the White Lady rather than at the man beside her. "She didn't say anything about love." Rowan put his hand on her shoulder. It was large, warm. Possessive? She wasn't sure whether she was threatened or comforted by the touch of it. "Does it hurt?" she asked.

"It does," he acknowledged. "No more than I can take."

She gave him a sideways look. "Are you babbling stoic warrior stuff?"

"Of course." He gave her one of his devastating, fleeting smiles. "It is a warrior's duty to be stoic."

"And you do the duty thing better than anyone I've ever met."

"I'll take that as a compliment, wife."

"You do that." Wife. What did he really mean when he called her wife?

Trust, Maddie thought. *It's a matter of trust.* It was more than that. The insight was sudden and frightening. It wasn't just a matter of trust, though that was hard enough to come by. It was about belief. About love. She glanced around the witch's cottage and attempted to logically take one concept at a time, for she wasn't up to taking them all in at once. Not yet, and maybe never. Rather than letting her emotions slide away from the point, she forced herself to concentrate.

After a few moments she said to Rowan, "I believe that you believe."

"You must believe in the magic yourself," Rowan answered, understanding just what she'd meant. "It's not enough otherwise."

She had to trust him. She had to believe in magic. And then there was that love thing. She knew she certainly felt something strongly for Rowan Murray. Was it love? "Those are some pretty tall orders."

Maddie stared into the fire, very aware of Rowan when he moved to stand behind her. The pot bubbled and steamed, throwing a rich herbal scent into the close, warm air. Maddie took deep breaths and tried to steady her nerves. The herb scent went deep into her lungs, tickled the back of her throat, and seemed to clear her head. It was sort of like camphor for the brain; it seemed as though it helped her to think. But while the thoughts that came to her were clear, they were not necessarily orderly.

They tied her in knots and left her in a welter of confusion. She knew she couldn't afford to be confused. Something told her that what happened in the next few hours was going to determine the course of the rest of her life, that she and Rowan would walk out of here with things settled or they wouldn't walk out of here at all. This premonition was foolish, but she believed it in the depths of her mostly practical soul.

She didn't realize she was trembling until Rowan's hands began to move on her shoulders. His presence had been so welcome, so comforting, she'd almost forgotten he was there. An hour ago she might have stepped away; now she leaned back against him and let her body accept the sheer animal solace in another body's warm touch. He stood solid as a wall at her back, serious, certain of who and what he was. Rowan Murray knew where he belonged. He knew what he believed. What was right. What was wrong. Who his friends were, who were his enemies. For him it was all so simple, easy, a world tied up in a plaid ribbon in a time when the sun revolved around the earth and people really cared how many angels danced on the heads of pins.

And believed in fairies.

"Let us not forget the fairies," she murmured.

"I wish we could," he answered. "The world would be better off without them."

He really, really believed. And if the White Lady was right, she had better believe, too, if she wanted to get the necklace off and live through it. And why was it she didn't have as much trouble dealing with the White Lady's mumbo jumbo as she did when Rowan went on about it?

"You have to trust that magic is real," Rowan said, before she could think any more about the wisewoman.

"And how am I supposed to do that?"

"And why are you such a skeptic? Can you not *feel* the truth of it in your very bones and blood?"

What she was feeling in her bones and blood was the presence of Rowan Murray as his thumbs made slow circles over her shoulder blades. It was melting one and firing the other, though she tried very hard to ignore the physical sensations that tempted her away from clear thought—or any thought at all, for that matter.

It wasn't time for letting physical reaction rule, not just yet. "Belief. Trust." She said two of the three things that needed to get settled out loud.

"Love," Rowan said, contributing the third.

"Let's start with the other two, shall we?"

"Aye."

She felt the tightly controlled pain in that one small word. Though she didn't know if he was afraid of rejection, or simply as reluctant to explore that mare's nest of conflicting emotions as she was.

"You're a stubborn one, wife," he went on after a long silence.

A smile lifted the corners of her mouth. "You sound almost proud of my stubbornness."

He laughed, a soft, breathy chortle. They were standing so close that she felt as much as heard the sound as his chest vibrated against her back. "At least you're consistent about it. You've a steadiness about you that I like fine, wife, even if what you believe is dead wrong."

"Thank you very much for that backhanded compliment—husband."

He put an arm around her waist. "It's good to hear you acknowledge the fact."

She didn't recall ever denying it, though she supposed she didn't even begin to live up to his standards for wifely behavior. All she could manage in the way of a reply was a soft, sad, sigh.

"I like you fine, Maddie," he whispered in her ear, as though he wanted no one else in the world to know. "Though too stubborn and hardheaded for your own good you be."

She wasn't certain of his grammar, but the hint of affection in his voice was inordinately pleasing. He pulled her closer, making her all too aware of the solid muscles of his thighs and how neatly her softer curves fit against that rock-solid, masculine, hardness.

"You're making it very difficult to think, Rowan Murray." And to breathe, she added to herself.

His answering chuckle was deep and dirty. It made her laugh, and blush, and want to turn around and fit her body against his in an even more intimate way than they were already joined.

This was all very interesting, but it wasn't getting anything accomplished.

Maddie took a deep breath and made herself move away from Rowan. She turned to face him. She touched the entwined gold and copper chains on her throat. "I'm willing to admit that this thing is eventually going to kill me. I want it off. Now, *I* think that there is some property in the metals that sets up an electrical charge. For some as yet unexplained reason, the longer the metals are in contact with each other and some other element, possibly body heat, the more powerful the charge becomes."

"And I say it's magic."

She held her hands up and said matter-of-factly, "Then we're in agreement."

His brows came down over his ice blue eyes. "I thought all those words were your way of denying the truth of it."

Maddie sucked in a long breath between her teeth. "No," she told him. "All those words are a just a different way of explaining reality. I look at it as science, you see magic. Maybe we're both right."

"And how can that be, lass?"

She grinned at him. "Because I just remembered something I read once. I think it's attributed to Arthur C. Clarke, who is Scottish, I believe. Anyway, it goes something like, 'Any sufficiently advanced technology is indistinguishable from magic.'" She touched the necklace again. "This thing might as well be magic for all the sense I can make out of how it works. So," she went on firmly, as Rowan frowned in confusion, "I declare that I believe in magic." Once she'd said the words, she felt as though a weight had been lifted from her. She smiled. "That wasn't so bad." When none of her former college professors appeared out of thin air to swat her on the back of the head for spouting such heresy, she even managed to laugh. She grabbed Rowan's hands. "Magic. Why not?"

"Why not indeed?" he answered. He matched her smile with one of his own, and drew her to him.

"Now, I'm not going to go overboard on this, or

anything," she hastily told him, babbling to try to ignore the sudden rush of her heartbeat. "Not going to admit to alien abductions or the Bermuda Triangle or anything like that. I'm just going to acknowledge a few specific instances where it's possible—okay, definite—that some sort of magical field energy is in operation in my life. Time traveling and lethal jewelry are as much as I am willing to declare magical at this time."

Rowan's eyes were full of merriment as he drew her even closer. His arms came around her. "You talk too much, lass."

Maddie found that she couldn't look away from his gaze, even as the expression in his eyes turned from amusement to something far more intense. A shiver ran through her, leaving a hot ache in its wake. She licked her lips. "I know."

He ran one hand up her back until his fingers tangled in the hair at the nape of her neck. Warm sensation spread out from the line his fingers traced. He used his hold to gently draw her head back. "Hush," he said, and kissed her.

It not only effectively silenced her, it took her breath away. The pressure of his lips against hers was insistent, and she answered it with an eagerness that surprised her. Her lips parted, and it was her tongue that sought the warm intimacy of his mouth.

Her reaction surprised him. Rowan drew back his head, eyes bright with both teasing and desire. "Can it be that you want me, lass?"

"Could be," she answered, though it took her a moment to get breath enough to speak. She wanted to recapture the pure, glorious, delightfully uninhibited sensations they'd shared by the lake shore before the pain came between them. She looked deep into his eyes while the words came up, unbidden, by her soul. "I want you, Rowan."

I've wanted you all my life, she thought. She didn't know why, or how, but it was true. The reason she'd been so alone in her own time was because Rowan had not been there.

He searched her face. "Do you trust me, then? For I think you have little trust in the kindness of men."

Sudden tears filled her eyes, while her throat constricted with pain. "Not men. It's me." She wanted to draw the words back as she said them, but instead, more spilled out. "I've always wondered why any man would want me." *Until now,* she thought. *Until you.* She found that her hands were resting on his chest, tightly balled into fists. She was shaking, her vision awash in tears. "What is the matter with me?" She was as confused as she was in pain. "Even you don't want me for me, but for the help I can give your people."

A moment ago she'd been tingling with desire, now she felt like she was a heartbeat away from falling into a thousand fractured pieces. This Humpty Dumpty feeling frightened her out of her wits. So much so that she found herself clinging to Rowan as though he were a rock on the very edge of the world, and without him she'd be lost. Hadn't she been the most self-sufficient person in the world not that long ago?

And hadn't the world ignored her as she went her own way? Or was it that she went her own way because the world ignored her? And what did it matter, since she wasn't in her own world anymore anyway? She was in Rowan's world. All she wanted was to be with him, even if—

"I want you for you, lass." His voice was a soft, gentle whisper. "I always have."

He sounded surprised by what he'd said himself.

It certainly surprised her. She was afraid to believe him. It meant too much to her. It frightened her to have gone almost instantly from self-sufficiently comfortable with her lonely existence to being so in need of love. Of companionship. Of intimacy. Not with just anyone, but this one specific, stubborn, difficult, dour Highlander.

"Trust," he told her, "that what I tell you is true."

"I don't know what trust has to do with anything," she said, with her head tucked in the crook of his arm.

He barely heard her for the way her words were muffled by his saffron shirt. He pushed her head up and made her look at him. "Ye've got to trust in yourself lass. Trust that you're woman enough for a man to want you, for you are."

She blinked, and tears spilled. Maddie crying was a thing it broke his heart to see. "I am?"

He ran his thumb gently across her lower lip. He kept himself from brushing the tears away, for it was not right to acknowledge such momentary weakness in a woman who needed to learn her own strength. "Are you not?" he questioned in reply. "Do I not hunger for you every moment of the day?"

"Me?" Her voice was barely a whisper.

He pulled her closer, so that their bodies fitted together, man to woman. "Can you not feel the heat of me? The swelling hardness that wants to rest no place but within you?"

A deep red blush darkened the fair skin of her face and throat. Her breath quickened, and a dazed expression widened her eyes. "Uh . . . yeah. I . . . feel . . . you."

He rocked his hips against her, subtly, suggestively. It nearly drove him mad to have so many layers of clothing between what his words conjured and his body craved. He wanted to do, not talk, but words were what his Maddie needed now. Words were what she would have.

His Maddie.

The realization struck him hard. It had been rocking him with both fear and wonder since nearly losing her to the fair folk hours before. Awareness of her rushed through his blood and being. His. His. His. This woman like no one he'd ever wanted had insinuated herself into his heart and his life through no fault of her own, and there he wanted her to stay. It made his grip on her shift to sudden harshness. It made his mouth come down on hers with a fiercer hunger than he'd ever known.

They were both panting by the time he lifted his lips from hers. She was wild-eyed, but not all of it was fear. "I want you." The words rasped out of him as he fought hard for control. "Waking and sleeping. In my dreams I touch you, though in the daylight I keep my hands away."

His hands were on her now, and he intended for them to stay on her until he'd touched his fill, until he'd taken his fill. He would learn every secret place on her soft, sweet body, and mark it as his own. He ran his hands up and down her back and cupped her buttocks. She was taut muscle under lush softness, solidly made, and a fine size for bearing bairns. And bairns he wanted from her, and the joy that came from making them. He wanted that joy first, and many many times before he heard the first strong wail of his son.

"Trust me to make love to you," he pleaded with her. "Trust that you're woman enough to make a man mad with wanting you, for you are. Trust that there—"

She kissed him before he could say another word, kissed him so hard that she very nearly broke his nose when she pulled his face next to hers and planted her mouth over his. Rowan didn't mind the pain one little bit, for he was instantly caught up in the intensity of the moment.

Okay, Maddie thought as their lips touched and tongues met and surged together. *If I'm going to do this sex thing, I'm going to do it. Right now. Before I lose my nerve. Before I—*

He cupped her buttocks with one hand, grinding his hips against hers, and Maddie completely lost her train of thought. Despite her techincal knowledge, she had never been sure how this making love thing was supposed to work on an emotional level. How did one put motion and emotion together? Why was she asking? She suddenly felt absolutely no need for an instruction manual. It all just sort of came naturally. Like it had back at the lake. At least some basic urges seemed to take over as Rowan *did* things and she responded and everything between them was hot and tingling and urgent. Things spun out of control so fast Maddie didn't have time to be awkward, or shy, or scared. She just went with the moment and forgot all about being analytical, or even being coherent, for that matter.

She barely noticed when his hands tangled in the hair at the nape of her neck. His fingers stroked her neck, moved whisper-softly against her skin. It sent a shiver through her, sent a sigh from her mouth to his as they kissed. She was too caught up in the ascending spiral of pleasure to pay much attention when the necklace slipped off and fell to the floor.

She had no objections when Rowan picked her up and took her the few steps to the nearby bed. She wasn't going to object to anything but the absence of his touch, and that didn't seem likely to happen. Her arms twined around his neck as he lay her on the bed. She drew him willingly down on top of her. She couldn't have let him go if her life depended on it.

The heat of their joined bodies brought more than warmth. It was pure fire. She tugged him out of his clothes. Her own became rumpled and disarrayed. He freed her breasts and nuzzled them, licked and nipped at them until she moaned with pleasure. Rowan pushed up her skirts and she wrapped her bare legs around his muscular thighs. Her breasts crushed against his chest, the rigid points of her nipples in electric contact with Rowan's hard, hot body. She reveled in the feel of the soft fur of his chest hair against her sensitized skin.

Rowan spoke, panted out words between fiery kisses, but Maddie was too wild with need to understand a thing he said. She made noises herself, deep expressions of pleasure and wanting, but there was nothing rational about the sounds. She rolled her hips against his, felt the hardness of his erection against her belly, told him how much she wanted him with her movements and small, begging cries.

Maddie knew an instant of devastation when he pulled away from her, but he didn't leave her. He rose above where she lay. She looked up at him in needy wonder. Rowan took her face between his hands, spoke in a lust-roughened whisper. Maddie had no need for words, but she recognized the concern that matched the fire in his eyes. His need was as strong as her own, but he was asking permission. In that moment she loved him more than she loved life itself. She reached up, touched his cheek, nodded.

"Aye, Rowan. I want you. You're all I want."

He recognized only his name in her words, but her tone and the soft smile that lit her face told him all he truly needed to know. She was his, freely. It was time for the two of them to become one. Rowan straddled her, stroked the soft insides of her thighs for a moment, fitted himself to her. He thrust into her, claiming the depths of her heated softness.

Maddie cried out when Rowan entered her, then cried out again as his hips began to pump and grind against her. The sounds were made up of equal parts delight and surprise. The surprise was at the heat that raced through her, at the sleek, smooth, perfect way his hardness fit so perfectly into the pulsing center of her, at the mixture of satisfaction and raw hunger that drove her to rise up to meet each hard thrust. She found utter delight in the same things that surprised her. She had never felt any pleasure like this before.

It was a pleasure that kept getting wilder, better, with each passing moment. In fact, time meant nothing. There were no such things as moments or minutes or any other increment of time as the heat built between her and Rowan. There was nothing but the consuming fire they made together. Their hands roved over each other's bodies, trailing flames. Their mouths found each other's, sharing short, hot kisses. The taste of sweat and need was salty on their tongues as they searched out many more places where they kissed and suckled and licked. Maddie soon lost all ability for thought. All she could do was respond to his touch with a wildness she'd never known before.

Each time he ground his hips against hers, Maddie's responses were more needy and eager; she was out of control, living completely on the heady sensory input. Her breath came in short, hard gasps as her fingers dug urgently into his shoulders. She tried her best to pull him closer, to somehow become even more engulfed in the shared conflagration. She wrapped her legs around his waist as he buried himself over and over inside her. She held on for dear life. What they were doing was the pure essence of being, this firestorm was the reason for life. She soared, taken over by the primal need. She flew away from herself as the pleasure screamed through her. At the same time every nerve ending strained through the fire, building to a final, blinding, frantic solar flare of sensation that set her shuddering with ecstatic release.

For a moment she thought she'd died.

And was perfectly happy to have done so.

Then she felt the comforting weight of Rowan's body as he collapsed on top of her, and she was happy that she wasn't dead. She was happy to be with him, to have made love with him, to cradle him in her welcoming embrace and whisper her joy and thanks and love as his arms came around her. He lifted his head long enough to give her the most brilliant smile she'd ever seen on the fine, handsome features of the usually grim laird of the Murray clan. Then he kissed her on the forehead and collapsed again.

21

Maddie put her hand on Rowan's bare flank and said suggestively, "I don't suppose we could do that again? I mean, it was my first time and I have a lot of experimenting to do and things I need to learn and I want to find out if it's always that intense or if it was just because it was the first time." She gave him a hopeful smile as she ran her fingers boldly up and down his thigh. "I don't know when the White Lady's due back, but . . ." Her words trailed off at the oddly puzzled look on Rowan's face as he propped himself up on his elbow. "What?"

They were lying side by on the little bed, facing each other. The heather-and-moss–stuffed mattress beneath them was soft and comfortable. She'd been having a wonderful time alternating between dozing off and studying Rowan Murray's long, rangy, mostly naked body. Rowan had been involved in an equally lazy examination of hers. She ached in some places she wasn't used to, but found those aches to be pleasant reminders of what she and Rowan had done not so long before. The silence between them had gone on for a long time, but it had been a comfortable one. At least, Maddie had thought it was.

"What?" she asked again.

He answered. In fact, he gave her a far longer answer than was usual for the taciturn laird. She listened carefully, but didn't understand a word that he said.

Without any further consultation, they both sat up and readjusted their clothing. One thing Maddie noticed as she tied her chemise over her chest was that the necklace was missing. She touched her throat. Her hand was still on her throat as she turned to Rowan.

"The necklace is gone."

He put his fingers over hers and said something. The words sounded, to her ears, like a guttural yet somehow lilting growl.

She wasn't wearing the lethal necklace. She wasn't dead. She couldn't understand a word Rowan said.

It made no sense. Didn't these people understand that she *needed* rational order in her universe?

The world had gone insane again. Every time she thought she was finding a bit of sense to hang onto in this time and place, the world tilted on its axis and tossed her off the side. She couldn't take much more of this.

A shiver of fear went through Maddie.

Rowan saw the look of confusion in Maddie's eyes, confusion that was close to panic. He instinctively understood the fear that was overtaking her. He swiftly put his hands on her shoulders and said as reassuringly as he could, "Any sufficiently advanced magic is indistinguishable from technology."

Or had it been the other way? He didn't know. He only knew that she'd used some such words to convince herself of the reality of all she'd been through. He wanted to remind her of them, to comfort and calm her. For the most important thing in his life right now was seeing to Maddie's happiness. Rowan wanted to shelter her from all pain and danger.

He stroked her cheek. "Don't look so frightened, beloved. We'll deal with it."

Of course she couldn't understand him. With the fair folk's chains off her and lying harmless on the floor, she had lost a gift for understanding the Gaelic language that came with wearing the necklace.

"The fair folk are wickedly whimsical in their gift-giving, but we'll find a way around them," he assured her, though his talking just seemed to make her more upset.

So he said no more. Instead he took her by the hand and led her to the bench by the hearth. The scent that rose from the little iron pot that bubbled and steamed over the fire was both sharp and soothing. Though his stomach rumbled, Rowan suspected that this brew the White Lady had left to simmer in her absence was not intended for dinner.

"I think there's a spell at work here," he told his uncomprehending wife. He pointed at the pot. "For once I don't mind the woman's interference. I think the herbs boiling there are meant to loosen tongues. For I've talked more in the last hours than I normally do in a year."

Whether it was a spell, or simply having been overwhelmed with the need to communicate his feelings at last, Rowan didn't know. He almost preferred believing in the spell, because he hated to think that he'd let love for Maddie make him weak in any way.

He settled Maddie on the seat and put his arm around her waist. Her fingers knotted together nervously in her lap while Rowan fought the urge to hold her, to rock her like a babe in his arms and promise to keep all harm at bay. He wanted to shelter her, but a solution to this new problem would be better. Besides, fixing things was probably more to Maddie's liking. She would not like to be coddled, he told himself. She was too strong for such nonsense. So he sat beside her, stared into the fire, and kept the words that wanted to spill out tightly held inside for now.

Maddie was glad of the silence. It was comforting not to hear Rowan's voice speaking in a language she couldn't understand. She needed time to calm down, to adjust to this new situation. Rowan's presence beside her, as calm and solid and quiet as a piece of Scottish granite, helped. She didn't have to give in to the urge to cling to him to draw comfort from him. His arm around her waist was comforting. So was the warm contact of their hips and thighs as they squeezed together on the narrow bench. Gradually, she felt the tension easing a bit. She even let her head rest on his shoulder and dozed off for a while. She told herself that everything must be going to be all right if she could fall asleep knowing that she couldn't communicate with the wild Highlanders she was forced to live among. How wild and scary could the situation be if she could sleep through it?

After what seemed like a long time, Rowan said, "You're feeling better, I think." Her response was to sit up straight and stiff, and look at him wildly. She said something in her own tongue. From the accusing tone, he thought that she'd just told him that she wasn't ready for conversation just yet. Perhaps she'd discovered that silence was not a bad thing. Rowan couldn't help but chuckle. "I know how you feel, lass, but we might as well begin solving this problem."

First he reluctantly pried himself away from Maddie's side and searched the floor of the small house until he found the fairy necklace. He was prepared for a jolt of pain when he scooped it up, but found that the magic in it seemed to be dormant when not fastened about Maddie's soft throat. He silently damned the fair folk who'd made the necklace as he stuffed it into a pouch, though he supposed they had done him a favor by bringing Maddie into his life.

He looked back at her after he'd put the necklace out of sight, and told himself that her presence was indeed a blessing. Oh, a mixed one, as most blessings tended to be. He remembered how she'd been as they'd made love, wild and free and a glory to touch. He saw her now, leaning forward, watching him intently, her flame-colored hair framing her anxious face, with her hands clasped nervously in her lap.

"You're nothing but trouble, Maddie Murray," he told her. "But I love you."

Maddie considered covering her ears when Rowan spoke, because she just didn't want to deal with this new problem. Then he stepped in front of her, and, smiling encouragingly, rubbed his stomach and spoke. *"Arcas?"*

He'd spoken the one-word question slowly and distinctly. Maddie continued to watch, somewhere between puzzled, annoyed, and frightened as Rowan pointed at the pot, at his mouth, and rubbed his stomach again.

"*Arcas?*" he asked again. And again.

Eventually she repeated the word. It sounded odd in her mouth, but she laughed after she said it. Light was beginning to dawn. Maddie jumped to her feet.

"Rowan Murray, you are married to an idiot!" she declared. "You're brilliant, and I love you! Here I've been sitting here wrapped up in feeling sorry for myself and frightened by all this magical claptrap when there's a perfectly logical solution to the whole thing. So what if we can't magically understand each other anymore? Magic-schmagic, I can learn the local language." She rubbed her stomach. "*Arcas* means hunger, right? Or hungry, or some variation of the concept."

Seeing that all Maddie's babbling boiled down to her understanding what he'd been getting at, Rowan threw back his head and laughed. Then he grabbed her by the waist and swung her around the tiny house.

They laughed together, and kissed, and then she said, "Hungry," in his language firmly enough so that he'd know she wasn't parroting his words, but that she wanted her dinner.

"Aye," he agreed, and began looking around, for he doubted what was in the pot was edible. "*Aran,*" he told her when he found a loaf of bread wrapped in a cloth on a shelf.

"*Aran,*" Maddie repeated. "Bread," she said in her own language.

"Bread," he said, as it occurred to him that they could teach each other.

A smile lit her face, and affection lit her eyes. The sight of her sent a flush of warmth through him, and

Rowan felt another sort of hunger stir in his blood. He put the bread back on the shelf and took a step toward her. She tossed her head, and gave a low laugh, as silvery bright as a swift-running mountain burn, yet deep as the wild ocean. The throaty sound held a newborn sensual awareness that set fire to his blood.

Maddie didn't quite know what had gotten into her. Maybe it was the way Rowan looked at her that made her feel so boldly sexual. She felt as though her body had taken on an erotic life of its own. No, it wasn't just her body; her whole being felt new, awakened. She felt—female. She was beginning to accept that all the physical cravings she'd always told herself were no more than hormonal imbalances were an intimate, important part of her being. All it took was Rowan looking at her the way he was at the moment and she forgot to feel awkward and unlovable.

As he came closer, she held out her arms in eager welcome.

The door opened before she could take him in her embrace. "Well," the White Lady said as they both jumped back and turned toward her. "I see my house is still here. And so are the pair of you," she added as she came in and put her basket on the table. The White Lady gave Rowan a thorough, critical look. While a deep blush colored his face, she turned her scrutiny on Maddie. "Easy to see what you two have been doing."

"We're man and wife," Rowan pointed out.

The White Lady leered at him. "So you are." She touched a spot on his throat. "She's a wild lass, I see."

"D'ye enjoy seeing me blush, woman?" She wasn't in the least put off by his growl, and within moments he found himself leering too, as memories of love-making filled his mind. "Aye, it's a wild wife you found for me."

"For which you should be grateful. I hoped that I'd give you enough time to find that out while I was gone. With any luck you planted a bairn in her belly in the last few hours."

"I pray so."

Maddie didn't understand what the White Lady and Rowan said, but their expressions and tones were not hard to read. They were discussing her and Rowan's having had sex, and Maddie was shaken by both outrage and shock. How dare they be so open and frank about something meant to be private? The embarrassment she felt singed Maddie to the core. She looked at the floor as she muttered, "This has been a terrible mistake. I'm sorry. We shouldn't have—" She covered her mouth before she finished, overwhelmed at the realization that she and Rowan had made love in this woman's house, in her bed, and the other woman knew it.

"Oh, God," Maddie whimpered. She covered her face with her hands. "Please, could I just curl up and die from the embarrassment right now?"

"What did she say?" The White Lady asked Rowan.

"I haven't a clue," he replied. "The necklace came off, you see," he told the wisewoman. "She lost the understanding of our tongue."

The White Lady nodded thoughtfully. "I suspected some such change might come over her when she was freed of the spell."

"And were prepared for it?" Rowan asked. He pointed suspiciously at the bubbling pot on the hearth.

"That has a fine and fancy smell to it. Did it set our tongues to wagging?"

She gave a dirty chuckle. "Your tongues have been doing more than wagging, Rowan Murray."

"No potion was responsible for that," he declared of his and Maddie's lovemaking. "Of that I'm certain."

She patted his shoulder. "True, lad." She looked around her small house. "The spell is broken, the necklace is off, and you and your wife have consummated your marriage. Not a bad night's work."

Rowan frowned at her satisfied smile. "You act as though it were all your doing."

She put her hands on her hips. "I'm making light of serious subjects, lad. You'd do well to see the humor in life upon occasion."

"I do. Upon occasion."

"Not on any occasion I've heard of. Och." She waved a hand at him dismissively and concentrated on Maddie. "He's your problem, lass, not mine."

Rowan fought the urge to step between the two women. He knew he had no reason to protect Maddie from the White Lady, yet the protective urge was strong in him for her. Though Maddie was the larger of the two women, she seemed to shrink before the White Lady's gaze. In fact, when the White Lady looked at her, Maddie clutched her arms tightly around her waist and backed into the shadows away from the fire. "She doesn't understand your words," he defended his wife's behavior. "It frightens her."

That her earlier dismay at the loss of the language had returned was the only explanation he could think of for Maddie's touchy response to the other woman. He didn't understand such backsliding, since she'd been eager to learn Gaelic before the White Lady had returned. Though he was puzzled by her behavior, Rowan didn't hesitate to go to Maddie. He stood behind her, his arms circled her protectively, but he made her face the White Lady.

Maddie was both annoyed and shaken by her own emotional shifts. She wanted Rowan to touch her, but wanted to slip out of his embrace as well, at least while the other woman was looking at them. "I am so confused," she muttered. "Maybe it's just because too much has happened too fast tonight."

Rowan felt as if he were hugging a stone, but he didn't let Maddie go. "It is late," he said. "Perhaps we should all just rest."

His hope was to take Maddie off to a dark corner of the house and settle down for the night beside her with their bodies snugly wrapped together in his plaid. In the morning they could leave, and spend the ride back to Cape Wrath learning to speak to each other. He had a vision of a secluded place where they could stop along the way to make love.

"It's early enough," the White Lady said. She turned and took the bread back down from its shelf. "No guest goes to bed hungry in my house." She gestured for them to sit.

Maddie managed to get over her embarrassed shyness long enough to steal a look at Rowan. He looked annoyed, but he nodded at something the woman said, and stepped forward, pushing Maddie before him.

"Hey!" she protested.

He sighed, pointed at the bread, then at the White Lady. The other woman set plates on the table then a dark yellow wedge of cheese. There was a bowl of berries, as well. It all looked delicious. *"Dìot mhór,"* he said, and urged Maddie toward the table.

Maddie decided to interpret this as dinner, and let her empty stomach override her awkward feelings.

Before Maddie could sit down, the White Lady put a hand on her arm. Maddie turned to the woman while Rowan moved past her to take a seat. The White Lady gave her a reassuring smile, then took down a cup made of carved horn. She put a dipper full of liquid from her the pot on the hearth and held it out to Maddie.

Maddie reluctantly took the cup, and realized just how cold she'd become when the warmth from the liquid radiated to her palms.

The White Lady said something, then smiled and nodded at Maddie, before giving Rowan a quelling look as she gestured him to stay seated.

Maddie heard Rowan grumble out a question, but most of her attention was on the lovely little cup cradled in her palms. It was dark brown and shiny, the outside carved in a delicate Celtic knotwork pattern. It was very pretty, but what it contained was what drew her complete interest. She'd gotten used to the delicious aroma that permeated the house, but now she breathed in fresh scents as steam lifted from the cup. She couldn't keep from holding it closer to her nose.

"Wonderful." Her mouth began to water.

Anything that smelled so good must taste fantastic. She heard the White Lady urging her to, but didn't need anything but the fascination with the lovely aroma to lift the cup to her lips. She was suddenly terribly thirsty. Hot as the liquid was, she found herself gulping it down.

While Maddie drank, she heard the other woman speaking reassuringly to Rowan. The Gaelic was lilting and lovely on her tongue. ". . . *leighis copan* will do her a world of good."

Leighis copan, Maddie thought, *means the healing cup.* She had trouble switching the words from Gaelic to English. "I'm thinking in Gaelic," she said. The cup—the healing cup—dropped from her numb hands.

Rowan grabbed her by the shoulders, though she wasn't aware of his moving from the table. She looked up at him. He was managing to glower and grin at the same time; a combination she was sure only Rowan could manage. "You're speaking Gaelic," he said.

She had no trouble understanding him. The room, quite disconcertingly, began to spin around her. "I'm dizzy." There were also small explosions being set off in her stomach, behind her eyes, and in the dense matter between her ears where her brain was supposedly located. "All my nerve endings seem to be celebrating the Fourth of July," she said. "I can't feel my feet. Are you holding me up, Rowan?"

"Aye."

"That's good." She blinked. It was a slow, laborious, process. "This is magic, right?"

"It's magic," the White Lady said, her voice sounding very distant. "A simple spell to replace the understanding the fair folk took away. I saw in a vision that you would need this when you came to me."

Maddie giggled. The room had stopped spinning. It was now melting. The low ceiling had been replaced by an arch of exploding stars. Maddie's head fell slowly back as she became enthralled with watching the light show going on above her. She tried to reach up and touch the stars, but her body was turning into a mass of boneless putty.

"Wow."

"She's ill," Rowan said.

She sort of felt him lift her in his arms. His worry slid over her, shadowlike. His concern was more like a comfortable warm blanket.

"She'll be fine."

"Magic," Maddie said. "Real magic. I get it."

"Of course," the White Lady answered as the stars rippled and shifted overhead. "I see that you believe at last."

"Yeah. This is great," Maddie said. She giggled, and passed out.

22

"*Drugs.*" The word came out of her sore throat in an almost choking rasp.

I was drugged. I don't know what was real from what was hallucination—because I was drugged.

How could she do that to me? Why?

A sense of betrayal was the first thing Maddie became aware of when she woke up. She regained consciousness and instantly knew that the crazy, so-called *wisewoman* had given her drugs. She didn't try to open her eyes. She didn't want to know anything about her present situation. She had to analyze what had happened prior to her having passed out. Then she would try to deal with the secondary knowledge that she was lying on a dirt floor, tightly wrapped in warm wool and Rowan Murray's snug embrace. She didn't have to actually look at him to recognize the soft sound of his breathing and the firm feel of his body. Even when she'd been unconscious she'd known she was safely sleeping beside his large, lean form.

She wasn't going to think about Rowan's body even

though they were cuddled up together spoon fashion in a way that had her buttocks pressed against his bare thighs. She wasn't going to dwell on this unseemly arrangement or try to edge out of it. Not yet. She didn't try to move away. She was far too warm and comfortable to consider the situation in solitary seclusion. She felt protected. This might be a false assumption, but the physical comfort was real enough.

Maddie recalled everything that had happened the night before quite clearly. She just didn't know how much of it was real. First there must have been the effects from the steam messing with her thinking, then she'd been foolish enough to drink the stuff in the pot. She had taken a drink, hadn't she? Yes. She was pretty sure that part had been real. As for the rest of it—well, the necklace had come off, and she and Rowan hadn't been able to understand each other. Right?

She'd actually been looking forward to learning Gaelic from Rowan. The thought threaded through her mind, leaving a melancholy sadness in its wake. It would have been a way for them to grow closer, something for them to share. *How foolish you're being,* she chided herself. *Everything that happened last night was just a dream.*

Everything?

The sadness lifted somewhat as memories—memories she was sure were not false ones—flooded through her. For a time last night she had been wild, uninhibited, and so had Rowan. Only—had he wanted to make love to her, or was it a side-effect of the hallucinogen?

Then again, maybe she was just imagining that she remembered making love. How could she be sure it wasn't something she'd dreamed? Because she *knew* she had done all those lovely, sensual, sexual things, she decided after considering what she remembered and how she currently felt. It wasn't just how she reacted emotionally, but her body was—different. Yes, definitely different. Awake. She was somehow more aware than she had ever been. How could making love make one feel more alive? Not to mention a bit bruised and strained in places, and definitely a bit sore in one specific very private spot she wasn't used to even thinking about that much, let alone using.

"I don't think I'm a virgin anymore," she found herself muttering.

Rowan's arm tightened around her and he chuckled in her ear. "No, lass, that you're not."

He sounded inordinately pleased about the whole thing. Which led Maddie to believe that he actually had been there during the process, which was how she remembered it having happened.

She was glad that they'd made love, even if it had been under the influence of some sort of drug. Maybe it was even a good thing that the drug had lowered her inhibitions enough to let her do something she wanted. Because she really had wanted Rowan. She wasn't going to pretend that she hadn't wanted last night's events to happen. She'd been waiting all her life for someone like—no, she'd been waiting all her life for Rowan—to make her feel like she had in his arms. It was nice that for once nothing had happened to stop them from getting together. On the other hand, wasn't using a behavior-altering substance, even inadvertently, cheating?

Who had it cheated? Him or her? Both. Yes, definitely, both of them. The so-called witch had created a situation where neither Rowan or she had behaved or responded in their normal manner. They'd been higher than kites and had behaved like a pair of oversexed bunnies because of it.

Then again, she hadn't needed a drug when they'd started to make love by the lake. That had been a very natural high. Who knew what might have become of it if the pain from the necklace hadn't knocked her out?

And what about the necklace? And had they said the things to each other that she recalled, or had she imagined a conversation about trust and love and believing in the reality of magic?

"Magic," she complained, and threw off Rowan's encircling arm.

"Aye," he agreed with her annoyed tone, and helped her untangle from the makeshift blanket. "Magic's hard on a body, that's for certain. Does your head hurt from the potion?"

She rolled over to look at him, and propped her head up on her hand. Her breasts were making a serious attempt to escape from the confines of her chemise, and she noticed that Rowan noticed. While he looked down her dress, she looked at him. He needed a shave, and a shower wouldn't have hurt, either, but he was absolutely gorgeous. Was that an aftereffect of the drugs? Or maybe Rowan was absolutely gorgeous.

When he finally drew his gaze up to her face, he touched her forehead. "Are you in pain?"

"No."

"Good. The White Lady said you'd take no harm from her potion."

"Did she?"

"Aye. I think we've slept overlong. Time we were up

and doing, wife," Rowan added, though he didn't rush to get to his feet. He was oddly content to just be side by side with Maddie for a while longer.

Maddie looked tousled and wanton, with her hair wild about her face, looking at him through half-closed, heavy lids, and with her lips a bit swollen from the many kisses they'd shared last night. He liked her looking this way, soft and ripe and womanly. He kissed her now, no more than a soft brush of lips against lips that left her looking startled and him feeling pleasantly warmed.

He wanted to get her home to Cape Wrath and into the bed they should have started sharing days ago. In order to do that they were going to have to get up off of the White Lady's floor, get out of her house, and get on with the journey. What he wanted to do even more than get home to Cape Wrath was to roll Maddie onto her back and repeat last night's lovemaking right here and now.

Instead he made himself stand up. He held out a hand to help her up as he said, "We have a lot of time to make up."

"That's for sure," Maddie said as she sat up. "I've to get to work on the chimney, and the loom, and—"

"And the bairns. We can't forget the bairns."

Maddie had no idea what bairns Rowan was talking about, nor did she care to speculate on the subject. "Right." She adjusted her clothing and looked cautiously around the White Lady's house. She didn't see any bubbling pot over the fire. Or even any fire in the hearth. Or the White Lady herself. Maddie gave a relieved sigh.

"Let's get out of here," she urged Rowan. "Before the crazy lady gets back."

"Such disrespect!" Rowan gave her a playful pat on the behind. Actually, more of a caress than a pat. He liked the feel of the sweet, soft curve of her rear.

When she threw him a startled look over her shoulder he very nearly burst out laughing. He didn't know why, but he was as giddy as a lad this morning. Maybe it was just the sight of her lovely freckled face that set his heart singing and made his mind as bubbly as sea foam.

He tried to frown, tried to assume his normally serious manner, and found that he simply couldn't. "Maddie, lass, you've stolen my dignity," he said as he wound his kilt around his hips.

Maddie had found a comb. She was bent forward, with hair in front of her face as she made a desperate effort to untangle her thick curls. She parted her hair with her hands and gave Rowan a bemused look. "I think you're still stoned, hon."

Aftereffects of a drug or not, she had to admit she liked seeing Rowan this way. He was all bright and cheerful and bouncy. Cute. Yes, he was definitely cute. Not that she was fool enough to mention this to him. She had brothers. She knew how much they hated to be called "cute." It was as though the word desecrated everything their macho hearts held dear. She didn't imagine this sword-wielding Highlander would take the term any better than her Montana cowboy siblings. So she kept her thoughts to herself and went back to combing her hair.

"I'll find us something to break our fast," Rowan said, and actually cheerfully hummed while he set about searching the White Lady's cupboard.

Maddie enjoyed the sound of his voice. She enjoyed

the simple task of grooming. She even enjoyed the gnawing hunger in her stomach. All these things were real-time, solid, normal parts of life—except maybe Rowan's lively pleasure in the day. She told herself that his behavior might just be the normal consequences of his having gotten laid and had more to do with physical satisfaction than reaction to drugs. The thought gave her hope that Rowan might have a loving core beneath his usually dead-serious and downright grumpy facade. She liked to think that she'd brought that out in him, but also cautioned herself that it was too early to tell. They had been drugged, and who knew what the side effects were or how long it was going to take to wear off.

Right now, she told herself, the best thing to do was concentrate on normal activity. By the time she'd finished the normal activity of braiding her hair, Rowan had found the bread, cheese, and fruit they hadn't gotten to last night. He divided it in half, and they set to wolfing down the meal without any further conversation. Maddie didn't feel rude about breaking into the White Lady's store of food. She figured anything they took from the woman was in compensation for the bizarre happenings she'd put them through.

"Magic," Maddie muttered darkly, and reached for another wedge of cheese.

Someone began banging hard on the door before her hand reached the food. She and Rowan both whirled around. Rowan's hand went to his long dagger when a man outside shouted, "Lady! White Lady, we need your help!"

Maddie took a step toward the door, only to be halted when Rowan put a hand on her arm. When she glanced inquiringly at him, her heart sank. All the seriousness was back in his expression. Worse, his eyes were lit with a deep, consuming anger.

Seeing the man who'd been so happy a moment before like this sent a shiver through Maddie. "What?"

The man called out again. "Harboth," Rowan said. He looked, and sounded, more dangerous than she'd ever seen him before.

"That doesn't sound like Burke."

"It's not." He moved past her with a lithe, deadly grace.

Rowan made sure he was between his wife and the enemy before he flung open the door. The man standing before the door was Allen Harboth. The look of angry surprise on his enemy's face was almost enough to restore some of Rowan's joyful mood.

"Aye, it's me," he told the rival clan leader. "What are you doing on my land?"

"This place belongs to the White Lady," Harboth pointed out. "I've come to see her."

"She's not here."

"Don't stand there looking hard and evil, Rowan Murray! Get out of my way."

Rowan stepped closer to the door as Harboth tried to get past. "I said she's not here."

Maddie didn't understand Rowan's annoyed response to the man at the door. The stranger sounded desperate. Maybe he thought he desperately needed one of the White Lady's dangerous potions or her socalled fortune telling abilities. As misguided as people's faith in the woman was, Maddie didn't think Rowan had any business trying to keep the man out.

"Why are you being rude?" she asked, stepping up

behind Rowan. "Hello," she added as the blond stranger looked over Rowan's shoulder at her. "You look like Burke Harboth. Are you two related?"

The stranger's annoyed expression softened somewhat when she spoke to him.

"He's my brother."

"Then you're one of the evil Harboth clan. Would you be Allen?" The Harboth nodded. "Which explains all the hostility." She touched Rowan on the shoulder. He spared her one quick glance before going back to glaring at his enemy. "Why don't you let Mr. Harboth in?"

Allen Harboth smiled at her. It was a smile so charming Maddie couldn't help but smile back. He wasn't as gorgeous as Burke. Allen was shorter, thinner, his features more saturnine than boyishly attractive, but the resemblance was very clear. The Harboths certainly weren't an ugly family. This man also had a decided presence. It was the same sort of presence Rowan wore so well, an aura of command and responsibility. Facing off, the two men exuded buckets of manly aura at each other.

Or maybe it's just stubbornness, Maddie thought, and firmly used a hip butt to ease herself between her husband and the newcomer. She could have sworn that Rowan actually growled when she got between him and his foe. She didn't suppose what she'd done was a very good idea, but she was afraid Rowan was ready to draw the very sharp, very long dagger he wore on his belt. The last thing she wanted on this already difficult morning was bloodshed.

"I'm Maddie," she told Allen Harboth. "We don't know where the White Lady is." *And happy to keep it that way,* she added to herself. "You look like you could use some help."

"Woman!" Rowan snarled.

Maddie backed up a step, then another, forcing Rowan to move or get his feet trodden on. Allen Harboth followed them into the little house.

"I need help," he said. "And so do you, Murray," he added to Rowan. "So listen to me. Thank you, lass," he said to Maddie. "Are you the White Lady's apprentice?" he asked her.

"She's my wife."

Despite the threat in Rowan's tone, Harboth kept his attention on her. "Of course. I should have guessed. Burke told me that you were a fair, fire-haired beauty."

He took Maddie's hand, and kissed it. No one had ever kissed her hand before. It certainly wasn't the sort of thing likely to happen on Montana ranches or Scottish oil rigs. She wasn't even sure it was supposed to happen in the medieval Highlands, but then she remembered being told that the Harboths sent their sons off to France for as decent an education as it was possible to get in the Middle Ages. Allen had obviously returned with a bit of sophisticated polish along with a knowledge of the seven liberal arts.

She wasn't surprised when Rowan complained, "Keep your hands off my woman."

She wasn't sure she was flattered, either, since Rowan sounded more disgruntled than he did romantically possessive. It didn't help that Allen half smiled and lifted an eyebrow sardonically at her in response to Rowan's words. She forced her attention back to the original subject before letting herself become a bone of contention between two men who were already rivals.

From this point on, she decided, any attention paid to her by either man would only be because of their on-going family feud.

"What sort of help do you need?" she asked. "What do you mean about the Murrays needing help?"

"Burke's been hurt," Allen told her.

A cold shiver of dread went through Maddie. "How badly?" Damn. She wished she knew something about medicine.

"Again?" Rowan scoffed. "What happened to him this time?"

Allen scowled, but he kept his attention on Maddie as he said, "A blow to the head."

"He has a hard head," Rowan said. "And not much in it to be rattled."

"I found him not far from here," Allen went on to Maddie. "That's why I thought to bring the White Lady to him." He finally looked at Rowan. "When Burke came home from Cape Wrath, he told me he was deter-mined to wed your sister."

"He'll do no such thing!"

"That's what I told him. I told him that he'd not wed her without your permission."

"When hell freezes over."

Burke nodded. "I don't like their liking for each other any more than you do, Murray, but it's been going on all their lives. He's had most of the women in the Highlands, but that hasn't changed his feelings for the girl. Even three years in the stews of Paris weren't enough to cure him of her, though there was no end of his trying."

"No doubt he came home with the French pox from his manly efforts."

Maddie touched Rowan reprovingly on the arm. "Don't be mean, Burke's a sweet boy. Is he hurt badly?" She asked Allen.

He shook his head. "Rowan has the right of it when he says the lad has a hard head, but the Lady should look at him."

Maddie remembered the sweet, narcotic fumes of the concoction the woman had brewed last night. "Her idea of medicine is the last thing anyone needs."

The scent still lingered faintly in the air, reminding Maddie of all her strange dreams of magic, mystery, and love. Thanks to the potion, she might never be sure of the truth of what had happened between her and Rowan. Maddie mourned the fact that all her memories of conversations about love and trust might be false; nothing more than wish fulfillment brought up out of her own lonely psyche. Maddie truly hated the White Lady for putting a barrier of doubt in the already prickly relationship she had with Rowan.

"Her advice would be welcome as much as her potions," Allen said. "But since you're already here, Murray," he went on, finally looking at Rowan, "we'll have to talk face-to-face without her intercession."

Rowan stepped around Maddie. Standing toe-to-toe with Allen Harboth, he demanded, "What would you need the White Lady's intercession for?"

"To tell you that your sister and my brother ran away together to be wed across the border."

"What!" Rowan roared.

"They agreed to meet at Scammon Cove yesterday. Well, they met all right, and discovered that Scammon Cove is where another band of Norsemen from up in the Orkneys have made their summer raiding camp."

"Micaela."

Shock and dread went through Rowan as he said his sister's name. Fear for her completely wiped out any traces of anger at his sister or suspicious hatred of the Harboths. His head spun, and his knees told him that he very much wanted to sit down. It was only Maddie's strong hand under his elbow that kept him upright for a moment. He exchanged a quick look with his wife. He would have kissed her and thanked her for the support and strength he drew from her steady gaze had Allen Harboth not been there to see them.

If Allen Harboth—if all the Harboths—would just leave his family alone, there would be no crisis with Micaela to begin with!

It took Rowan a moment to bring the words out, but he swallowed and asked what had to be asked. "Does she live?"

Allen nodded. "Burke tells me they took her prisoner, and left him for dead on the shingle. He crawled away at sundown. I found him trying to reach Cape Wrath—trying to bring his plea for aid to *you*, Murray—just an hour ago. He's blood-soaked and frantic for the safety of his woman, but he's determined to get her back or die trying. The damn fool," he added, but Rowan thought the Allen sounded strangely proud of his brother despite his words.

Rowan was halfway to being proud of the fool himself. No, not quite half, but a man had to admire another man's daring and determination, at least a wee bit. Burke had always been so honorable in his courtship of Micaela and in his assertion that there could be peace between the clans that Rowan had never expected him to run off with the girl like a normal man.

There was something about Burke that was likable—for a Harboth, but he was still a Harboth who had put a Murray in danger.

"I don't understand much of this, you know," Maddie said. "What's going to happen to Micaela?"

When he looked Maddie in the eye, Rowan saw that she knew very well what could happen to a woman captured by a band of ruthless raiders. She was a woman herself, after all, one who'd been tossed into an alien landscape, vulnerable as all women without men to protect them were. She wanted to hear reassuring words about Micaela, he knew, not tales of rape and degradation and slave trading.

Fortunately, he had some hope to offer her. "Capturing and selling slaves is a good way to spend the summer for these Orkney traders. They think of their profits from these occasional raids before they think of satisfying their lusts."

"Occasional? You mean slave raiding is just a sideline?" she asked in surprise.

"Aye, they sell smoked fish and woolens most of the year," Allen answered. "But sometimes they deal in humans as well, especially if the fishing's been bad."

"How—Viking of them." She turned her worried gaze back to Rowan. "But?"

"Pretty young girls are more valuable untouched," Rowan explained. "Micaela's a beauty."

"A Moorish, Byzantine, or Italian lord will pay more for her if she's still a virgin," Allen explained.

"She better still be a virgin," Rowan said, as he turned a dark look on Allen. It was a threatening, brotherly look that Maddie was sure was really directed at Burke.

"She's going to be sold into a harem?"

"Or a brothel," Allen elucidated.

"I didn't need to hear that," she complained to the far-too-sophisticated-about-his-world Harboth.

"Nor did I," Rowan added. "Take me to your brother," he ordered Allen.

"Aye." Allen gave Maddie a quick, beseeching look. "He needs aid, lass."

She didn't bother explaining that first aid wasn't her strong point, but lifted her heavy skirts and followed the men out of the house and down the steep hillside.

Burke Harboth was propped up against a big boulder halfway down the track. The White Lady was already with him. So were a belligerent-looking group of men.

"Murrays," Allen Harboth snarled angrily. He stepped up beside his brother and put his hand on his sword. "Touch the lad and I'll take a dozen of you down with me."

The White Lady, from her position kneeling next to the prone Burke, swatted Allen on the back of one bare leg. "Hush. Besides, there's only eight Murrays standing there for you to try to kill."

"Still pretty stupid odds," Maddie said quietly. She couldn't help but exchange an amused look with the White Lady at the display of male bravado. Then she remembered that she was furious with the bogus wisewoman, and looked away.

Rowan heard his wife's word and put a hand on her arm. "Allen Harboth's not to be underestimated," he warned her quietly. "Be careful of him, lass."

She had the obscure feeling that he meant the words in more than one way. He stepped up beside his men before she could ask what he meant. No one paid her any mind as Maddie stepped back and leaned against another of the many gray boulders that strewed the mostly barren hillside. The sky overhead was typically gray with low clouds, and wispy white fog clung to the hilltops in the distance. A cool wind blew inland from the sea a few miles away, mixing the scent of salt with that of pine and heather. She was left feeling alone and left out as the Murrays began to talk.

"Micaela's gone," Father Andrew reported.

"For nearly two days now," Walter added.

"Ran off with the Harboth lad," Angus reported. "Left a message for you with Rosemary about not being able to wait any longer."

"We tracked him here." Father Andrew said. "Micaela's not with him, but we thought we might kill him anyway after we found out what he did with her."

Weapons were drawn at the priest's words. Rowan held up a hand. "I know what happened. I know where she is. We need a plan to save her."

After a bit more grumbling and sword-rattling, it was the usually cheerful Aidan who pointed grimly at Burke, who had struggled to his feet, and said, "You stole my sister, and I mean to see you dead."

"Save your anger for the Norsemen," Burke suggested. He had leaned on his brother when he first stood up. Now, Burke stood straight, and put a hand on his head. "The White Lady's fixed this. The pain's gone."

"If your head's working," Allen Harboth said sarcastically, "perhaps you can think of some way to get your lady back from the raiders."

Burke looked around. "You should have brought

more men after me, priest. It would have saved time in gathering more to attack the raiders."

"We have eleven men and no time," Rowan answered. "This will have to do."

"There's at least forty of the sea raiders," Burke said. "With two ships beached at the cove."

Rowan scratched his chin. "Eleven against forty. How many prisoners?"

Burke shrugged. "I caught a glimpse of a group under guard, but I had no time to count heads."

Maddie thought hard while the men talked. They looked determined and doughty, tough and ready to fight, but there just weren't that many of them. She anxiously looked over the gathered group of warriors, and murmured, "Eleven against forty. Bad odds — unless . . ." As an idea struck her she went quickly up to Rowan. "Do you know what you need?"

The gaze he turned on her was so angrily intense she almost took a step back. "I don't have time for you now, woman."

He meant neither rudeness nor disrespect to his woman, but he needed to think like a warrior now, not like a husband. Maddie blushed at his words, but he saw that it was with anger rather than womanly chagrin. "Go back to the house with the White Lady," he instructed, trying to sound as gentle and forbearing as he could. More than anything else he wanted to keep her safe. "I'll come for you when this day's work is done."

Maddie squirmed inwardly at Rowan's condescending tone. Even if this was the Middle Ages and he had switched from normal human being to laird of the fighting clansmen mode, she didn't have to like it. She wasn't able to put up with it, either. Maddie put her hands on her hips. "By 'this day's work,' I assume you mean that you're off to fight a superior force with only eleven men?"

"Aye. I mean just that."

"It won't work."

Rowan could not let anyone, even someone he loved, challenge his authority in front of the Harboths. "Don't meddle in things it's better for you to not know about."

"I do know something about strategy and tactics, sweetheart." The word dripped with sarcasm rather than endearment. It shamed Rowan to hear her speak so before the other men. "Enough to know how you can get Micaela back without losing all your men in a stupid, head-on assault."

Rowan took her by the arm, intending to lead her away. "We've no time for your fool ideas now."

"Fool?"

He saw that she took his words as a deep insult, but he could not call them back. When she tried to pull from his grasp all he could think of to do was grasp her tighter.

"Ow! Rowan!"

"Come along, lass."

"Wait," Allen Harboth called out when Rowan tried to pull the struggling Maddie from the group.

When she jerked violently away from his grasp, it was Allen who caught her by the elbow to keep her from falling. Rowan would have pushed Allen away from his wife, but Maddie stepped aside herself. She whirled to face Rowan, but again Allen got in the way.

"What would you have us do, lass?" the laird of the

Harboths asked. He flashed a warning look at Rowan. "I'm willing to listen even if the Murrays are not. Burke and I are anxious to help Micaela."

With the reminder that his sister was in danger and that time was wasting, Rowan swallowed both pride and misgivings and looked to his wife. "What have you in mind?" he demanded. "And be swift about it."

Maddie tried to tell herself that it was concern for his sister that had Rowan acting like a jerk. She tamped down her own annoyance, at him, herself for not being more diplomatic, and at the White Lady for simply existing. It took her a great deal of effort, but she managed to look at the other woman and ask politely, "Do you have any more dresses we can borrow?"

23

"*'Tis not right for a man* to be dressed like a woman," Walter complained as he adjusted the cloth over his hips. His kilt had been replaced by a long plaid skirt. "I'm ashamed to be seen like this."

Over the murmurs of agreement from several other members of the group as they approached the hidden cove, Maddie said, "Right. As if you all don't normally dress like a bunch of hairy-legged Catholic school girls? What's a kilt if it isn't a skirt?"

"It's not the same," Father Andrew said. He tugged on the long white veil that covered his tonsured head. It was arranged to also cover his full beard, so his voice sounded a bit muffled behind the cloth. "Wearing a priestly robe is all very well for me, but a warrior ought to show his knees to the world."

Maddie knew very well that Father Andrew was considered the finest, fiercest fighter in the Murray clan, so his reasoning really didn't make much sense. Nor did any of their complaints about skirt lengths. "Who'd have thought the Highlands would prove to be such a fashion-conscious place?"

"I just don't think Walter and Andrew like my wardrobe," the White Lady said. "Pink and green don't suit them. Though I think you look quite lovely in what you're wearing."

What Maddie was wearing was a black velvet number embroidered in silver. The dress had a close-fitting, low bodice and yards and yards and yards of skirts. It was a lovely dress, and she had to admit that it showed off her—assets—of round hips and full breasts better than anything she'd ever worn.

She'd been told, gallantly, by Allen Harboth, that the black and silver suited her red hair and pale skin. All she'd gotten from Rowan was a tight-jawed, stern once-over and a curt nod. He'd also given Allen a similar look, at which Allen had laughed. It was all very weird. The reaction from the two men left her completely confused as to how she really looked.

She'd always been fairly certain that there was nothing appealing in her looks, nothing interesting. Last night Rowan had made her feel beautiful, desirable, loved. This morning she didn't know if he'd meant any of it or if it had just been hallucinations. Maybe she'd only dreamed hearing him tell her things she wanted to hear. Still, they had made love, he'd seemed interested in doing it again, but the moment he got the chance to get back to being the serious laird of the clan he'd jumped at it. Then Allen came along and acted like she was a *girl,* and Rowan seemed vaguely jealous, which gave her a certain sense of power. Which was not a very nice way to react, she told herself. She should be ashamed.

Maybe later, after they'd rescued Micaela, she'd take the time to give herself a good, harsh lecture and sort out just what it was she was feeling. Especially what she was feeling about and for Rowan Murray. Anger, she told herself now. Lots of annoyance at his trying to brush her off as a mere woman when she came up with this harebrained scheme. Then again, after he'd heard the harebrained scheme, he'd been the first to agree to it.

"What is with him?" she murmured with a dejected sigh.

It was Aidan who came up behind her and said, "He fears enjoying himself, lass. He fears being in love."

Maddie paused to give the teenager a puzzled look. "Why?" As she waited for an answer she noticed for the first time the slightly slanted shape of his aquamarine-colored eyes and the sharpness of his high-set cheekbones. He'd braided his hair and arranged it on top of his head, saying it looked more maidenly to Norsemen that way. When he tilted his head to one side, she noticed something else about him and just barely managed not to gasp. In her surprise, she almost forgot her concern over Rowan Murray. She couldn't keep herself from saying, "I don't mean to be rude, but do you know that you have pointed ears?"

Aidan gave her a wickedly teasing smile. "Oh, aye. They're my best feature. Very sensitive to a lady's caressing touch." He bent his head toward her. "Want to touch?"

"She does not," Rowan said as he came up behind his wife.

Aidan chuckled and stepped back. Maddie gave him a stinging look, and Rowan almost flinched waiting for her response. Instead of showing any sort of protest, her expression swiftly changed to one of alert attention as all the fighters gathered around him. He was grateful that she didn't waste time arguing that she had every right to talk to her brother-in-law if she wanted to. She seemed well-aware that so close to a battle was no time to argue. Rowan almost hugged her and told her he was proud of her, but he had no time for that, either.

He could hear the roar of the nearby sea, and knew it was loud enough to muffle their voices from the raiders on the shore. They had chosen a narrow break in the cliffs above the cove for their ambush. It was one of many spots where thin rills of rainwater ran down to join the ocean. Gorse, ferns, and a few seedling pines grew here, protected from storm winds by a tall granite outcropping.

Rowan pointed to the top of rocks that overlooked the cove. "The six of you ladies go up there, show yourselves, and lead the Norsemen down here." He pointed to a scattered group of boulders on the other side of the trickling stream. "The rest of us will wait behind those."

Maddie nodded. "Okay, girls," she said. "Let's go." She turned and set off briskly, without waiting to see if the men would follow. The White Lady laughed and hurried after her.

Rowan didn't know if his heart was ready to burst with pride or fear as his wife walked away. Her magnificent hips swayed tantalizingly beneath her full skirts. He found himself watching her movements longingly for a moment. Then he noticed that all the other men were watching her as well, some with the same rapt eagerness in their expressions that he felt. He growled a warning, and waved the decoys forward with his sword.

"Anything happens to her and you're all dead," he told them.

At his words, the men picked up their skirts and ran to catch up so they could surround and protect his lady. Rowan gave a satisfied nod, refused to let his worry for either Maddie's or Micaela's safety prey on his mind, and hurried to hide himself behind the nearest boulder.

Maddie tried not to worry as she, the White Lady, Aidan, Burke, Walter, and Andrew stationed themselves on the flat top of the spit of rock. She mentally braced herself against the coming bloodshed with the knowledge that there was no other way to rid the people of the Scottish coast of the immediate danger of the Norse raiders. "Negotiations aren't going to get prisoners back from slave traders," she said as the camp and beached boats came into view.

Burke Harboth put a hand on her shoulder. "That's true. To try to ransom the prisoners would only cause the Orkneymen to return and try the same trick of stealing then selling back our own people next season."

Maddie nodded and glanced at Micaela's handsome boyfriend. She suspected he and Aidan looked better in a dress than she did. A jeweled sword belt rode low on his hips over a costume of lavender and purple, and his silvery blond hair flowed magnificently around his face and down his back. Except for his broad shoulders, from a distance he probably looked tall and willowy and gorgeous. They had to count that from a distance the Norse wouldn't notice anyone's broad shoulders or beards. She and the White Lady were here to stand in the front and look like real girls. The White Lady might be a charlatan, but she was certainly attractive enough. She and Burke, with their pale good looks, could easily pass for sisters. It also turned out that the White Lady had a great wardrobe, which certainly came in handy for this little adventure.

A guard down on the shore saw them, pointed, and called out a warning. When faces turned toward them, Maddie took a few steps closer to the camp. "Hey!" she called out as she waved her arms. "We're the women of clan Murray!"

She'd been told during the planning of this operation that everybody, including the raiders from up in the Orkney Islands, knew how bossy and brash the Murray women were. It was one of the reasons Rowan had gone along with the idea. He'd said that if any females were fool enough to march off to rescue one of their own, it would be the women in his family. Down on the shore, men grabbed their weapons, but the sound of rude laughter mixed with the clang of drawn steel.

Maddie moved closer to the camp while the other woman and the warriors stayed on the top of the hill. She straightened her spine, then leaned forward a bit to give the men at the bottom of the hill a better view of her cleavage. She wasn't sure whether to be terrified or gratified by the lewd shouts that greeted her movement. She felt herself blushing hotly as she called out, "We've come for Micaela Murray. Let her go and no one gets hurt!"

The plan hadn't been to do any talking, but Maddie didn't think it could harm anything but her conscience if she didn't at least offer to negotiate.

It didn't do any good, of course.

"Women!" someone called from down below. "Get them!"

The raiders came howling up the hillside like a small swarm of wasps. Maddie lifted her skirts and turned and fled. So did the White Lady. The men waited a few seconds longer, to put themselves between the women and the raiders, then they ran themselves, before the Norsemen could see that they were being led into a trap. Maddie sprinted down the hill, and jumped the stream. She was looking for a big rock to hide behind when Rowan darted out from in back of a boulder, and pulled her down to the spot where he'd been waiting.

"Stay here," he ordered, as Burke and Aidan hurtled past in a flurry of pastel skirts. They were followed closely by a hairy, shouting Norseman. Rowan gave her a hard, quick kiss, then ran after the raider.

Maddie had no intention of doing anything but staying put. As a battle began around her, she closed her eyes, covered her ears, and prayed for it to be over swiftly. She agreed this had to be done, she'd helped plan it. She didn't have the stomach to witness it. Besides, she was too frightened for Rowan's safety to actually watch him fighting. Or so she thought. After a few moments, worry drove her to raise her head. She heard the clang and clash of weapons, shouts and heavy breathing, but she couldn't see anything from the shelter where she crouched.

"Rowan," she whispered, and shivered in fear.

Not for herself, but for him. She had to see that he was all right. Her stomach churned at the thought that he wasn't. Maddie got to her knees, and looked cautiously around the side of the boulder to where the noise of fighting was coming from. Rowan was in the thick of it, of course, unwounded and swinging his claymore at a pair of opponents. She couldn't take her eyes off him. She wanted to call out to him, but wasn't foolish enough to try to distract him in the middle of a battle.

When he killed both men, she was actually glad. Glad he was alive and that they weren't. She didn't know if she had become as barbaric as the people she lived among, and for the moment she didn't care. All that mattered was running to throw her arms around the vibrantly alive Rowan Murray the instant the fighting was over.

Rowan's heart sang with joy when he saw Maddie rushing toward him, a smile on her lips and unshed tears gleaming in her eyes. The battle was done, he was victorious, and he shouted with triumph as he took his woman into a tight embrace. Her lips were soft and pliant beneath the demand of his kiss. Her body was soft as well, perfectly fitted against his hardness as he pulled her closer.

He might have had her then and there, he might have forgotten his duty, and that his sister and others were still prisoners, if Allen Harboth hadn't slapped him hard on the back and said, "The ruse worked, Rowan! And not a man or lassie of ours wounded! And have you a kiss for me, Maddie Murray?" the laird of the Harboths added as Rowan lifted his lips from his wife's.

"She does not," Rowan informed the lecherously smiling Harboth.

He wanted to put his arm possessively, protectively, around Maddie's waist. He was so proud of her. Proud of her courage, her cleverness, her beauty. He was very nearly blinded by the things he felt for her.

The one thing Rowan knew he could not allow himself was to be so drawn to a woman that she became his entire world.

The world around him went cold and dead at this thought. His happiness turned to ashes. He had no right to feel the things he wanted to feel, dared not take more than a small taste of the joy Maddie offered. He'd had two days with her. That would have to be enough for now.

He moved a pace away from her instead of drawing her closer. It was the hardest thing he'd done today, far harder than fighting a skirmish to the death with a band of Norsemen. What he wanted and what needed to be done were separate things. What had to be done must always come first. Love was a trap. He didn't blame Maddie, but she was a danger to his resolve. Just having her by his side out in the light of day was a lure away from performing his duty to his people.

It was hard to do, the hardest thing he'd ever done, as he wanted to share the triumph of the victory with her as much as she'd shared the danger with him, but he turned away from Maddie. "We'll burn the dead raiders in their boats after we've freed the prisoners," he told Harboth as they walked together toward the camp.

Rowan pretended not to see Allen Harboth glance back and give Maddie long, appreciative look.

"Yes, I am!"

"No, you're not!"

Variations of this conversation could be heard on both ends of the camp. Maddie sat by the fire in the

middle of the clearing and shamelessly eavesdropped
on both arguments. Actually, it was impossible to do
anything but overhear the fighting, as both the Murray
and Harboth contingents were shouting at the tops of
their lungs. As she sat alone among the Murrays gathered by the larger of two campfires, she fervently
wished they'd gone on to Cape Wrath rather than settling down for the night in this rain-soaked glen. She
found it a wonder and a marvel that the men had managed to make fires, albeit smoky ones, out of wet wood.
She was absolutely delighted that a hunting party had
brought down a deer to cook over the big fire for dinner. She was really glad that the White Lady had gathered up her extensive wardrobe, with the exception of
the black dress that Maddie had reluctantly accepted as
a present, and headed back to her isolated cottage.
Maddie was convinced that the less she had to do with
that woman, the better.

She was also ecstatic that neither Micaela nor the
other three women they'd rescued had been physically
harmed by their captors. In fact, Micaela seemed to be
having a much more traumatic experience dealing with
Rowan than she'd had being held prisoner by slavers.
The other women had gone with the White Lady to
spend the night at her house before returning to their
own homes.

As for Rowan—Maddie wasn't sure what to think
about Rowan. The man hadn't said a word to her since
the rescue. He hadn't ridden by her side as they headed
toward Cape Wrath. She didn't know what to think, so
she tried not to. She tried to concentrate on eating her
share of roast deer, but all the shouting got in the way
of even that. Finally, she got up and marched to the

edge of the campsite, where Rowan and Micaela stood belligerently toe-to-toe.

She stepped between them, stepping on Rowan's foot to do so. She gave her sister-in-law a sympathetic look. "Let me talk to him," she suggested to Micaela. "You get some supper. That girl's been through a lot," she angrily reminded Rowan. "This is no time to badger her."

He looked after his sister, sighed, and turned his annoyed expression on Maddie. "I'm no badgering the lass, I'm laying down the law to her. She'll not marry a Harboth and that's final. If she wants to go south," he added darkly, "it'll be to join a Sassenach convent."

Maddie couldn't keep from laughing. "The girl practices magic and claims to be half-fairy. I don't think a convent's the place for her."

"Married to a Harboth's no place for her."

"She doesn't want to marry a Harboth. She wants to marry Burke."

Rowan put his hands on her shoulders. His touch sent warmth through her. Maddie tried to ignore the longing to have him draw her close. His touch was gentle enough, but his features were hard. "This is a family matter," he told her.

Maddie held very tightly onto her own temper. Somebody had to remain reasonable in this bunch. Her tone was still sharp when she reminded him, "I may not have asked for it, but I am family."

Rowan ducked his head. He looked a bit contrite when he looked at her again. "I'm sorry. Of course you are family, Maddie."

He glanced anxiously once more toward Micaela. Maddie followed his gaze and sighed when she saw that Burke was trying to reach the girl's side, but Father Andrew, Aidan, and Walter had formed a protective circle around her. It didn't help that Allen Harboth was clinging tenaciously to Burke's sleeve.

Maddie's frustration at the situation boiled out of her. "This thing is so incredibly stupid! I do not believe the way you people are acting. Let's discuss this like civilized people, shall we?"

Rowan nodded, then drew her further into the darkness beyond the firelight. When they found a nearby bench-high boulder, they sat down on it. Rowan put his arm around her shoulders. He sighed. "My mind's made up, but you'll say what you have to whether I give you leave or not. So, talk to your heart's content, Maddie, but mind that I'd like to get some sleep tonight."

Maddie was annoyed with what Rowan said, but drew hope from the weariness she heard in his tone. He talked as if he were adamant and completely unswayable, but his voice betrayed misgivings she knew he wouldn't outwardly admit to. She put her arm around his waist, and leaned her head against his shoulder.

From this seemingly relaxed position, she said, "How did this feud start, anyway? Some Harboth steal some Murray cattle?"

He sighed again and conceded, "Or some Murray stole some Harboth cattle. Whoever started it, people died. Until then our clans were friends and allies."

"And how long ago was this?"

"In my grandfather's time."

"Which makes it your grandfather's fight, if you ask me."

"Which I did not."

"No, but you said you'd listen to what I have to say."

Rowan couldn't help but admire the calm way she spoke. Her determination, her sheer stubbornness, the way she constantly bedeviled him with her ways ought to infuriate him—and sometimes it did. For some fool reason, what he should have found inexcusable behavior from another woman he often found commendable in his wife. She stood up for herself and what she believed in no matter how wrong she might be.

"And here I wanted a meek and mild little wife," he said as he gave her a quick hug. "Go on, then, say what you will."

Maddie appreciated the hug, but she wasn't sure what Rowan's words meant. Did he really want a mealymouthed yes-woman, or was he saying he liked her the way she was? This wasn't the time to ask, not when she was being given the chance to discuss solutions to the Murray-Harboth feud. She'd have to put the questions concerning her and Rowan's relationship on hold for the sake of helping find peace.

"We Scots are good at holding grudges," she said. "Maybe all humans are. When does it stop? When do we let go? What's the point? Even in my time people divide themselves into us and them and fight each other over quarrels started hundreds of years before. Why?"

"Revenge," Rowan said promptly. "Honor. Duty to the dead."

"I don't think we owe any duty to the dead," she snapped out. "At least not to someone who died a hundred years ago. We're alive, our ancestors aren't. Let's just get on with living, okay? Let the dead bury the dead—I think that's in a gospel, and I also think it's pretty good advice. The living ought to have peace and get married and have babies and not fight with each other just because their grandparents couldn't get along." She lifted her head to look Rowan in the eye. "You hear what I'm saying, Murray?"

Rowan frowned deeply, but said, "I'm listening."

"You have an opportunity here to make peace," she went on. "Don't let it pass you by. Please. Those two are determined to have each other. I think Micaela tried hard to put the clan before her own feelings for as long as she could, but she can't take it anymore. Give her your blessing, because it's going to happen anyway."

"It? It? By it you mean that she and Burke are bound to have each other no matter what I say?"

She nodded. "No matter what you say. No matter what Allen says. Don't make it into a breach with your sister. Don't toss her out of the Murray clan or make her life miserable because of an old quarrel. Don't make it into another excuse to fight the Harboths. Just forget their last names and let them live together in peace."

"Do you think that's possible?" His voice was soft, but very cold.

Maddie worried that she might as well be trying to convince a slab of granite to change into a flesh-and-blood man, but she persisted. "Please, Rowan. Swallow your stiff-necked pride and take the opportunity to make peace. There," she added as she slipped out of his embrace. "I've had my say."

She stood up. Without the touch of Rowan's body to keep her warm, Maddie felt the chill of the night air.

Or maybe the shiver that ran through her was from the cold look she saw in her husband's eyes. She was almost grateful when he looked beyond her to Micaela. Maddie wondered if he'd listened to a word she'd said. Not that it had been all that eloquent a speech, she didn't suppose. He didn't say anything. He didn't move. Maybe he *was* a piece of unfeeling granite. Maddie gave up trying to persuade him any further. She walked away to get her cloak, to sit next to Micaela by the fire and try to get warm, to give him time alone to think.

For all that she left him to think, she couldn't keep her gaze off the spot in the darkness where he sat. Even though she was many feet from Rowan, she felt as if she could hear him breathe, imagined she could make out his face though it was concealed by the distance and the dark. She felt as though she were with him, as though he were in her blood or something. She could feel his anguish, his indecision, his groping for answers, though she told herself the connection was all in her imagination. She tried to be rational, but her soul told her that she was part of Rowan, that his pain and pleasure were as important to her as her own. Maybe more important. She didn't know why. She didn't want to admit that she'd fallen in love with him.

Maybe she didn't want to admit it, but her heart began to pound and her blood race when Rowan walked from the darkness into the firelight. Maddie jumped to her feet, barely able to restrain herself from running forward to throw her arms around him. She felt as if she'd been deprived of his presence for days, when she knew that it had been less than an hour since she'd left him alone to think.

Rowan didn't even look at her. He didn't look at anyone, though everyone's attention focused intently on him. He strode past the people gathered round the largest fire and walked to the smaller fire, a second camp Allen had set up nearby, but separate from the Murrays.

"We have meat and mead," were the first things Rowan said when Allen and Burke stepped toward him. "We fought together today. There's no reason we should fight each other tomorrow."

Maddie heard the reluctance in the words as Rowan spoke them, and she gaped along with every other Murray at their peaceful import. She gaped for a moment, that is, and then began to grin. Growing pride filled her. She couldn't take her eyes off her husband.

Allen Harboth looked suspicious, but not angry. "What are you saying, Murray?"

"He's saying we're invited to dinner," Burke said, and hurried to the Murray side of the camp before his brother could stop him. He took Micaela's outstretched hands and said, "I love you. Let's eat."

Several Murrays grumbled, but room was made for Micaela and Burke by the fire. Rowan filled Maddie's awareness. She barely paid attention to anything else going on around her.

She nearly burst with joy when Rowan said, "It's time we talked about my sister's dowry, Allen."

Allen Harboth stiffened. For a moment it looked as if he might draw his dagger. Rowan didn't make any aggressive move; he didn't flinch. He waited. He'd swallowed his pride and thrown away tradition. He didn't know what he was feeling, but he'd made the offer. He did know he could feel Maddie's gaze on him.

When he glanced her way, he saw the open caring on her face, the deep glow of emotion in her eyes. It was a look of love that was for him. It made his blood and heart sing.

He did know that this was not the moment to listen to the song rising in his soul. He forced his attention on Allen Harboth.

After what seemed like an endless moment, the laird of the Harboths gave a short, breathy laugh. "You're offering a dowry, eh?" He shrugged. "Well, why not?"

Every Murray by the fire let out a tense sigh. Some began to grumble, but no one openly protested. Maybe they were more tired of feuding than they wanted to admit.

Maddie sighed too, but not from relief of tension. Her sigh was one of pure romantic response. As he made the effort to make peace, she thought Rowan Murray was the bravest, handsomest, most wonderful man in the world. She couldn't have been more in love if she'd tried.

24

"You work too hard, lass."

"I know," Maddie agreed as Rowan's hands kneaded the stiff muscles of her shoulders. He had very gifted fingers, as she'd learned very well. She smiled and very nearly purred, not just at what he was doing to her now, but at memories of all the sensual, sexual encounters she'd shared with Rowan in the last few weeks. Trouble was, those sensual encounters were circumscribed by a set time and place. He was only this way with her when they were alone. That made this time precious, but it was also disturbing. She tried not to worry about it now, though.

"You're turning me to butter," she told him.

"You don't sound as if you mind."

"Not a bit," she answered around a yawn. It was hard to sound sexy around a yawn, but his answering chuckle told her she'd managed.

She had slept well, but not enough, and woken up just about as tired as when she went to sleep. This had a lot to do with what she and Rowan had done in bed before settling down for the rest of the night. While Rowan wasn't much of a talker, she reveled in the discovery that he could communicate very well without words when he wanted to. Or maybe communication and sex had nothing to do with each other; she didn't know. What Maddie knew was that when they were alone in the dark together with their bodies entwined and driven by mutual desire, she was happy, whole, complete. In the dark he gave her the confidence to believe that she was a woman that a man could love. In the dark she believed they were made to be together forever. It was when they got out of bed that things got complicated. Or at least they got a heck of a lot quieter.

They'd been lovers since the night spent at the White Lady's. Maddie knew she was in love with him since the night he'd shown the strength to make peace with the Harboths. Though they didn't talk about it, they'd created their own little world in the darkness of the laird's private chamber. Outside this room, in the daylight, Rowan acted as if she didn't exist.

Apparently she couldn't keep from thinking about it. Maddie told herself her last thought was an exaggeration. She just felt as if he acted as if she didn't exist. Sometimes feelings were more important than facts, even if they weren't very logical. Sometimes, even though she was surrounded by people and certainly wasn't sleeping alone, Maddie felt as lonely as she used to on her long walks by the ocean. There was a new part of her that wanted to burst out and be in the open all the time, but was circumscribed by rules Rowan hadn't bothered to explain to her.

She tried not to feel lonely now, this instant, or to think about problems that were possibly all in her insecure head. Except that she no longer felt all that inse-cure. Right now, she was sitting on the edge of the bed with Rowan kneeling behind her giving her a back rub, neither lonely or insecure. She just wished it could be that way all the time.

"You have a gift," she told him as he kneaded her muscles. "A real gift."

"Aye."

"And you're modest, too."

Rowan bent forward to kiss the side of Maddie's throat. She smelled good, and the soft springiness of her hair against his cheek was delightful. After he kissed her, he ran his thumb over the light line of scar-ring on the back of her neck. The mark was fading evi-dence of the fair folk's perverse interference in his lady's existence. He was grateful they'd brought her to him, but furious that it had nearly cost her life.

As for the necklace, to show his respect for the fair folk, he'd put it in a finely embroidered silk pouch that had belonged to his mother. Then he had sent the pouch to the people under the hill. He hoped that the necklace was what they sought, not the woman who'd worn it as it was drawn back through time.

His messenger was Aidan, who had the gift for trav-eling in both the daylight and moonlit worlds. Rowan had told him not to linger. He hoped the boy did not lose track of time on the magical journey. It had been a month since Rowan had sent the lad on his errand. With luck, Aidan would be home in time for their sis-ter's wedding tonight. Then again, it might be years before the lad put in an appearance at Cape Wrath, as unchanged as the day he'd left. Rowan didn't think that would happen, but it was a faint possibility. One he didn't mention to Maddie. He hadn't discussed magic with his wife since their night together at the White Lady's. He sensed she was more comfortable that way, and if truth be told, so was he.

He was also far too comfortable with Maddie. He felt the danger and fought it every time he looked at or touched his wife. He almost wished he hadn't given in to the temptation to touch and taste and be with this woman at all. He recalled that he had initially thought that he could slake his lust with this handfasted woman but feel nothing for her on any but a physical level. He should have known he was too much like his father, too full of romantic notions to be satisfied with simple carnal pleasure.

Sex should be enough for any man, or so he had firmly made himself believe for years. With Maddie he wanted to comfort and cozen her, to discuss all her wonderful plans, to be by her side every moment of the day, to make her laugh, to let her coax him to laugh, to cry with her pain, or better yet, to keep her from any kind of pain. That he found himself wanting to take care of this woman, to spend his days as well as his nights with her, terrified him.

He *would not* let himself become a besotted fool. He *would not* abandon his responsibilities for the sake of his own gratification. He did not blame Maddie because he was so very tempted. She was not the cause of this weakness he felt when he was with her. She was indeed the savior of his people, he was certain of that. He was the weak link. For her sake and the sake of the entire Murray clan, he vowed not to let that weakness show.

So, when she leaned back against him and tilted her

head so that she was practically looking at him upside down, and said, "I don't suppose we could take the day off, do you?" Rowan did not respond as he wished.

Instead, he got up off the bed, away from her warmth, and said, "It's past dawn already."

Maddie took Rowan's withdrawal, both physically and emotionally, to mean that she'd said the wrong thing. He didn't want to spend time with her when they weren't having sex. She wished she'd kept her mouth shut. A few minutes ago, she'd only suspected that all he wanted was to get laid. Now, as she studied his shuttered face in the frail light of one candle and the room's one small window, she was certain that all he wanted her for was her body. Oh, he wanted her for her mind, too, at least to use her mind for his blasted clan.

He just didn't want anything to do with her soul. He didn't want *her*.

She didn't know why.

She did know that she wasn't going to put up with it. Or so she told herself now. She also knew that when he touched her again she wouldn't have any resolve to say no. She loved the way she felt when he touched her. She loved touching him.

She loved him.

She just wasn't sure why.

Rather than asking him or herself, she got up, got dressed, and went to work. Rowan, who'd been so eager to be up and doing, was still standing half-dressed in the middle of the room when she silently walked out past him. She felt his gaze on her back, but had no idea what he was thinking.

"Probably something to do with sheep or cattle," she

muttered on her way to the hall. "Because that man certainly doesn't think about me."

"Do you know what you remind me of?" Rosemary asked. She thumped Rowan on the shoulder to get his attention when he didn't immediately look her way.

Rowan turned a deep frown on his cousin. "I'm busy," he told her. He was seated in the hall, a parchment and tally sticks spread out on the table before him. "What do you want?"

Rosemary took a seat on the bench beside him. "Busy?" She laughed. "You've been staring for the last half hour."

"If I've been staring, it's because I'm working out sums in my head."

Rosemary pointed to where Maddie was seated among a group of women across the hall. She was showing them how to use some new device she'd made. Rowan thought that his wife had very clever fingers, but then, he knew that from the things those fingers did to him in the dark.

He sighed. Rosemary prodded him again.

"Working on sums, you say? While your eyes have been following every move she makes? I doubt there's room in your head for such arcane things as numbers when it's lust and longing that's showing on your face. I've been watching you," she went on before he could protest. "You're lovesick, and too stubborn to know it."

"I know it," he acknowledged quietly to his cousin. "I'll not let the sickness rule me." He picked up the parchment and began to read. The Latin words blurred together on the page after only a few seconds. He looked up, and his eyes focused clearly—on Maddie. He wanted to go to her, but he looked at Rosemary instead. The woman beside him was gazing at him with an expression of disgust. "You look like you just drank sour milk," he told her. "Or one of your own healing potions."

"It's a healing potion you need," she countered. "Or some sense knocked into you."

He glared. "Why?"

"She's your bride," Rosemary answered. "See sense and spend some time with her. You're entitled. All newly married folk are entitled to dote on each other at first."

He stood, stiff and proud and unyielding. "I'll dote on no one. There's a wedding and a visit from our overlord for you to see to." He waved a hand toward the records he was studying so he could report accurately on the state of the holding to the Lord of the Isles. After waiting nearly two months for the visit, a messenger had finally arrived the day before to tell him that his overlord was within two days' distance of Cape Wrath. "Be about your own business, Rosemary, and leave me to mine."

Rosemary rose to face him. "You're not your father, but you are a fool. There's no talking sense to you." She walked away, shaking her head in disgust.

No, he was not his father, nor was he going to let himself be a fool. Rowan tightened his resolve, looked at the parchment again, and made himself concentrate harder. He couldn't help but look up occasionally to see what his wife was accomplishing. He told himself that it was her work that interested him, even if he did appreciate the fine swell of her bosom when she stretched and arched to work a kink out of her back, or if he did bask in the reflection of her bright smile when she turned it on one of her pupils. Finally, he convinced himself that even glancing at Maddie was a waste of valuable time.

An hour must have past before he looked up again, then stood up abruptly as shock and rage shot through him. "What the devil is Allen Harboth doing in my hall?"

More importantly, what was Allen Harboth doing sitting among the womenfolk and talking to his wife? Rowan strode quickly across the hall to find out.

He remembered that he'd made peace with the Harboth clan before he reached them. He still kept his hand on his dagger hilt as he joined Maddie and Allen. "What are you doing here?" he growled as the laird of the Harboths stood to greet him.

Instead of an immediate answer, Allen smiled down at Maddie. "Didn't I tell you that's how he'd greet me?"

She laughed. "I'm glad I didn't bet on it."

She stood at Allen's side, Rowan noted. He longed to put his arm around her shoulders and draw her safely close, but she chose to face him instead of join him. He knew that the hurt he felt was unreasonable, for he certainly gave no indication that he wanted her near. It was better not to touch her, he reminded himself. His head would be clearer without the distraction of Maddie's soft, warm body so close to his.

"As for my business," Allen said, "my brother's marrying your sister in a few hours. I've come for the wedding. It's taken long enough to work out the marriage contract. Now it's time to celebrate."

"Aye. So it is." Though the words nearly choked him, Rowan added, "You and your clansfolk are welcome at Cape Wrath."

Allen laughed again. "That's good, as my whole clan is out in the courtyard."

"That they are," Rosemary added as she came up. "And they brought ale and beef to add to the feast. For which we are grateful, Allen," she told the laird of the Harboths.

"So your formidable cook has told me, Mistress Rosemary."

She touched her hair, and smiled widely as she gave the laird of the Harboths a long, assessing look. "Welcome to Cape Wrath, Allen," she said. "It is good that our clans are friends once more. And it's glad I am that you're still unwed."

He nodded. "That I am, lass. I hear you've turned down every offer yourself since we met at the Glasgow fair six years ago, Rosemary Murray."

She laughed. "Do you think it might be for your sake, laddie? When I've a holding to manage and people who need me?"

"Pity. I've often thought it would be fine to have a woman pining for me the way Micaela did for Burke."

"Aye, but you'd have to pine back the way Burke did."

"There's not many worth pining for, lassie."

"Murray women are worth it."

"Perhaps they are."

Rowan didn't like the lascivious look on Harboth's face, but before he could complain, Rosemary tossed her head and walked away. Rowan chose not to notice that there was a bit of an extra sway in his cousin's hips. That she might be thinking of making a match with a Harboth was unthinkable. That the Harboth was now smiling at his wife, Rowan found even more untenable.

That his wife was smiling knowingly back infuriated him. He would not call what he was feeling jealousy. Better not to name any possessive urges. Best still not to acknowledge them at all. He'd seen too many of his father's jealous rages to ever let that destructive emotion color his thoughts.

Yet he found that he'd taken a step closer to his wife without noticing doing so. "What are you doing with Harboth, woman?" he demanded of her.

"We were just discussing the changes in this place," Allen answered. "I was complimenting your lady on her cleverness with her hands."

"She's clever enough," Rowan conceded.

"You're so generous with your praise, laddie," Allen mocked.

Rowan was more than pleased with his wife's handiwork, but he saw no reason to say so to someone who had recently been his worst enemy. To himself he even conceded that he had made peace with the Harboths because Maddie had made him think about the future instead of day-to-day pettiness. His heart was filled with nothing but pride for the woman, but he didn't think it was safe to let the world know that. His every urge was to protect her. He thought it might be easier to shield her from any who might mean the Murrays harm by not drawing attention to how important his lady was to him and the clan. Allen Harboth was no longer an enemy, but he certainly wasn't yet a friend.

"We'll soon be family," Allen said. It was as though he had read Rowan's thoughts, but his words were addressed to Maddie. "Perhaps you can teach this new type of spinning and weaving you mentioned to our womenfolk?"

Rowan was pleased that Maddie looked to him before she gave an answer. It showed that she was well aware of the value of the new things she brought to the world. "Perhaps," he answered for her. He reluctantly admitted to himself that a bit of openness might prove beneficial to this new alliance. "You are going to be family," he told Allen. "We have many things to discuss after the wedding."

"Speaking of which," Maddie spoke up, "I promised Micaela I'd help her get ready. I better go."

"Then be off with you." Rowan meant the words as tender and teasing, but they came out gruff instead, tainted by his wanting her away from Allen Harboth.

Once again, only more strongly than before, Maddie felt as though she had married two men, or at least that he'd been split into daylight and nighttime halves. Rowan had been disagreeable when they were first married, and she'd accepted him that way. She hadn't actually minded his dour Highlander routine because beneath it there had been constant flashes of wit and humor and caring. She was beginning to think of him as Good Rowan and Bad Rowan.

She was just about fed up with Bad Rowan, especially when she knew that tonight he would be all kissing and cuddling and would make passionate love to her. She was tempted to say something right now, to tell Bad Rowan off, but decided it wasn't polite or politic to fight with her husband in front of a guest.

Especially since the guest was someone Rowan disliked and barely trusted.

So she did the only thing she could think of to show her annoyance at her husband and perhaps pay him back a little for his rudeness. She ignored him and turned the most friendly smile she could manage on Allen. "It's been lovely talking to you. I'll see you at the wedding."

Allen bowed to her, and returned her smile, while Rowan stood beside them and frowned. "I look forward to sitting by you at the feast, dear lady." He turned quickly to Rowan and pointed toward the courtyard door. He said over his shoulder as he began to walk away, "Come along, Murray. We've much to talk about and little time before the festivities."

Without so much as a glance her way, Rowan immediately followed.

"Micaela made a lovely bride."

Maddie sighed after she spoke, the way women always seemed to sigh over weddings and brides. All Rowan could do was frown in confusion over such sentimentality—even though his sister was indeed a beautiful bride. A pity she'd married a Harboth. Rowan also thought it a pity a Harboth was seated on his wife's left; she was between himself and Allen at the feast table. The happy newlyweds were seated on Rowan's other side. They were too lost in looking into each other's eyes to pay him any mind.

"Aye," Allen agreed with Maddie. "But was my brother gazing fondly at his bride or at her gown? After the way those Orkneymen chased after him a week ago,

I think he might fancy wearing a dress over armor for battle."

Maddie laughed. Rowan saw no wit in the man's words. Perhaps she only laughed to be polite, he told himself. Or perhaps she laughed to show her interest in Allen, a small, ugly voice deep in his mind added. Rowan chided himself for such an unkind thought, and tried to banish it.

It was turning into the longest day of his life. Rowan had wanted to spend the day alone with his wife. He wished—well, never mind what a man wished, it was what he did that mattered. Duty had kept him from that pleasure, and was prolonging the time they must spend apart.

Maddie was seated beside him, but he might as well not be there for all she seemed to care. There was that pettiness again. He couldn't fault her for ignoring him; she was doing her duty by being gracious to the most important guest at the feast. The feast might be in celebration of Micaela and Burke's wedding, but Allen Harboth was the dominant force at the high table.

He certainly dominated Maddie's attention. Allen could easily talk and joke. Maddie enjoyed these things, and Rowan could do none of them, at least not with the cleverness and charm exhibited by the laird of the Harboths. He felt like a lump of dull rock, lichen-covered and weatherbeaten. Allen was like a finely cut and polished sculpture who'd stepped straight off a French cathedral, fine to look at, glib, and full of learning.

Maddie was full of learning. Even if she had no understanding of Latin or instruction in rhetoric or the other liberal arts as Allen Harboth and his brother had, she was well educated for a woman. Rowan was barely able to read and do sums, though that was more learning than most men had. He was still no match for Allen. Nor match for Maddie, either, though he enjoyed learning the practical, mechanical skills Maddie was so eager to teach.

It seemed faintly wrong to take instruction from a woman; he certainly had to deal with complaints from the other Murray men on the subject. He hadn't taken their side in any dispute yet, and they were slowly coming around to following their lady's lead and ways of doing things as time passed.

Was that because she was always in the right? Rowan found himself wondering while the celebration went on around him. Or had he been showing his father's brand of doting devotion by backing his lady wife in every quarrel with his own people? Was he giving Maddie her head about building, changing, and tinkering with every part of their lives for the good of his people? Or was he spoiling her the way his father had his fairy wife when he encouraged her teaching of spells and divination because such intrusion in mortal affairs made her happy?

These questions shook Rowan down to the bone.

Before he had time to pursue these disturbing thoughts, Allen said, "During his sermon at the wedding ceremony, Father Andrew mentioned that your marriage to Rowan is a handfast one, and that he hoped you and Rowan would follow Micaela and Burke's example in the future."

Maddie blushed at the memory of Father Andrew's exhortation to her and Rowan earlier in the day. She'd been embarrassed then, and she was embarrassed now, though she wasn't sure what she had to be embarrassed about. Father Andrew's words had been spoken jokingly. Everyone had laughed, except her and Rowan. They had shared quick, almost furtive eye contact. Then he'd looked away. She hadn't known what he'd been thinking. She still wasn't sure what she'd been thinking, though her emotions had run a dizzying, confused gamut at the time.

She supposed she just hated being reminded that her relationship with the man she loved was not a permanent one. She hadn't thought about the reasons they were together for what seemed like a long time. She was the one who'd insisted on the temporary marriage. In fact, she hadn't wanted to get married in the first place. The truth was, she'd had to be forced into any kind of marriage with Rowan Murray.

She shouldn't have let herself become so complacent and halfway content with her situation in this world. She should treat the whole thing with Rowan as an affair, maybe even be relieved that he only wanted a physical relationship. Maybe he was doing her a favor and her heart wouldn't be broken when she left. She was from a different time. She was supposed to be looking for a way back to that time. She should go.

Shouldn't she?

Allen gently touched her hand. "Did my words offend you, lass? You look pained, and are far too quiet."

Since Rowan hadn't said a word to Allen all evening, and didn't appear to be about to now, she made herself turn to the laird of the Harboths. Maddie found him gazing at her with genuine concern.

"Rowan and I are wed for a year and a day," she told him.

His eyes glinted with sudden mischief. "Well, then," he said. "You and I will have to have a talk the day after that year and a day is up."

Maddie was sure that Allen was only teasing, but Rowan surged angrily to his feet. His voice was deadly cold when he said, "Will you, indeed, Harboth?"

Allen jumped to his feet. So did Maddie. All eyes in the room turned to them. All the latent tension that Harboth and Murray kinsmen had suppressed seemed to be on the brink of surfacing.

"Rowan," Maddie warned. She put a hand on each man's shoulder. The two of them glared at each other. The silence in the hall grew deep and ugly. Hands went to dagger hilts. Eating knives were grasp tightly in tense fists. "Stop it," Maddie pleaded. Neither Rowan or Allen seemed aware of the growing danger that filled the room. "Remember that you're friends now and offer a toast to the happy couple, or something."

Fortunately, a diversion presented itself before either a Harboth or a Murray did anything both clans would regret. The door to the hall was open, instead of shut and barred as it normally would be after sundown, for the feast was going on both indoors and in the courtyard. As a guard ran into the hall, everyone's attention shifted to him, including the two men who'd been glaring at each other a moment before.

"What?" Rowan demanded as the man hurried up to the table.

"The Lord of the Isles," the man announced loudly.

"The Lord of the Isles is at the gate. He says he heard of the celebration and he and his men came to share in it rather than making camp for the night."

Rowan forgot any quarrel with Harboth as he focused on this new development. He'd been waiting for anxious weeks for this moment, but didn't feel ready for it. There was nothing he could do but say, "Well, let the man in!"

25

"What's going to happen with us?"

Maddie asked the question too softly for anyone but
herself to hear. She was afraid to speak any louder, for
Rowan was sleeping beside her and she was terrified of
how he might answer. Truth be told, she thought she
was too afraid of the answer to ever voice it. She hated
being afraid. It wasn't her nature to fear the unknown,
but this time she did. This time she wasn't worrying
about a scientific or engineering problem. She was
worrying about her own future—more importantly, she
was worrying over the future she might or might not
have with the difficult man she'd come to love so
deeply it hurt.

It had been a very long night. First Laclan MacDonald,
Lord of the Isles, and his entourage showed up, which
had served to dissipate the tension. MacDonald proved to
be a boisterous, charismatic man. He had a big personal-
ity and a high opinion of himself. Conversation during
the rest of the meal had centered exclusively on
him. Maddie hadn't minded a bit. In fact, she'd actually

managed to relax enough to enjoy the rather lewd and crude spectacle of escorting the newlyweds to bed at the end of the evening. Even Rowan laughed and joked as the couple was undressed and settled side by side in a bed set up in a flower-strewn, curtained-off area of the hall.

After the festivities were over, Rowan drew her into a dark corner, and they shared a fierce kiss and quick caresses. It fired her blood, but didn't last long enough. When she took Rowan's hand and tried to lead him to their room, he shook his head. Then he told her that there was man's work to be done, that he must speak with the Lord of the Isles, and sent her to bed. The hard look on his face brooked no argument. That she was his wife and lady of the castle made no difference. Women had no place in political discussions in this day and age. She recalled that they barely had a place in her own time, and made herself leave the hall without any protest.

She'd gone to bed but she hadn't slept, even after Rowan came in and lay down beside her. He took her in his arms, but was faintly snoring before she could say a word. She held him, let him rest, took as much comfort as she could from his warm, solid presence, but there was no rest in her.

Now, as morning came, all her thinking and worrying could be summed up with one frightening sentence.

"What's going to happen to us?"

"What?"

This time, she had spoken loud enough for the man so close beside her to hear. She stroked his cheek, heard as well as felt the faint scratch of beard stubble against her palm. "Nothing. Go back to sleep."

Rowan hardly felt as if he'd slept. He was a man of regular habits who didn't function well on little sleep. During battle situations it was different. One slept and ate when one could while chasing raiders and cattle thieves. But in his own stronghold he liked an orderly routine. Between wedding his sister to a Harboth and last night's conversation with his overlord, Rowan felt as if he'd brought a battlefield into his own home. As he woke and became aware of the tension radiating from Maddie, he feared that his wife was going to prove to be one more source of conflict in his life. Having to fight his own desire for her was hard enough on him. It was as if she were a part of him, for he could feel that she was sad and worried, and perhaps a bit angry. He feared that that there was a battle brewing and that the enemy was the woman beside him. It pained him, more because he hated that she was hurting than for any injury her anger could possibly inflict on him.

Was that the way love should be? he wondered. Did it mean worrying more for another than for one's self? Or was this ache and need to keep Maddie safe and happy some perversity he'd inherited from his father along with the light brown color of his hair and the rangy way he was built? How was he to tell what was the right amount to love?

He wished they were back at the White Lady's house or roaming the heather-covered hills together once more. It had been so much easier to give of himself, to concentrate all his emotions and attention on Maddie when there had been only the two of them alone together. Even such a fanciful wish was wrong, he warned himself. Fair folk could be fanciful, but he was a mortal man, with a mortal man's responsibilities.

Among his responsibilities were those he owed his wife. With this in mind he stopped pretending to sleep, looked at Maddie and asked, voice rough from lack of sleep, "What?"

"Do you love me?" Maddie hadn't meant to ask, but once the words were out she could hardly call them back. So she sat up, took a deep breath, and demanded. "Well, do you?"

Rowan propped his head up on his pillow and watched her. To her he seemed not only grumpy, but wary of the question. He took a bit longer than she liked to answer. "Have I not told you so once already?"

Maddie crossed her arms beneath her ample bosom. "When?"

Rowan sat up. "At the White Lady's. Do you not remember?"

Maddie hated to tell him that she wasn't sure what she remembered. He believed so strongly in fairies and magic that telling him she wasn't certain about anything that had happened that evening would just lead into an argument she didn't want. This was no time to go off on a tangential debate that probably could never be resolved.

She stuck to her central point. "Do you love me?"

"Aye."

The fact that Rowan was scowling when he said it didn't help. "Why?" She undid the drawstring at her throat and pulled her nightgown down to expose her breasts. Once she would have suffered a full-body blush as she did it, but weeks of loving had made her able to flaunt her body with assurance, even pride.

Rowan's gaze immediately shifted from her face, and Maddie arched her back and demanded defiantly, "Is it me, or these, that you love?"

A smile quirked at the corner of his mouth. "That's a fine amount of freckles you've got there, lass."

Maddie almost laughed at Rowan's dry response. Almost. "You haven't answered my question."

His gaze met hers once more. "You expect a man to be able to think when you're showing him one of the finest views in the Highlands?"

She yanked her gown back up over her shoulders. "How about now?"

"Give me a moment." Rowan closed his eyes.

"What are you doing?"

"Thinking of something unpleasant to get my . . . mind . . . off what I'd rather be doing just at present."

What he was thinking of was that it was daylight, with all the duties and tasks that came with the day if he was going to remain a good laird to his people. What he wanted to think about was lying down with his woman and resting his head on those fine, soft, freckled breasts. It wasn't even making love that he wanted just now as much as he wanted to rest a while with their bodies nestled lovingly together.

If a knock hadn't come on the door he might even have given in to the powerful longing that pulled at him. Instead, he swung his legs over the side of the bed and got up to answer the knock. "What?"

Maddie recognized the voice that answered as Father Andrew's, but she didn't catch the softly spoken conversation that followed. She stayed where she was while they talked, arms tensely crossed, and waited for Rowan to return to her. Somehow, she wasn't surprised when he wrapped his kilt over the shirt he'd slept in and left instead.

Without a word or look for her as he did so, of course. With Father Andrew waiting just outside the half-open door, Maddie didn't say anything, either. She just sadly watched her husband, not that he noticed that she was disappointed or upset or anything.

"Men," she murmured after he was gone. "Mom told me they preferred my boobs to my brain. I guess she was right."

Maddie just wished she knew if that was a good or bad thing in her relationship with Rowan.

" 'Tis only women's work."

If he says that once more, Maddie thought. *I'm going to kill him.*

Rowan was being more than usually dour today, and Maddie was about ready to strangle him with his own kilt.

"Designing such fine-drawing chimneys is hardly what I'd call woman's work," Lord Laclan MacDonald answered. He looked from one corner of the freshly whitewashed room where a fire blazed in one of the new stone fireplaces to the corner diagonally across from it where a second blaze warmed that side of the room. "I've never seen such an efficient way for heating a hall, nor been in a warmer one."

"It's a Southwestern design," Maddie found herself explaining.

She couldn't help but speak up at last, though Rowan had firmly ordered her to stay in the background and hold her tongue when the Lord of the Isles had gallantly requested the presence of the lady of the hall on his inspection tour of Cape Wrath. She'd done her best to remain unobtrusive, but the role had been hard on her justifiable pride in the improvement projects that were under way at the castle. If the Lord of the Isles had scoffed at the things he saw—the new windmills that powered the forge and newly constructed laundry; the compost heaps that were making soil to be used in the greenhouse she'd contrived out of oiled hides lashed to a wooden framework; the distillery she was building to process pig droppings into methane; the loom and the spinning wheels; the new rudder and sail designs for the fishing boats—she might not have been so frustrated by Rowan's deprecating replies to his comments.

In the last few weeks Rowan had encouraged and enthusiastically participated in all the improvements at Cape Wrath. She had thought he was proud of them, that they were working as a team to improve his people's lives. Now he was acting as if he were uninterested, or even ashamed at all the newfangled gadgetry that littered his property. He was also downplaying and downright ignoring the part she'd played in the changes. In fact, the only person who seemed to remember that she was involved in bringing technology to the Murrays was Allen Harboth. Somehow it didn't seem right or fair that Allen was the one who cared to give her credit.

Now that they'd returned to the hall after traipsing all over the castle and village in a misting rain, Maddie was too wet, tired, and furious with her husband to obediently follow his orders any longer. Which was why she spoke up when Lord Laclan mentioned the fireplaces. All gazes turned to her when she did. Rowan's look was furious and warning. She ignored him to concentrate on curious stare of the Lord of the Isles.

"Southwestern?" he asked. "Southwestern where?"

Since there was no reason to confuse the man by explaining that she'd come from the future and she'd adapted a Southwestern architectural style of the United States for her Scottish fireplaces, she replied, "It is a Spanish design, my lord. Placing a rounded fireplace in a corner rather than putting it flat against a wall is a more efficient way to heat a building. More warmth, less fuel." Since Lord Laclan was still staring at her when she finished, Maddie gave him the most reassuring smile she could manage, and asked, "You see?"

Rowan stepped between her and the Lord of the Isles before he could reply. "Come and warm yourself by the fire with a goblet of honey wine, my lord," he said loudly, as though shouting would somehow drown out what she'd already said.

Maybe he was just trying to negate her presence altogether. Maddie studied his fine, flat butt for a moment. She was tempted to kick him squarely in the center of it. Instead, she leaned forward and half whispered in his ear, "Rowan! What is the matter with you?"

Rowan began to wish that his wife had been a bit closer to the Lord of the Isles on the tour. Rowan realized that if he hadn't relegated Maddie to the background she might have seen the covetous look on Laclan MacDonald's face that grew greedier and greedier with every new wonder he was shown. Rowan had felt danger growing around Cape Wrath all day. It was bad enough that there were three boatloads of MacDonald's warriors camped outside the gates of the fortress. The things he and Allen had discussed with the Lord of the Isles the night before weighed heavily on Rowan's mind, fueling worries for his clan's future. Now he feared that a more personal danger loomed in his overlord's growing interest in Maddie's clever handiwork.

It didn't help Rowan's darkening mood to hear Allen Harboth eagerly praising Maddie every chance he got. It didn't help that he caught Maddie giving Allen grateful, appreciative looks every time he spoke. Rowan didn't know whether Allen was playing some game or genuinely admired his wife and her accomplishments. Rowan did know that he didn't like the attention the Harboth was paying to the woman who belonged to him.

It had nothing to do with jealousy, he told himself, and everything to do with keeping Maddie out of harm's way. Just because his blood burned with rage every time Allen or Maddie looked each other's way wasn't causing *him* to behave with less sense and more rancor toward his wife as the day wore on.

She seemed to think so, though, as she glared fiercely into his eyes. "What is the matter with you?" she demanded again in a hissing whisper when he didn't answer her immediately. "What have I done to deserve this?"

They were surrounded by a gaping crowd. Rowan felt everyone in the room's gaze on them, and the curious silence pressed against his nerves. He was acutely aware that there were Harboths and Lord Laclan and his men as well as Murrays among the watchers. He could not afford to look weak to any of them by engaging in a public argument with his offended wife.

He put his hands on Maddie's shoulders. "Hush," he ordered. "We'll talk tonight."

Her laughter was loud, and angry. "We never talk. I think that's the problem, don't you?"

"Don't be foolish."

"Foolish!"

She jerked away from him, and stumbled. She would have fallen if Allen Harboth had reached out to steady her. Fury shot through Rowan at the sight of the other man touching his wife, but Maddie shook off Allen's touch as furiously as she had Rowan's. Her stormy gaze never left Rowan's. "I've about had it with you," she told him.

Then she stalked, as regally as a queen, out of the hall. It broke Rowan's heart to let her go, but since having her out of both Harboth's and Lord Laclan's sight was for the best, he forced himself to let her leave.

26

"I've had it. I'm out of here. I don't know how, I don't know where, but I'm gone." She'd been standing in the middle of the rainy courtyard for at least five minutes, hands clenched into tight fists at her sides, her fury and humiliation boiling up into words she couldn't hold back.

"You're talking to yourself, lass."

Maddie whirled to face Rosemary. "I'm not a lass. I'm twenty-eight years old. I've got a master's degree, you know. I'm not some *foolish* little girl whose only functions are to provide sex and technology to a man who doesn't appreciate either unless I keep my mouth shut when I'm doing both. Actually, there are times when he likes having my mouth open, but that's only when he's putting parts of his anatomy in it."

It was the realization of the crudeness of what she'd just said, coupled with the fact that she'd said it very, very loudly in a courtyard full of playing children that brought Maddie's tirade to an abrupt halt. A flush instantly heated her skin. She ducked her head in shame under Rosemary's disapproving frown. If her mother had been there, Maddie knew that that formidable woman would have washed her mouth out with soap.

She began to cry.

She wanted her mommy! She wanted to go home. She wanted Rowan to acknowledge that he loved her, and then this would be home. She was certain now that that was never going to happen. She didn't have anything to live for here any more than she'd had in the twentieth century. She didn't know what she was going to do, and she just couldn't take it anymore!

Once the tears started, Maddie was overwhelmed with the terror that they weren't ever going to stop. She wished she'd stayed angry. Anger was so much easier than heartbreak.

Children stopped their games and gathered around, asking worriedly what was wrong. Adults stopped their tasks to do the same. A small crowd quickly gathered around her, and Maddie was helpless to do anything but sob.

After a few seconds, Rosemary handed the full basket she carried to a nearby girl, instructing her to take it to the kitchen. After the girl ran off, Rosemary took Maddie's hand and led her toward the chapel. "Let's have a little talk in private, lass—my lady."

Maddie didn't want to go to the chapel, but she knew she couldn't stay out in the courtyard and just cry herself to death, tempting though that was. Tears blinded her, and the sudden increase in the rain from mist to downpour didn't help her vision either. Her skirts dragged in the courtyard mud. She was glad of Rosemary's sure guidance by the time the church door had closed behind then. It was cold in the chapel, and dark, but it was dry and private.

Rosemary settled Maddie onto a stone bench next to the crudely carved statue of the Virgin and child, and handed her a dry cloth. "Here. Dry your eyes and blow your nose. Our Lady will not mind your using the cover from her offering table."

Maddie didn't care where the makeshift handkerchief came from, but she was grateful for it. Grateful for Rosemary's kindness. The gratitude sent another wave of emotion through her that brought even more tears. It was quite a while before she was under control enough to actually dry her eyes and blow her nose.

Rosemary waited patiently the whole time. Maddie heard her moving around the small church and became aware of a soft glow from behind her squeezed-shut eyes when Rosemary set down a lit candle from the altar next to the Virgin's statue.

Eventually Maddie looked up to find Rosemary standing patiently in front of her. Maddie had to blink to bring her vision into focus. Then she sniffed and wiped off one last tear with the back of her hand. "Sorry."

"Why? We all need a good cry now and again."

Maddie sniffed again. "That was full-blown hysteria."

"Murray men will do that to you." Rosemary sat down beside her and took her hand. "It's a wonder it didn't come to this sooner. You're a strong, stubborn woman, Maddie Murray."

Maddie looked down at the floor. "I want a divorce," she mumbled.

Rosemary laughed, softly, though with no mockery

in it. "Only kings and queens can afford to pay the pope for such a thing. You're handfasted, my lady, and you owe Rowan Murray a year and a day."

"But no more," Maddie vowed.

A hand seemed to tighten painfully around her heart at her words. A desperate voice cried in her mind that she didn't want to leave Rowan. But what choice did she have when Rowan didn't give a damn about her?

"It's for you to choose. Remember there's many months you and Rowan have to live through together before the day comes when you can make that choice."

Maddie wished Rosemary didn't sound so pragmatic, so sensible. Normally she would have welcomed anything that sounded even vaguely sensible from a Murray woman. Now she looked at Rosemary and asked, "I don't suppose you have a spell or potion or something that'll give me amnesia until the time's up? Or how about something to put me to sleep for a few months? Yeah," she went on with pained enthusiasm. "That sounds good."

Of course, if she slept through the rest of her so-called marriage, she would no longer be able to make love to Rowan Murray. Then again, her life was a nightmare, so she might as well be asleep for it.

"Magic isn't what you need," Rosemary told her.

Maddie snorted. "Never thought I'd hear a Murray say that."

"Well, you just did. Look at me, my lady."

Maddie turned her head to gaze into Rosemary's eyes. The woman looked sympathetic and thoroughly exasperated at the same time.

"What you need," Rosemary went on, "is some sound advice, and perhaps a bit of family history to explain how Rowan Murray turned into the biggest fool the Highlands has ever seen."

Maddie decided she didn't have anything better to do than listen to Rosemary. Twenty minutes later, she stormed out of the church and headed for the hall. She was ten times angrier when she entered the castle than she had been when she left it.

"All right!" she shouted when she marched in. "Where is he?"

All Rowan wanted was to go after Maddie. He needed to make things right with her, to apologize for acting the fool, even though he'd done it for her own good. He needed to talk to her, he needed to touch her. He just *needed* her. Instead, what he had was a private meeting in his bedchamber with Allen Harboth and a belly full of worries over the demands their overlord had made of them. Rowan sat on the edge of the bed while Allen moved restlessly about the chamber.

"We're allies now," Allen said as he paced back and forth across the bedroom. "Kinsmen. We should stand together in our answer to MacDonald of the Isles."

Rowan's gaze had strayed to the door, but he turned it back to Harboth. For all that he wanted to run after his woman, he still put duty first. The Lord of the Isles was leaving with the tide, and an answer had to be given to him before he left. "I'm troubled about what that answer should be," Rowan admitted to Allen.

Allen stopped pacing and gave Rowan a respectful look. "It's hard for me to confess my uncertainty on the matter to you as well, Rowan. I'm glad you trust me enough to speak frankly. It's not that I don't have the stomach for a good fight," he went on. "I'm just not sure this is a good fight."

"Nor am I," Rowan replied, making himself continue this new-formed trust. The words came grudgingly, but Rowan said, "We stand or fall together. We're kinsmen, Allen." *But stay away from my wife,* he added to himself.

As he thought the words, the door opened and Maddie stepped inside. He sprang to his feet while her gaze settled on Harboth. "I was told you couldn't be disturbed. I'm disturbing you. Would you mind leaving us alone, Allen?" she asked.

Allen looked from Maddie to him and quirked an eyebrow questioningly. Rowan was torn with guilt and indecision, but this meeting was important. Rowan stepped forward and did the one thing he didn't want to do. "Whatever you came for will have to wait, Maddie. We haven't much time."

Maddie's features went very still, very cold. She said, "I wasn't talking to you. I was talking to Allen." She turned a chillingly furious glare on him. "I'll talk to you when we're alone."

Allen put out a hand, but he was wise enough to glance at Rowan before he touched Maddie, and let his hand fall. "Please, my lady. This truly is important."

"I'm not going anywhere until I've had it out with Rowan." She looked from one man to the other as she stood white-knuckled before them. "But for your information, I already know what the Lord of the Isles is planning. He's about to invade the south, burn Glasgow, and declare himself overlord of the Highlands. King, actually."

Both Rowan and Allen moved swiftly to her side.

"How do you know that?" Allen demanded. "Is she a seer?" he asked Rowan.

"No. Lord Laclan spoke to us in private. He claims only a few of his men know his plans, and that they are sworn to secrecy. How do you know, Maddie?"

She was fuming and furious and full of far more important problems than politics, but she made herself say, "Because of where I came from. Because I know Scottish history. I should have realized who he was and what was going on sooner, but I'm not really sure what year this is. That it's sometime early in the thirteenth century is all I've been able to work out."

Maddie didn't want to take the time to give a history lesson. She wanted to have a knockdown, drag-out fight with her husband, but she supposed the safety of the clan had to come first for both of them. That meant she'd better take the time to explain to the gaping men, even though the explanations forced her to hold onto a calm she didn't want.

"MacDonald's gathering troops right now. He's going to burn Glasgow. He wants you to gather your warriors, leave your homes unprotected, and come with him to win a glorious new future for the Highlands. He just wants power for himself," she added. "It won't work. It's a waste of men and resources to follow this mad dream the MacDonalds had of making the Highlands a separate country. The Campbells are just going to make life hell for the Highlanders when they come after the MacDonalds. Eventually it'll lead to English troops stationed all over the Highlands and most of the native population exiled to Nova Scotia and America and Australia—living everywhere but in Scotland. Eventually the English and their pet lairds are going to replace all of you with sheep, this land is going to have pastures rather than a population. All because of a power struggle between two families. It could be stopped right now if the other clans just tell MacDonald that they don't want to play."

There. She'd explained everything. Now Allen could go away and she and Rowan could get down to important matters.

Instead of being grateful, Rowan took and angry step back and said, "Must you know everything about everything, woman?"

Maddie's head came up sharply. "What?"

"Am I head of this clan or not?"

She faced Rowan, toe-to-toe. They looked deep into each other's eyes for a long, tense, moment. Maddie told him, "You are head of the clan, Rowan. I'm just telling you what's going to happen."

"You told me what decision I should make."

She shook her head. "No, it's your choice—as laird of the Murrays—to decide whether the clan goes to war or not. I told you the logical thing to do. The logical thing is to stay home and take care of your people."

"Stay home with you, you mean?"

Maddie had no idea why he looked and sounded so dangerous, why his closeness was suddenly threatening. She wouldn't be bullied. "Yes. Please don't get involved with the Lord of the Isles' mad scheming."

Behind them, she heard the door close as Allen left them to deal with their problems in privacy. It didn't help when a brief look of exasperation crossed Rowan's face when Allen exited. Then he looked accusingly at her.

"He left because of you."

"Maybe he left because he saw that we have things to settle."

"He's attracted to you," Rowan replied. "That makes him vulnerable."

Maddie laughed. It held hysteria, and was hard to stop. "Attracted to me? No way."

Rowan nodded at her shocked protest. "Allen wants you. I can see it."

"Well, I certainly can't."

"It's true, and he has na the strength not to give in to a woman's whims."

"Whims? I don't do whims. I am the least whimsical person you are ever going to meet. In fact," she went on, "you are the person who's having the problem with an excess of whimsy, not me."

"I?"

"You."

He glowered. She was used to it. She'd come to find it endearing. She certainly didn't find it intimidating. She reached out shoved hard against his chest. She pushed hard enough for him to stumble backward to sit on the bed. Maddie took the opportunity to loom over him.

"I'm not sure what a fairy princess looks like." She spread her arms and slowly turned all the way around. "This isn't it. I'm a flesh-and-blood woman, Rowan Murray."

He looked her up and down. "Aye. So you are."

"I'm not beautiful."

"I'd argue with that."

"Thank you, but I know I'm not. I'm not ugly, either. When we make love, I know I'm not ugly, or unlovable. You've taught me that what I've got is a perfectly serviceable, acceptable variation of the female form. It's not hardware that's important." She touched a finger to her temple. "You've taught me that once a woman—this woman—figures out how to work the preloaded software for sex, the actual operation is the most wonderful thing in the world. You're the perfect partner for me, Rowan Murray, and I love you." *Even if you don't love me,* she added to herself.

Rowan's eyes lit, then he smiled, but the hard mask shut down over his features once more. "Making love to you is a joy," he admitted.

"Making a life with me would be better."

There was a significant silence after she spoke. She waited, tense as a bowstring, for his answer. She almost felt the slow seconds passing, like sand flowing over her tender flesh.

After a long time, he said quietly, "What more life can I give you?"

"You could love me." There, she'd said it. She almost wished she hadn't. The subject was so touchy she very nearly ran from the room after bringing it up, even though love was at the center of this confrontation she had forced.

Rowan didn't look as though he'd heard her, or at least not the desperation she was feeling. He was as still as a man-shaped granite boulder on the bed, his face half in shadows, his eyes giving nothing away. "You're my wife, you are the lady of Cape Wrath," he told her.

"For a year and a day," she snarled. "Then what? You'll trade me in for some other woman the White Lady tells you to look for on the side of the road?"

"I will continue to protect you," he answered.

"For the sake of my helping your clan."

"You are a part of the clan. And handfasted or wed by a priest, I honor you above all other women, I protect you with my body and sword, I hope to have a child with you. That is our life."

She was snarling at him, and she hated the calm way he answered. His words were gallant, but they didn't match anything she'd experienced lately. "I'm not your partner anywhere but in that bed. I don't think even your stupid White Lady meant for us to just screw around together."

"A wife's duty is to serve her husband."

"And a husband's duty is to serve his wife. All you care about is serving your damned clan!"

"That's not all I care about."

"If that's true, why don't you show it?"

"I canna."

"What are you afraid of?"

His hands rested on his thighs, clenched into white-knuckled fists. "It is not you I fear." Then he went pale, and added hastily, as if he'd just made a major slip, "I fear nothing and no one."

"You fear for your people," she countered.

He gave a grudging nod. "Aye. It is right that I have concern for my clan."

"They're my family now, too." Suddenly she found tears blurring her vision. Her voice nearly choked with pain as she went on. "I've lost my world, Rowan—a world you haven't asked me about since we came back to Cape Wrath. For a while I thought you cared enough to get to know me, to find out the things that are important to me. I see now that I was wrong."

"I fight battles every day with my people to help you

put a bit of your world into ours," he protested. "You're building the things that are important to you."

She shook her head, and fought back sobs so she could get out words. Her voice still shook when she spoke. "I'm building things because I've bought into this prophecy about saving your clan—and I don't even believe in prophecies. I don't even know what the prophecy I don't believe in meant. And I don't have anything better to do," she added as she dashed tears away. "I'm lonely, Rowan. I'm sick for a home, and I have to do something to occupy my thoughts or go crazy."

"You love what you do. I've seen the pleasure it gives you to work like a man."

"Hold it!" The words came out close to a scream. She pointed furiously at him. "How is it that in front of your jock friends what I do is 'woman's work,' but in here it's 'man's work'? Never mind," she said before he could answer. "I came here to point out to you that I am not your stepmother. You are not your father."

Rowan's eyes glittered with cold anger. It was as though all the light in the room was suddenly concentrated in his gaze. Maddie couldn't have looked away if she'd wanted to. "I know I am not my father."

"Do you?"

"I will not let myself become like him."

"Rosemary says he was a good man."

Rowan's gaze slid away from hers. His tense shoulders slumped a bit. "He was a good man. He was a fool as well."

"From the way Rosemary tells it, he got in over his head with the wrong woman." Rosemary had told of fairy enchantment and spells, and all the other stage dressing the natives used to embellish the world around them. Maddie had still managed to weed out the relevant points in the narrative.

"He fell into the trap of being in love," Rowan said, "and nothing could save him." Rowan looked grim and unforgiving, and his voice held an undertone of long-suppressed fury.

His pain ripped at her heart, but she couldn't give in to the fierce stab of sympathy. "You think love is a trap?"

He looked at her, and she saw the sorrow that shone deep in his eyes beneath the stalwart determination. "I'm sorry to say it to you, lass, for you deserve a man stronger than me. For men of my line, love is indeed a trap. I dare not fall into it, even for your sake."

"Then that night we spent together at the White Lady's was a dream."

"It was no dream."

"It must have been. Because I dreamed that you told me that love was about trust. I had to have dreamed it all—because you don't trust me, or yourself, or even the idea that love can exist."

Rowan slowly got to his feet. When he would have come to her, Maddie backed toward the door. She didn't want him touching her just now. Even as angry and hurt as she was, she feared that Rowan's touch would make her forget everything but how much she cared for him. She wasn't unaware of the irony that Rowan felt that way all the time, but he took the concept so overboard she feared she could never reach him.

She couldn't give up trying, though. "I'm a mortal woman, you're a mortal man. Right?"

He nodded. "That we are."

"I'm not some ethereal little thing who'd rather drag you off on picnics and dancing in the moonlight. I'm more likely to force you help me build that methane converter than I am to do whatever it is fairies do when they're in love with mortal men. I'm not your step-mother," she repeated adamantly.

"But I am too much like my father."

"Oh, for God's sake!" She wanted to beat down the walls he'd put around his heart with her bare hands. She did snatch up a candlestick and throw it at him.

"Aye," he responded as he ducked. "I pray to God every day for the strength my father lacked. I'll not abandon my people."

"Who's asking you to?" Maddie brightened at a sudden idea. "Maybe the White Lady thought you were the savior of your people and all you needed was the right woman to loosen you up."

He almost smiled. "If I loosen up, Maddie, I'll fall apart."

She was ready to pound her fists against something in frustration. Preferably Rowan. She thought it was a monument to *her* restraint that she didn't. Actually, there was nothing immediately handy to throw.

"I'm a lot like my father, too," she told him. "He was an army sergeant before he came back to take over the family ranch. There's a military joke, a non-com's joke. Whenever somebody'd call my father 'sir,' he'd say, 'Don't call me that, I work for a living.' That's how I am. Whatever else you think I might be, I work for a living. I like working for a living. I'm used to working around some of the toughest men in the world in howling storms and other conditions that makes the life at Cape Wrath seem almost comfortable by comparison."

She didn't know why she was telling him this, except that he looked interested, interested in her for the first time since that night at the White Lady's. She wanted desperately for him to be interested in her the way she was interested in everything about him.

"And what is it you're trying to tell me with this tale, lass?"

"That I'm not the sort of woman you're afraid of. That I wouldn't let you become the sort of man you're afraid of being."

"You can not stop me from following his path."

"You're the only one who can do that," she agreed. "*We* can love each other without spending our entire lives locked in some kind of self-involved, selfish, passionate, sex-induced haze. Rowan, I love you, but I don't spend twenty-four hours a day thinking about you, at least not consciously. You're always on my mind, I'm always aware of you. You've seeped into my bones and blood and thoughts, but that doesn't mean I'm going to run off and have my way with you when I'm in the middle of an important project." She put a hand to her throat. "I can restrain my excess of passion for your manly touch for a few hours out of every day, you know."

"Can you, indeed?"

She shrugged. "Mostly."

He smirked. She wasn't used to Rowan Murray smirking. She liked it. It disappeared all too quickly. Maddie wanted desperately to bring it back, even as Rowan's features settled once more into hard-held control. She wanted to run to him, to throw her arms around him, press her body to his and kiss him until they were both consumed with need. He never looked so stern when they were making love, but this wasn't about making love, it was about making a life. She stayed where she was despite strong temptation to do otherwise.

He had to come to her. He had to prove he wanted a wife, not just a lover. It didn't look as if he was planning on moving any time in the near future. He was probably just waiting for her to get out so Allen could come back and they could get on with their little talk.

He probably hadn't listened to a word she said. His mind was on going off to make war with the Lord of the Isles. His mind was always anywhere but on them. She wasn't so selfish that she wanted him to think of nothing but her, or them, but right now she needed some proof that *they* even existed.

It was time to play hardball for the sake of what they could have. She'd tried waiting for him to show her the man she'd come to love when they were away from Cape Wrath. She couldn't wait any longer. She took a long, deep breath in a vain attempt to steady her nerves while all too aware of his watching her out of those cool, calm, ice pale eyes.

"This is the deal," she said looking straight into his icy gaze. "Discussion, such as it's been, is over. I'm going to turn around and walk out of here. Whether or not I ever come back into this room is entirely up to you."

She was hurt, disappointed—heartbroken—when he didn't leap to stop her, or even say a word to call her back. She wasn't surprised.

27

There was no doubt in Rowan's mind that he was a fool. The question wasn't so much whether he was one, but whether he was right or wrong to be one. He knew that Maddie was the most wonderful woman in the world, and that he was a dolt and a villain, for hurting her.

He was barely able to stay still long enough for the door to close behind his sad, disappointed wife. He was up and after her in an instant, but he stopped at the door. Duty—no, fear of his own nature—kept him from following the impulse to chase after her. Every fiber of his being told him he was making a horrible mistake, but the discipline of control held. It was shaky—he was literally shaking with the pent-up emotions—but he forced his body and heart to obey his will.

"This is driving me mad. Damn you, Father! Damn me for being your son!"

Rowan wanted to howl, to rage, to break every piece of furniture and crockery and anything else he could get his hands on. Instead he let out some of his rage as he banged both fists against the unyielding wood, hard enough to raise bruises on his already roughened hands.

He found himself looking at his hands, the fingers spread wide before his face—as though they'd just let something precious slip right through them. He recalled watching Maddie's still form bent over a clear mountain loch, hands carefully poised to quickly snatch a fish out of the water. The image brought a smile to his lips, and helped ease the tight fist of control squeezed around his aching heart. He remembered standing in an abandoned house and thinking that she was no fairy woman, but a practical, wonderful mortal. It seemed he'd instantly forgotten those thoughts on the dawn he had them, for he'd been chagrined at his foolishness when she pointedly reminded him of her true nature.

His lass didn't conjure fairy feasts out of midair; she went fishing for her breakfast.

He remembered holding his hand out to Maddie and speaking to her of trust and love. That had been in a protected, safe place far away from the cares of the world. Back in the world, he dared not trust himself to show more than a minute part of the love that burned through him for the woman who'd come to save his people.

Or perhaps he was frightened to love for fear that he didn't deserve someone as wonderful as Maddie. What if she did disappear back into her own time once her work at Cape Wrath was accomplished? Could he live with losing her? Or did he, perhaps, hold himself from her out of guilt for having forced the marriage on her? All he knew was that he'd overreacted, that he'd run from his own feelings, and that his overreaction was likely to destroy the one wonderful thing that had ever come into his life.

Had the White Lady sent her to save him as well? Was Maddie here to bring him back from the emotionless prison he'd put himself in to save his clan? *Would* saving him be the saving of the Murrays? Or were these thoughts excuses he made to himself to give in to his hot-blooded, selfish nature?

Or perhaps he wasn't as selfish as he feared. Perhaps he was just a man, and she was just a woman, and they needed each other.

He wanted desperately to be kind to the woman he loved, to be more than kind. He wanted to be loving, to show her how much he cared every minute of every day, not for just a few guarded hours when they were alone in this room. After what Maddie had said before leaving, he knew that they would not even have the time together in this room anymore. She was a strong, stubborn woman; she would not come back to him unless he bent to her in this.

It wasn't even an unreasonable demand. Maddie was no princess of the fair folk who asked for roses in winter and expected them to appear. She was merely asking for her rights as a wife. He found no blame in her actions. He simply could not give her roses, even in summer. He could not bend, for to him the slightest bend would surely lead to breaking.

He wished with all his heart that he could call back the magic of the night they'd shared at the White Lady's. He wished that there were some safe place for them, but he would not abandon his people to find that haven for his heart and his heart's desire.

And was the magic between us that night not the sort mortals make?

The thought was his, but it seemed to come from outside himself. "Magic," he said. "That was not magic, that was love. It was trust. It was the way a man and woman are meant to be together."

And can you not find that love every time you look into your Maddie's eyes?

He could, he knew, if he dared.

"But how to control that love?" He looked around wildly, at the room he had not destroyed no matter how strong the desire to smash his circumscribed world into oblivion. "How do I control myself?"

I'm not some ethereal little thing who'd rather drag you off on picnics and dancing in the moonlight.

No matter how much his pain, Rowan couldn't stop the laugh as he suddenly recalled Maddie's words. An image formed in his mind of her dragging him off, hoisted over her shoulder, for she was indeed *not* some ethereal little thing. She was a big, strong, capable mortal woman, and he wanted her no other way.

I work for a living. I like working for a living.

As did he. They were a fine match. Together they could indeed fulfill the White Lady's prophecy of saving his people. If he was just strong enough to be the partner Maddie deserved. She wanted and deserved more than a lover. Was he being strong by denying her the partnership she deserved, or was he being a coward?

You've seeped into my bones and blood and thoughts.

Just as she had seeped into his. Had his father ever truly been a part of his fairy wife? Had their thoughts and feelings, hopes, plans, and deeds been as well matched as his and Maddie's? He knew for a fact that they had not. Maddie was a part of Rowan's world, while his father had tried in vain for years to be a part of his fairy lady's, and had failed in the end.

"What do I have to lose by letting myself love this mortal woman? Am I not as mortal as she is? As attached to the world? Her cares and mine are the same. So are the joys. Why have I not seen that before?"

But that doesn't mean I'm going to run off and have my way with you when I'm in the middle of an important project. I can restrain my excess of passion for your manly touch for a few hours out of every day, you know.

Rowan laughed again at the memory of her words. He laughed long and hard, until his shoulders shook and his knees went weak and the laughter turned to wracking sobs that he feared would never end. He lost control of his emotions and didn't even try to gather them back. He cried, he shouted, he laughed wildly, he pounded on the wall and the bed and broke a piece or two of crockery.

It felt wonderful.

It didn't last very long, either. He discovered that once let loose, the flood of emotions were quickly spent. The storm was violent, but soon over. When calm returned, he gazed around the empty room and shook his head.

"I've no time for private frenzy," he realized. "What I need is to shout back when Maddie shouts at me." He smiled. "She can't have a proper fight all on her own. Now, *that* would be a satisfying way to have a roaring fit, the two of us letting ourselves say the things that need to be said and then making up in that big wide bed."

Only he had to convince her first that he was worth fighting with. He had to prove to her that he could be the man she needed and wanted, that he loved her as much as she did him. He was still afraid that he would follow in his father's excessive footsteps. He had to trust himself, and try not to. He had to trust in Maddie and in the love they shared.

When had he forgotten that love was about trust?

"And where has that woman gotten to?" he demanded as he threw open the bedroom door to find Rosemary, Micaela, Burke, and Allen Harboth waiting on the other side. "Well?" he demanded of the startled lot. "Where is she?" He glared at Allen. "Don't you get any ideas about harboring my wife if she's smart enough to run away from me, either. She's *mine*, Harboth."

Allen stepped forward and put a hand on Rowan's shoulder. "I don't want your woman, Murray. I've got a fine woman of my own." He glanced at Rosemary. "Why do you think I made peace with you, man? I've been trying to get Rosemary to run off with me since we met in Glasgow. Unlike Micaela, she wouldn't give in while our clans were enemies."

Rowan looked from Allen to the smiling Rosemary, then back again. "If you're in love with my cousin, why have you been making cow eyes at my wife?"

"That was my idea," Rosemary spoke up. "I thought if he made you jealous you might see that you've been acting mickle odd lately."

"Acting like a fool," Micaela said. "Honestly,

Rowan, you're not a thing like Father. You never have been. Thankfully, Maddie's nothing like Mother. Did the White Lady put a spell on you to make you think otherwise?"

"No," Rowan admitted. "I did that myself." He looked sheepishly at his family. "The spell's broken now. Where is she?"

"The Lord of the Isles asked her to come down to his camp," Rosemary answered. "To look at ship rudders, of all things. She was crying, poor dear, but she went."

"She said she didn't have anywhere better to go," Burke added, with a dark frown at Rowan.

Rowan squirmed under his family's disapproval, but he didn't stay to try to defend or discuss his foolhardy behavior. He went in search of his wife.

He was more than annoyed when Allen caught up with him near the castle gate. Rowan rounded on the other laird. "What?"

"The Lord of the Isles' war," Allen reminded him. "What do you want to do about it?"

It was a decision he had to make, one that couldn't wait even for love's sake. A tiny smile curved his lips as he recalled that Maddie had granted that it was his decision. She offered information but didn't try to bend him to her will in this. How had he been so blind as to think she was trying to turn his—their—home into her private fiefdom?

"What do we tell him, Rowan?" Allen questioned.

"We tell him to go to the devil."

Allen thought for a moment, then nodded. "Aye, but with sweeter words than that. We can't forget that he has a fine beginning, for his army is camped outside your gates."

"And outside they'll stay." *They'll be gone in a few hours, anyway,* he thought. "You find sweet words and plausible excuses to keep our folk out of the fighting," he told Allen. "It's Maddie I need to deal with right now."

He had his own life to set to rights before he could concentrate on his people. For once, he didn't feel guilty about that. In fact, it felt as if a weight had been lifted from his soul. The new lightness growing in his being aided the sure speed of his steps. He rushed forward, holding onto hope for Rowan Murray for the first time in his life.

Never mind the Lord of the Isles today. It's Maddie who'll be here for a lifetime. Please let it be so, Rowan prayed as he hurried out his heavily guarded gates. *Please, God, let it not be too late to win her back.*

He hurried through the village and down to the shingle where the Lord of the Isles was camped. The ocean roared on one side, and Murrays and visiting Harboths streamed down the narrow path behind him. On the shore there were beached ships, tents, and a great many people about. Rowan took no heed of anyone as he went along, until he caught sight of Maddie. That she was surrounded by soldiers he didn't he even notice at first. What he saw was that she was tall and dignified as she stood with MacDonald next to his ship, the flame brightness of red hair dulled by the rain. The rain seemed to kiss her face but could not hide her tears from him.

Tears he had caused. Tears he would stop. He never wanted to make her cry again. "Maddie! I love you!"

A smile as bright as sunlight broke across her features. It warmed him even from a distance. "Rowan!"

"Lord, woman," he called as she turned his way. "I'm a fool!"

"No, you're not!" she shouted back.

Behind him Father Andrew said, "Yes, he is."

Rowan lifted his voice to shout over the roar of laughter, the roar of the ocean, and a questioning murmur from MacDonald's men. He wanted to the world to hear. He stood in the center of the camp and proclaimed, "You know very well I am. You said so, and you were right. I've come to my senses, lass!"

She held a hand out to him. "Just come to me!"

He hurried forward. "I love you! I've loved you from the moment I saw you. I'll love you till my dying day. Let the world witness that I'll do whatever it takes to make you happy if you'll have me."

He hoped she'd run to meet him, but Maddie did not move. She smiled at him, but still dashed away tears with one hand. Rowan saw that the Lord of the Isles had his hand grasped about her other wrist. When Rowan was within a few feet of the shore where Maddie waited, a trio of soldiers blocked his way.

"Let me by."

One of the men looked at MacDonald.

The Lord of the Isles shook his head. "Stay where you are, Murray, and your lady will stay by me."

There was a stillness, a tense alertness about the men surrounding the spot where Maddie stood. Rowan knew that he should have sensed trouble before. He knew now that Maddie was in danger, and he knew exactly what it was. What he had feared might happen had come to pass. It was all his fault.

"She's not going with you, MacDonald."

"Ah, but she is, lad."

Maddie tried ineffectually to pull away from her large captor. "I already told you that I'm not going with you."

MacDonald paid her no mind. Even though he winced when she kicked him on the ankle, he more than outmatched her in size and strength. She was no more than a nuisance to him.

She was Rowan's nuisance, and he wanted her back. Terror shot through him at the thought of losing her just as he'd begun to hope to build a life with her. Terror shot through him just because she was in danger. He let himself have that moment of terror, then he forced it down and replaced it with the steely calm that came to him before every battle.

"I'm going to kill you, MacDonald," Rowan said. At his words two of the guards grabbed him by the arms. Behind him the Murrays set up an angry shout. Murrays, MacDonalds, and Harboths all had weapons in their hands by now.

Maddie watched the change come over Rowan, from apologetic lover to concerned husband to stone-calm leader, and she didn't regret the transition one little bit. He had bared his emotions not only to her, but to the world. She had seen the love, heard it, practically felt it as his words caressed and eased her aching heart and mind.

There was more than hope for them. They were going to make it. He loved her. She loved him.

All they had to do to be together was get through the Lord of the Isles' army.

Maddie couldn't stop the grin as she looked deep into Rowan's eyes. "No problem. Right, babe?"

Rowan knew exactly what Maddie's encouraging

look meant, and her confidence in his ability to protect her filled him with jubilation. He wished for a moment that he had the magic to fly to her side and spirit her away, but magic was not going to save them this day. He knew spells for dealing with fairy armies, but with other mortals he must use sharp steel, muscle, and cunning. He noticed that Burke and Allen had arrived, claymores in hand, but he knew that even though the Murrays and Harboths would stand together, they were outnumbered.

It didn't help that he was a prisoner himself, with a man holding tight to each arm. It didn't help that there was many an unarmed woman and child scattered among the fighting men. His best hope right now was to get Maddie away from MacDonald and get her and his people behind the thick walls of his fortress. There they could easily withstand a siege. Getting his people out of MacDonald's camp was very likely impossible. The shining look on Maddie's face told him he could do the impossible.

For you, lass, he thought, *I will.* First he tried talking. "Why are you doing this, my lord? What do you want with my wife?"

"I mean no dishonor to your wife, to you or your clan," MacDonald replied. "I am your overlord, am I not?"

"You are. Or, rather you were. I'll not follow a man who takes my most precious possession from me."

"We need not fight over a woman, Rowan," the Lord of the Isles responded.

He made an effort to look reassuring. He even let go of Maddie's wrist, but a guard clutched her by the upper arms before she could dash away. At a gesture

from their lord, MacDonald's men released Rowan.
They continued to flank him, however. Rowan didn't
bother to try to draw the long dagger on his belt, but he
rested his hand on its hilt.

"Rest assured I don't want her for my bed,"
MacDonald went on. "She'll be a honored guest at my
stronghold on Skye. She'll dwell among the women of
my own family and receive all the honor due her rank."

"And why will she be honored on the isle of Skye
when she should be with me?" Rowan asked. He
spoke quietly, but with a great deal of menace.
Though he remained very calm, he made no effort to
hide his hatred. The time for shunning his emotions
was past.

"Don't fret for your woman, Murray," MacDonald
answered. "Taking hostages to ensure loyalty is done
all the time. I felt that you and Harboth were a bit luke-
warm in your enthusiasm for the coming fight with the
Campbells. Having your lady as hostage will ensure
your clans ride with me on Glasgow. Once you have a
taste of booty and power, you'll thank me for forcing
you to the fighting."

"And my lady will still be on Skye."

"That she will, lad."

"That is not acceptable, MacDonald."

"It is my right."

"You have no right to steal another man's wife."

"I hear that that you are but handfasted. If you try to
thwart me in this, she'll be a MacDonald's wife when
the time comes. I know she comes by her skills through
magic, but she can teach my artisans all her clever
ways. I'm no fool," the Lord of the Isles went on. "I see
how the things she builds can bring power to the man

who commands her skill. As your overlord, those skills rightly belong to me."

Rowan knew that though a great deal of water and a great many MacDonalds stood between him and the fortress where MacDonald planned to hold Maddie, he would get her back. He would swim the distance if he had to, and strike every MacDonald down one by one if he must to set her free.

"She's my wife, now and forever. I'll kill any man who tries to lay claim to her."

Maddie lifted her head and said proudly. "Rowan Murray is my husband, now and forever. I won't have anyone else."

"And I bless this holy union in the name of the Father, Son, and Holy Spirit," Father Andrew called out loudly. "Their marriage is a lifetime one, blessed by the church."

A high wind came up as the priest spoke. Instead of blowing his words away, it seemed to magnify them. The sky above darkened with thick, racing clouds, and a mighty wave crashed onto the shore. The restless sea darkened to black. The foaming waves thrown up on the shingle spewed deep green and purple foam.

MacDonald laughed and raised his voice over the growing storm. "She's still my prisoner. She's still coming with me. Look around you, lad, and see that you cannot stop this. Your wife goes to Skye, and you fight with me. That's how it will be, or I slaughter every woman and child that bears the name Murray. Your wife is mine whether you live or die. See reason, and I'll let you visit her after we win the Highlands. I'll be a king, lad," he cajoled. "And you and yours will share in the glory."

"I want no glory. I want my wife. I want you gone."

"Those sound like wishes to me," a light and lilting feminine voice said from behind him. Rowan spun around, and the world kept spinning when he stopped. He saw one clear image in the twirling world, that of an inhumanly beautiful woman. Tinkling laughter sounded at his startled movement. "I'm so glad to hear you wish for something, my dearling darling Rowan love."

She had always called him Rowan love. "Mother?" She was not his mother, but he'd always respectfully called her that. "What are you doing here?"

Her smile was still as serene and lovely as the moonlight. "Come to grant your wishes, of course."

"We've come for what is ours," another, deeper, angry voice interjected. "We've come to make war with mortals if we must."

Then the world stopped spinning, and an army of fair folk stood among the greatly outnumbered mortals on the shore. Their coldly beautiful faces shone though the day was wild and dark. Clouds and sea alike reflected off their gleaming silver armor and the swords of sharp crystal and obsidian in their elegant, long-fingered hands.

"Magic!" MacDonald shouted in alarm.

"Magic," Maddie repeated as she looked around in amazement. She was so shocked at what she saw all around her that for a moment all she wanted to do was have a little lie down, pinch herself, and know that it was all a dream.

She wasn't dreaming.

There really were fairies. Not itty-bitty winged creatures from children's books, but glorious, Tolkienesque magical beings. What she saw, hundreds and hundreds of them—though she didn't see how there was room to crowd mortal and immortal alike onto the shore—were the *Sidhe,* the fair folk of Celtic legend. They looked anything but legendary. They looked—and were—very, very real. Some were tall and so lovely it hurt her eyes to look at them. Some were short and squat and grotesque, with leathery skins. Some seemed to be made of stone, or wood, or moss or water or flowers. Some had wings, some tails, some both. There was nothing at all human about them, though many were human-shaped. She saw a few of the big, dark-furred animals Rowan called Questing Beasts among them.

One of the fair folk spoke, though Maddie had no idea who it was. The sound came from everywhere, and sounded as though moonlight had taken on a voice. It was a cold, wintery moon, at that. "This land belongs to the Murrays and the Harboths. We protect them. We've come to deal with them. All who wear the plaid of clan MacDonald are not wanted here. Be gone from this place."

Without a word, almost without a sound, slack-featured and moving as though connected to puppet strings, the Lord of the Isles and his men headed for their beached boats.

Maddie realized that no one was watching her but Rowan. He held his arms open, and she ran into his welcoming embrace. They kissed until they were breathless, then Maddie panted, "There really are fairies!"

"Of course there are," he answered. He kissed her again. "I thought you agreed to believe in magic."

She knew now that nothing that had happened that

night at the White Lady's had been a dream. Everything they'd said and done—and all the magic— had been real. Rowan really had risked his life to take the necklace off her. He really did love her, enough to die for her if he must. And she knew that she loved him enough to do the same. That was the real magic.

She owed the White Lady an apology.

And a thank-you for bringing her together with Rowan Murray.

"Who are they?" she asked as Rowan slipped an arm around her waist. They turned to face the fairy host. "What are they doing here?"

It was Aidan who stepped forward to explain. "They need the silver hawk." He had his arm protectively around the most beautiful creature Maddie had ever seen. "This is my mother," he told Maddie. "She's come to welcome you to the family."

The fairy woman turned an enchanting smile on her. "I knew you'd make him happy when I brought you to him."

"You brought her here?" Rowan didn't know whether he was more angry or surprised. "Why?"

"I promised to bring you love once, lad. Don't you remember?"

"I told you I didn't want fairy love."

A trace of annoyance entered her voice. "Well, she's not of the fair folk, is she?"

Rowan couldn't help but smile. He kissed Maddie's freckled forehead. "No, Mother, she's not. Thank you," he added after a long, grudging pause.

Another fairy woman stepped forward. She was far taller than Rowan's stepmother, dressed in armor rather than gossamer silks. She was dark-haired and deep-voiced, and her silver eyes showed no expression. She spoke to Maddie. "Where is the silver hawk?"

A chill of fear went through Maddie as the fairy spoke. She sensed the woman's power, and her anger. She had not been afraid of MacDonald, but this was someone she didn't want to cross. "Huh?"

"You rode a silver hawk when you were called into this world," the fairy said. "I claimed it as the price for letting such deep magic be performed. I intend to ride the silver hawk to your world. Give it to me."

"Silver hawk?" Rowan asked. He looked at Maddie. "What does she mean?"

"I have no idea."

The fairy gestured impatiently. "You flew here. The necklace guided you. We gave it to you."

Maddie touched her throat. "Gave it to me? It nearly killed me."

The fairy nodded. "When you did not come to us at first as you should have, we sent strong magic to make you come to us."

"But Rowan countered that magic," Rowan's stepmother said proudly. "I taught him well."

"It was love that countered the magic," Rowan spoke up. He tightened his hold on Maddie. "Mortal love."

"Of course it was," she answered. "What your father and I shared taught you the power of love, mortal or immortal."

Rowan didn't try to argue with her, not with the fairy queen glowering angrily at his wife. "If it is a silver hawk you want, then we will find it somehow."

Maddie thought furiously while Rowan talked to the fairies. What the devil did they mean? Silver hawk?

What hawk? She'd come here in an—"Airplane." Maddie leaned her head on Rowan's shoulder and laughed triumphantly. "I came here in an airplane. So much has happened that I actually forgot."

"Airplane?" the fairy leader said. "Is it silver? Does it fly?"

"Actually, it's mostly aluminum, but it looks silvery." She looked at the magical creature in confusion. "What do you want something as practical as an airplane for?"

"To fly to your time," the woman answered. "For the magic to work, I must fly in something from your world. Give it to me," she added darkly, and gestured at the fairy army she'd brought with her. "Or you will all die."

Rowan looked furious at the fairy's threat, but Maddie laughed to ease the tension. "Sure. No problem. It's all yours. I don't need an airplane. I don't even know how to fly an airplane. Of course, neither do you."

"The magic will fly the silver hawk."

Maddie thought about this for a moment, but conceded the point easily enough. "I don't doubt it. Of course, you have to get it down off the mountain first." She turned around, bringing Rowan with her, and pointed toward the highest of the nearby peaks. "I think I can find the spot. If not, you have enough people to spread out and search the whole mountain."

"We have hunted," the fairy told her. "My people do not see well in the daylight world."

"Then my people will find the silver hawk for you," Rowan said. "Aidan can hunt in both sun and moon worlds."

"That I can," the lad said proudly. He bowed deeply to the fairy queen. "I'll gladly direct both my people to the silver bird you seek."

The fairy nodded. She even smiled. "Then it will be done. I thank you, Rowan and Maddie Murray, and will stand fairy godmother for all your children."

Maddie didn't think this was a good time to mention to a would-be time traveling fairy queen that the last thing she wanted her future children to be involved with was magic. Actually, she just wanted to get on with the process of having those children. So she nodded graciously, and said, "Thank you."

When he realized what the fairy wanted with this silver hawk, Rowan drew Maddie aside. With his arms around her—with his arms where he always wanted them to be—he said, "You could go with her. If you wish."

He hated every word he said, but they had to be spoken. He had to give her the choice.

"You could go back to this Toby Coltrane you left behind."

Maddie blinked in surprise. "Who?"

"The one who looks like me."

"I know who he is." She'd all but forgotten Toby Coltrane. "What would I want with him?"

"He was the one you wanted."

She brushed her hand across Rowan's cheek. It seemed that when she'd wished for someone like Toby, she'd gotten someone better. "Why have the shadow when I can have the reality?"

"I've hurt you."

"Yes."

"I've put you in danger."

She nodded. "I've been in danger."

"Your world is a better place than mine."

"In many ways, yes."

"You'll likely be in danger again if you stay with me."

"The Highlands are a barbaric place," she agreed.

She sounded far too calm, as phlegmatically matter-of-fact as he usually did, in fact. It infuriated him. It frightened him. "Will you leave me?" he asked. "Will you go back to your own world and time?" He was desperate to hear her say no, but knew that it would be best if she said yes. He could barely say the words, but her forced them out. "I want only what's best for you."

"I know."

Then she kissed him. He had his answer in the fiery, demanding touch of her lips, in the way her tongue ravaged his mouth, the way their bodies fit so rightly together.

When she took her lips from his, she said, "I'm not going anywhere. My heart's in the Highlands. My heart's with you. We'll make our own kind of magic, Rowan Murray. And we'll live happily ever after. Besides," she added with a breathless laugh, "you can't start the Industrial Revolution without me."

CAPTIVATING AND HUMOROUS
HISTORICAL ROMANCE FROM

SUSAN SIZEMORE

Winner of the Romance Writers of America Golden Heart Award

AFTER THE STORM
When a time travel experiment goes awry, Libby Wolfe finds herself in medieval England and at the mercy of the dashing Bastien of Bale. A master of seduction, the handsome outlaw unleashes a passion in Libby that she finds hauntingly familiar.

IN MY DREAMS
In ninth-century Ireland, a beautiful young druid inadvertently casts a spell that brings a rebel from twentieth-century Los Angeles roaring back through time on his Harley Davidson. Sammy Bergen is so handsome that at first Brianna mistakes him for a god—but he is all too real.

NOTHING ELSE MATTERS
In the splendor of medieval Scotland, a well bred maiden is to marry a boorish young warrior. When tragedy strikes, the warrior's quest for revenge nearly tears them apart—until the lovers realize that nothing else matters once you have found the love of a lifetime.